Dancing with the Uninvited Guest

J Wallis Martin

Dancing with
the Uninvited Guest

Hodder & Stoughton

Copyright © 2002 by J Wallis Martin

First published in Great Britain in 2002
by Hodder and Stoughton
A division of Hodder Headline

The right of J Wallis Martin to be identified as the Author
of the Work has been asserted by her in accordance with the
Copyright, Designs and Patents Act 1988.

10 9 8 7 6 5 4 3 2 1

A CIP catalogue record for this title
is available from the British Library

Hardback ISBN 0 340 72818 3
Trade paperback ISBN 0 340 73412 4

Typeset in Sabon by Hewer Text Ltd, Edinburgh
Printed and bound in Great Britain by
Clays Ltd, St Ives plc

Hodder and Stoughton
A division of Hodder Headline
338 Euston Road
London NW1 3BH

For T.F.

I am indebted to Professor Robert L. Morris,
The Koestler Parapsychology Unit,
University of Edinburgh

Prologue

Claudia entered the room to find her son crouching in a corner, his knees to his chest, his hands across his eyes. He heard her come in, and yet he didn't move. She spoke to him, her voice unsteady. 'Nicholas, come away—'

He stepped over debris that once comprised a table, its legs snapped, its top scratched as if by the claws of a bear. Books lay beside it on the floor, their pages torn, the covers ripped from the text, but because experience had taught them not to clutter his room with items that could be broken, the damage on this occasion was less than in the past; just a light shade ripped from its fitting in the ceiling, and small, round wall lights torn from their sockets. They dangled on the ends of flex like eyes still fixed by the optic nerve, and the sight of them offended her, made her stomach lurch.

'Take me outside,' he said. 'But please – don't leave me.'

The garden was divided from the bleak Northumberland moors by granite walls. Trees formed a bower above their heads, and as they walked beneath them Claudia said, 'Perhaps if we got you away from here?'

'What would be the point?'

True enough, thought Claudia, for whatever it was, it followed him. Even when he left the house, it couldn't be persuaded to abandon him.

'I am its prey,' said Nicholas.

The path curved, and Lyndle came back into view. It dropped its walls clean into the waters of a moat, the parapets of a stone bridge leading the eye to a courtyard, its towers and gables deserted, the undergrowth closing in.

From this angle, and at this time of day, the house was at its

I

most bleak, its fortifications a reminder of savage times. It had fallen to her to preserve it, to keep it intact for future generations, but for two pins she would happily have put a torch to it. Perhaps, in the end, torching it would prove to be the answer?

'I'm not sure how much longer I can stand it,' said Nicholas, and in looking at him now it was difficult for Claudia to remember him as the bright, happy boy who climbed in these trees, and played on these lawns, and ran to her with sprigs of fern or tiny, fragrant flowers.

He suddenly winced in pain, and brought his hand to his neck, relaxing only to repeat the action a moment later, and as she watched him livid welts rose up on the skin of his throat. It took a moment for her to understand what caused them, but once she realised, she backed away in horror.

'What is it?' he said, and, still backing away, she raised her hand and pointed: 'It's biting you,' she said. 'Dear God, Nicholas – *it's biting you.*'

I

> 'There is a type of fish that lives three miles down in the
> western Atlantic. It spends its entire life in the pitch dark. It
> can neither see nor be seen by others of its kind. And that is its
> world. That is all it knows. If you were to ask it what lies
> above the surface of the water, not only would it have no
> conception of what the surface was, it could not possibly
> imagine the world of light and air that exists above it. And
> perhaps there is a comparison to be drawn between the
> existence of that fish and our own existence, for we are in
> the business of finding out whether there is a world, an
> existence, beyond that which we know, and whether certain
> of those who have passed over into that world are capable of
> diving three miles down to communicate with us, to tell us
> what it is like up there in the world of light and air.'

Such was Audrah Sidow's introduction to the course in parapsychology at the British Institute for Paranormal Research,
and few of her students ever forgot the analogy.

She coined it at a time when she was still prepared to
consider the possibility of unimaginable worlds just waiting
to be discovered. But that was before she realised there was
nothing on earth for which there was no rational explanation.

Having reached this conclusion, she questioned whether
anyone could justify spending their entire professional life
looking for something that didn't appear to *be* there. It was
a question she occasionally put to her students, and it invariably produced the response she expected. *She* might have
grown cynical, but *they* were prepared to keep an open mind.
After all, there was always the chance of being the one to prove

there was a spirit world, and that the concepts of a parallel universe, time travel, the ability to conceal or move objects at will or communicate with the dead were not merely the stuff of science fiction.

She supposed it might be her very cynicism which prevented genuine paranormal phenomena from manifesting in her presence. After all, it was well known that a bias towards or against belief in the paranormal had the ability to taint the results of any research. Those who *wanted* to believe that a psychic had just moved a rubber ball a fraction of an inch along a table were perfectly capable of neglecting to note that there was a slight slope to the tabletop. But equally, it would be impossible to convince someone such as herself that the ball had been moved by the power of telekinesis.

The problem was, she had yet to come across anyone who had managed to convince her they were psychic, and years of research had convinced her she never would. Therefore, she had let it be known that she intended to resign.

Leaving the Institute would mean leaving Edinburgh along with this elegant building, and the rooms that she had come to regard as home. They looked out on to a quad, and at certain times of year tourists came to photograph it. Few people saw it like this, when daggers of ice formed on the walls that surrounded the Master's Garden.

She turned from the window to face a room in which two comfortable sofas were divided by a long, low table. Space was at a premium at the Institute, and it was common for her to give tutorials here. Consequently, she currently had one of her students with her. Of all that year's intake, he was the one who interested her most, because he was one of few parapsychology students who claimed to have seen a ghost, though what he meant by a ghost, and what other people meant, were often two very different things.

During the interview that got him on to the course, he described the experience to her:

'Some months after my partner died, I was at the Chelsea

4

Flower Show of all places. Natalie never missed it, and I went more for her than for myself, though don't ask me what I mean by that – I'm not sure. I was walking round the displays, wondering what I was hoping to achieve by being there. And suddenly . . . there she was, looking at some fabulous succulent – a protea.

'At first, I didn't know what to think. I knew I had to be wrong, but the curve of her neck, the way her hair fell forward – I had to go up to this woman if only to get a proper look at her face. And as I walked towards her, she saw me, and smiled. And then she kind of . . . evaporated, I suppose.'

'How did the experience make you feel?'

'Initially, I was frightened. I'd had a bad time since Natalie died. While she was ill, I was fine, I was kind of holding it all together somehow, but after I lost her . . .' He paused, and then went on:

'It had been six months since she died, but I wasn't getting over it. I still couldn't ever see myself making a new life for myself – not one I wanted to live, put it that way. And I couldn't imagine ever meeting anyone who made me feel . . . I think what I'm trying to say is, when I saw her, well, to be honest, I thought I was losing it. But after the shock wore off, I found the experience comforting.'

'Had you and Natalie ever discussed how you felt about her dying?'

'We'd talked about it, sure. Not a lot, but enough. And we talked about whether or not we believed in an afterlife. I don't think either of us did. Not really. We were what you'd probably call fingers-crossed Christians. But Natalie said that if it turned out we were wrong, she'd try to make some kind of contact. So when I saw her . . . well . . . I felt that was what she'd done. And I felt . . . I felt I hadn't lost her.'

'What you're saying is, you believe you saw her ghost.'

'Yes – at the time.'

'And now?'

'And now I no longer believe it.'

'Then how do you explain it?'

After stating that he couldn't, but that he hoped one day to be able to, he was offered a place to read for an MA.

The notes relating to his proposed dissertation rested on the table in front of him. He picked them up as Audrah turned from the window and asked him to talk her through them.

'Essentially,' he said, 'I intend to propose that the manufacturing of what are *perceived* to be supernatural phenomena might be a psychological response to emotional trauma.'

'What kind of supernatural phenomena are we talking about?'

'Apparitions. Premonitions. And anything else that looks as though it might be relevant.'

It was part of her job to advise the students with regard to whether or not the idea they had in mind for their dissertation was suitable. Often, what they came up with had already been covered, in which case they needed to find a fresh angle if the work was to be regarded their own. What this student was suggesting sounded like a subject that had been covered by the scientific community, in which case she had to be sure he wasn't just going to regurgitate information gleaned from medical journals, but was going to provide fresh material. Also, she wanted to know what he meant by the term 'manufacturing'. She asked him, and he replied that the 'manufacturing' of supernatural phenomena was something a person might do subconsciously:

'I don't mean they start making ghosts out of cheesecloth without knowing they're doing it. I'm talking about people experiencing something they can't explain without realising it's come from their own subconscious.'

'You mentioned emotional trauma,' said Audrah. 'Are we talking about the trauma of bereavement?'

'Not exclusively. I intend, for instance, to include the transcript of an interview with the wife of a man who was taken hostage in Iraq. There were uncorroborated reports that he'd been executed, and she'd gone to church to pray. While she was

6

there, she suddenly saw her husband kneeling beside her – a momentary thing, but enough to convince her the reports were true. In fact, he was freed some months later, but the news that he'd been executed caused her to produce what I believe was a crisis apparition.'

It sounded as though this was going to be quite an interesting dissertation. 'Have you thought about what purpose these experiences might serve?'

'Only to the extent that they always seem to have one. They never just occur without there being an apparent benefit to the person experiencing them.'

'Such as?'

'Sometimes the apparition offers advice. Sometimes, as was the case when I thought I saw Natalie, it's a comfort in itself.'

'And what if the apparition or vision is demonic?'

'That usually only occurs when the individual concerned is suffering from some sort of recognised psychiatric illness.'

After thinking it through for a moment, Audrah said, 'Assuming we go with that. Assuming we accept that the manufacturing of phenomena *might be* a psychological response to trauma – are comfort and advice the only purposes they might serve?'

'To be honest, I'm not sure at this stage, but I suspect that in extreme cases they provide far more than that.'

'Can you expand?'

He replied, 'What if, in cases where a person's life is at stake, but where the odds against survival are overwhelming, some mechanism kicks in to motivate them into doing something radical to survive?'

Audrah played devil's advocate. 'What if logic dictates that the odds can't possibly be overcome?'

'Then maybe this "mechanism" gives people the courage to face death calmly. Maybe it convinces them that death is not the end—'

Death, thought Audrah, most certainly *was* the end. If

nothing else, years of researching alleged paranormal phenomena had convinced her of that.

For once Professor Mallory Wober had forsaken his tweed jacket in favour of a fleece-lined coat. 'Walk?' he suggested.

It wasn't the kind of weather people chose to walk in, but Audrah felt she could guess what this was about. Her resignation had come as a blow to Wober, who was bound to try to persuade her to reconsider.

She tucked a mass of auburn hair into a hat, grabbed a skiing jacket and zipped it tight as they stepped out into the corridor. Moments later, they crossed the quad to a gate that led to the park. In the distance, trees divided them from an ornamental lake. On the other side of it stood buildings similar to that in which the Institute was housed, the winter sun glancing off the windows.

It was a mere six years since she first saw those buildings, and a lot had changed since then. The days of sitting someone behind a screen and asking them to try to guess what shape was being drawn on a piece of paper were long gone. The parapsychologists of today were more interested in identifying what parts of the brain were responsible for producing the hallucinations that people perceived as supernatural experiences. Wober, for instance, was an authority on religious visionaries, and there were enough people out there experiencing everything from visions of Christ to premonitions of the apocalypse to keep him in research funds from now till the crack of doom. 'Let me guess,' said Wober. 'You've been headhunted—'

Audrah was now a Doctor of Parapsychology. It made her an attractive proposition. 'If I'd been made an offer I couldn't refuse, I'd have said so.'

'Then why are you leaving?'

Like Wober, Audrah specialised in an area that had more to do with pure psychology than with the supernatural. It related to the nature of psychic fraud with specific reference to pseudo psychics who courted media attention when a missing person

8

or murder investigation became high profile. Defrocking them had once seemed a worthwhile occupation. Not any more. 'Let's just say I feel I've achieved everything I can.'

'Not quite everything,' said Wober. 'What about John Cranmer?'

The comment didn't register because the trees had parted to reveal the ornamental lake. It was frozen, bewildered Mandarin ducks waddling over its surface like lacquered clockwork toys. They tottered on to the snow-covered grass as a man in a buckskin jacket strolled towards them. He was too far away for Audrah to see him clearly, but something about him reminded her of someone she once knew. She had no desire to go down to the lake and have her fantasy shattered, for he looked so very like him that she wanted to savour the image for a moment.

He, and what had become of him, had cost her a very great deal, and it was time to let go. Time to stop the constant hunt for something that couldn't be found, for a voice that would never be heard, a face that would never be seen, and a mystery that, in all probability, would never now be solved.

2

Late October was no time to be driving across the moors, but Tate didn't have much option. Police business had brought him to Lyndle, deep in the heart of Northumbria's National Park.

The sky above, though overcast, was currently keeping its cargo under wraps. But it wouldn't hold back for long. Over the past few days, flurries of snow had fallen intermittently. Soon it would start in earnest, and he wanted to be off the moors by the time it came.

Even so, when he reached a low stone wall at the top of a crag he stopped the car. Then he sat there for a moment, debating the wisdom of what he proposed to do. Those who miscalculated the risks sometimes died out here, their bodies found a few hundred yards from cars that were stuck in snow.

The events leading up to their deaths followed much the same pattern: engines were kept ticking over to keep the heater going; but after the petrol ran out, the temperature inside the vehicle plummeted.

People who were dying of hypothermia became confused. It was then that they tended to leave their vehicles and wander on to the moors, only to collapse, sink into a coma and die. Tate had no intention of being one of them.

He got out of the car, struggled into the kind of outdoor gear that was the choice of the professional, then reached into the back for a rucksack. In it were a survival blanket, maps, compass, chocolate, flares, a torch, matches, a candle, a mobile phone and a first-aid kit. As an added precaution, he'd made sure there was at least one person who knew where he was going. That person was Detective Sergeant Fletcher. Like Tate, he was a voluntary member of Northumbria's Mountain and

Moorland Rescue Service. It formed a bond between them. *If I'm not back by six, and if I don't phone to say what's keeping me, I expect you to come looking—*

He slipped his arms through the slings, then walked towards the low stone wall that divided him from a drop of two hundred feet. Beyond it was one of the most spectacular views in Northumberland. But Tate wasn't there to look at the view. Not today.

A gap in the wall led to a path fenced in such a way as to stop kids from squeezing through and plunging to their deaths. It zigzagged down the crag and came out at the foot of a forest of pines. None of the trees were growing as they should. They were planted too close together, and because the light and air that sustained them was at a premium, some were almost entirely without foliage. They had, however, grown tall and fast in their fight for life, and the end result was a crop of telegraph poles.

A road wide enough for lumber wagons dictated the way, and he followed it until he left the pines. They had sheltered him from the wind, but the minute he left them he jammed a pair of goggles over his eyes. Although they gave some protection, they dimmed the world around him, and he found the effect both depressing and unnerving.

A short while later, he was walking down a slope to the valley floor. Below him, ancient woodland spread away to the north, the trees that comprised it as densely packed as the pines.

He knew this woodland existed, but until very recently he hadn't known there was a house down there, largely because it wasn't visible from the road. But it was listed, and as recently as fifty years ago the architectural historian Bischel had mentioned it in a letter to a colleague. Some days ago, an excerpt had appeared in the press:

Despite that it has a moat, Lyndle cannot be classified a castle. It is, in fact, the earliest known example of a medieval English manor house. I wished to see it but, access from the road having been denied me, I approached it from a village on the other side of the wood. It was derelict, the cottages abandoned, but behind them was a sunken road that once linked the Hall to the village.

The trees now towered above me, their branches entwined and blocking out the light, but just as I began to fear that perhaps I'd lost my bearings, she rose up out of the waters of the moat . . .

Tate took the same route as Bischel until he came to the track that ran through the wood. There would once have been a time when it was wide enough for livestock, but over the years it had narrowed with neglect. Centuries of use had worn it to a depth of several feet, and it now resembled a ditch as much as anything, water having collected at the bottom. Bischel had made no mention of the water, but he came in summer. This was winter. Even so, Tate felt he had the advantage, because Bischel had come upon the house quite suddenly, whereas he could see it taking shape through the trees.

For quite some time, he stood at the edge of the wood, just looking at Lyndle, because this was what Bischel had done, and he wanted to compare his own impression with that of a man regarded as one of the great authorities on England's historic houses.

My friend, it was an obscenity, an offence to all that is right, and good, and clean. And yet it was possessed of a sinister beauty.

A sinister beauty. Tate hadn't known what he meant by that until now.

Bischel had mentioned lawns that were 'meticulously kept', but these were gone. All that remained were undulating meadows dividing the house from the trees. He walked across them, making for a bridge that spanned the moat. It led through an arch to the courtyard. Then the solid oak doors of Lyndle's Great Hall stood before him.

The wings to either side were built of the same black stone, their windows high and plain, many of them broken. But hard times, or perhaps just the fashion of the times, dictated that the wing behind him should differ. Its walls were wattle and daub around a solid timber frame. For this reason alone, it had fared less well than the rest of the property. The glass had long since fallen from its delicate latticed windows, and it leaned towards the moat, its great wooden beams having warped beyond redemption.

This was what happened to this kind of construction. The frames began to poke through the skin like bones. One day there would be nothing left to show for it. But the Hall itself would stand for another thousand years. The roof would go, and lichen would cover the walls. But the walls would remain.

No point knocking on those great oak doors. No point calling out. He had no intention of allowing whoever was in that house the satisfaction of knowing he had failed to make them answer. Better to let them realise that he could bide his time.

In the last half-hour, a warning tinge of purple had come to the sky. Tate knew what it signified. He took a last look round, then started to head back.

By the time he reached the car, snowploughs were coming out of the darkness, their headlights casting a dim yellow light on the road. He used the remote to open the central lock, and felt a stab of apprehension when the indicators flashed but the locks stayed frozen. He tried again, and this time he heard the welcome snick; then he opened the door, pulled out his shoes, and kicked off his boots.

He wasn't quite sure at exactly what point he began to feel he was being watched, but it wasn't unusual to feel you were being watched up here. It had something to do with the loneliness of the place, the certainty that at any moment anything might happen.

He picked up his boots, then slung them in the back. And as he turned round . . .

. . . someone was standing a matter of feet away, the hood of his coat throwing his face into shadow.

Over the years, Tate had dealt with any number of villains,

and his first reaction was to wonder whether this was someone who had deliberately set out to find him in as lonely, as remote a place as possible. If so, then they'd picked the right place. At this time of year, fewer than two cars an hour passed this way.

'Detective Inspector Tate?' he said, and the fact that he knew his name increased Tate's conviction that this was some face from the past. When he reached into a pocket, Tate took a step back, but he didn't pull a gun. What he pulled was a business card. 'John Cranmer,' he said.

Tate knew the name. Over the past few days, Cranmer had tried to contact him at the station, claiming to have information about the situation at Lyndle. He would have returned the calls if not for the fact that the copper who passed him the messages said, 'I wouldn't hold your breath . . . he say's he's psychic.'

Cranmer was persistent. When Tate didn't call him back, he phoned every hour, on the hour, until he got a warning. He was a nutter. Not that the realisation did anything to lessen Tate's unease. It was a relief to know he wasn't about to be shot by some face from the past, but it was wisest, for the moment at least, to regard him as potentially dangerous.

'You didn't return my calls.'

'I'm a busy man.'

'Well,' said Cranmer, 'now that you've put me to the trouble of finding a way to attract your attention, the least you can do is take my card.'

He held it out again, but Tate wasn't about to risk getting too close to him, and when Cranmer realised he had no intention of taking it, he walked over to the car and pinned it under a wiper. 'It gives the name and number of someone who can vouch for me,' he said. Then he turned away, and melted into the darkness.

Tate stared after him. And within a matter of moments he found it hard to believe he'd ever been there. He stayed where he was for maybe thirty seconds, then pulled the card from the wiper and got in the car, locking all four doors with the central lock.

The experience had shaken him, because although there was no violence involved, the seriousness of what had just happened couldn't be underestimated. Cranmer must have followed him when he left the station that morning. Either that, or he'd found out what his movements would be that day. And if he'd gone to the trouble of finding out what his movements were going to be, who was to say he hadn't also found out where he lived?

His home on the outskirts of Hexham was less than an hour's drive away. What if Cranmer was heading for his house . . .

Tate used his mobile to phone the station and ask for a patrol to be sent to his home. He then phoned his wife and told her what had happened.

'Where are the kids?' he said.

June was a calm, intelligent woman who taught in the local school. She wasn't given to panicking, but she didn't like the idea that someone had followed her husband on to the moors any more than he did. 'Becky's in her bedroom, finishing her homework. Steven's on the Play Station.'

'Bring them downstairs,' said Tate. 'Keep them with you until I get home. And try not to worry too much. Any minute now, you'll have two whacking great coppers dripping snow on to the kitchen floor. They'll stay with you until I get back.'

Tate disconnected and fired the engine, but he didn't pull away immediately. He turned on the overhead light and read what was on the card. On the front, it bore the emblem of the Los Angeles Police Department and the name 'Lieutenant George Iwanowski'. On the back Cranmer had scrawled his name. Beneath it, he had written 'The Grange Hotel, Hexham'.

The Grange was one of Hexham's better hotels, but Tate doubted that was Cranmer's reason for booking in to it. It was almost directly opposite the police station.

He did a three-point turn and headed in the direction Cranmer had taken as he melted into the darkness. There was no sign of him, or of a car.

It had taken a few minutes to phone June and the station. If Cranmer was parked up ahead, those few minutes would have been enough to give him a good start. Not that it mattered. He had no intention of trying to catch up with him. This was a B road that wound its snakelike way through rocky outcrops, and it was dangerous enough at the best of times. Besides, he had plans for Cranmer, and none of them included confronting him out here.

When he reached the station, he got hold of Fletcher, who assured him he hadn't told anyone what his movements would be that day. Tate had thought as much, but to have it confirmed was a relief. And although it didn't explain how Cranmer knew where to find him, that wasn't insurmountable: Tate intended to bring him in, and get it out of him.

Fletcher had the deceptively lazy eyes of a mountain lion. He yawned, and said, 'Where is he?'

'He's staying at The Grange.'

'Millionaire, then, is he?'

'He'd have to be,' said Tate.

The Grange catered for people who wanted gourmet food and an Elizabethan four-poster at the end of a day spent slogging up and down Hadrian's Wall. At this time of year, it operated on a reduced scale, but it was still the best place to stay for miles around.

He decided to phone to check that Cranmer was in fact staying there before turning up in reception and embarrassing the owners. Fletcher, at thirty-three, could just about pass for something other than a copper. Tate, at forty-four, tended to wear suits, or the kind of casual walking gear that didn't look out of place down the local pub. But he still looked like a copper. And the owners of The Grange wouldn't welcome a visit from the police without good reason. They didn't get the kind of guest that warranted that kind of embarrassment.

The receptionist checked the register and confirmed that Cranmer booked in five days ago.

'Is he around?' said Tate, and she said she'd try his room.

Moments later, Cranmer picked up the phone, which told Tate all he needed to know.

He cut the connection, then flipped the business card over. Coppers carried business cards, same as anyone else. They came in very handy. *If you think of anything, love, just give me a ring.*

He had no idea whether or not it was genuine. It looked it, but that meant nothing. Cranmer could have had it printed up. There was only one way to find out, and that was to phone the number, so he dialled it.

A few moments later, a mechanical voice told him he was being put through to Lieutenant Iwanowski's voice mail, but that if he needed to speak to someone urgently, he should dial another number . . .

Tate was surprised to find that Iwanowski existed. But the fact that there was a Lieutenant Iwanowski serving with the LAPD meant nothing. It didn't prove that he'd given his card to Cranmer, or that he'd be able to tell him anything about him when they spoke.

Tate would have preferred to have talked to Iwanowski before pulling Cranmer in, but since he wasn't there it looked as though it was going to have to wait. He left a message asking Iwanowski to return his call, then disconnected. 'Let's go see what Cranmer has to say for himself,' he said, then he and Fletcher left the station together.

3

Tate and Fletcher walked into The Grange, showed their IDs to the girl on reception, and asked her to put a call through to Cranmer's room.

'Don't let him know there are police down here wanting to speak to him,' said Tate. 'Just ask him to come down to resolve some minor query on his account. We'll do the rest.'

When he realised she wasn't listening, but was looking beyond them, Tate turned round to face a couple of sofas arranged around a coffee table. As he did so, someone rose from one of them and approached him.

'Inspector Tate,' he said. He held out his hand. 'John Cranmer—'

Back on the moors, Tate's impression had been that Cranmer was big. He was now obliged to reconsider, because Cranmer wasn't as big as he'd first thought. He was maybe five foot ten or eleven, no more than that, and his strong facial features, his solemn, half-hooded eyes, weren't what Tate would have expected to find behind the scarf and hood he was wearing earlier. The clothes he wore now couldn't have been farther removed from the mountaineering gear that had made him seem twice the size and concealed his features so effectively. Now, he was dressed in a slate-grey suit and cashmere turtleneck jumper. The belt was Italian leather, a darker grey than the suit, and the shoes were a match for the belt. They looked hand made.

When Tate ignored his offer to shake hands, Cranmer withdrew it, and said, 'Let me guess – you'd like a word about what happened earlier?'

The accent was that of someone who had been privately

educated, but there was the suggestion that Cranmer might have lived in the States for a while. It would fit, because he looked American. The clothes, the grooming, even the mannerisms. It was going to be interesting finding out what a man like this was doing in Northumberland.

Cranmer nodded towards a doorway that opened out on to a well-stocked bar. 'Why don't we find a quiet corner.'

'There are plenty of quiet corners down the station,' Tate replied.

Cranmer smiled. 'Whatever you prefer—'

He grabbed a coat that was draped on the back of a sofa, put it on over the suit and arranged a cashmere scarf around his neck. Fletcher watched him do these things as if he were some exotic animal preening itself. Like most men born and bred in Newcastle, he seemed almost impervious to the cold. He wore little more than a jacket over a short-sleeved T-shirt and jeans. No gloves. No scarf. No interest in the fact that, outside, snow was beginning to fall in flakes the size of a fist.

He held the door for Cranmer, and as Tate followed both men through and on to the street, he glanced back at the hotel. It wasn't large by modern standards. There were maybe twenty rooms, half of them at the back. The rooms at the front looked out on to a row of shops. They were divided from the station by a side road, and although it wasn't possible for anyone in the hotel to see into the station, it had long been a cause for concern that the station's main entrance was exposed to the kind of place that would enable a villain to sit at one of those windows with a semi-automatic, waiting for their favourite copper to emerge.

He pictured Cranmer sitting in one of those rooms and watching out for him. Not that it would have been likely to pay off. He rarely used the main entrance. He used it now, however, and as he and Fletcher escorted Cranmer in, Tate was surprised by how calm he seemed to be. Most people in his position could have been forgiven for getting a little anxious about what was happening. Cranmer didn't look anxious. He didn't even look particularly put out.

They led him down a flight of concrete stairs to an interview room adjacent to the cells. It stank of disinfectant, because earlier in the day someone had pissed on the floor in protest at being charged with aggravated burglary. There was no heating to speak of. No window. Just a table, two chairs and a dent in the wall where the piss artist tried to escape by jumping through it.

'Make yourself at home,' said Tate, nodding in the direction of one of the chairs.

Fletcher closed the door, then leaned against it as Cranmer sat down, the table between them, its legs bolted to the concrete floor.

'Well,' said Tate. 'Now that you've got my attention, perhaps you'd like to tell me what you were playing at.'

'Look,' said Cranmer. 'What I did today was out of order, but you gave me no choice. I kept leaving messages. You didn't return my calls.'

'Where are you from?' said Tate.

'Originally?'

'It's a start.'

'Home Counties.'

'That doesn't answer my question.'

'I'm not sure there *is* an answer – I've moved around a lot.'

The character who had pissed on the floor earlier in the day was currently down in the cells, no doubt pissing on his bunk. If he didn't watch out, Cranmer, in his Italian suit, would find himself keeping him company. 'If you want to spend the night in the cells, you just carry on—'

'I'm merely trying to answer your questions honestly.'

'Where do you live?' said Tate.

'States.'

'How long have you lived there?'

'Almost twelve years.'

'Why the States?'

'I was invited to take part in certain experiments.'

'Who by?'

'The US government.'

The guy was a fantasist. 'Where's your passport?'

Cranmer pulled it out of his pocket. Tate flicked through. It had been renewed within the past five years, but what information there was suggested that Cranmer lived in the US but travelled extensively throughout Europe.

'You lead a busy life.'

'Then that makes two of us,' said Cranmer. 'And you probably don't like your time being wasted any more than I do, which was why I stopped trying to phone you and started trying to find you.'

Fletcher smiled and lowered his eyes as Tate weighed Cranmer up. On the one hand, what he'd done was outrageous. On the other, he didn't come across as a crank. He sounded plausible, well educated and, above all, calm, as if he might be accustomed to dealing with the police.

'You say the US government invited you to take part in certain experiments. What kind of experiments?'

Cranmer looked down at the desk, his eyes passing over the scratches and burn marks that marred its surface, and finally coming to rest on Tate's drumming fingers. 'Have you ever heard of people who can project their astral selves to places they can't access physically?'

Fletcher had to stifle another smile.

'It's a gift,' said Cranmer. 'The US military asked me to go to the Gulf to penetrate a building, then report back on whether it was a hospital or a military depot.'

This particular room had witnessed the telling of some extraordinarily tall stories over the years, and it looked as though this one was going to be particularly memorable. But as far as Tate was concerned, the most interesting thing about what Cranmer was saying was the *way* he said it. He sounded so sane. 'Let's forget about the Gulf for a minute,' said Tate. 'Because what I want to know is, what are you doing here, and why are you following me around?'

'I flew in from the States specifically to help you.'

'What with?'

'The investigation.'

'What investigation?'

'Lyndle.'

'What's your interest in Lyndle?'

'I was walking through the wood—'

'When?'

'A while ago. But I didn't know where I was until I read about it.'

'What do you mean – you didn't know where you were?'

Cranmer replied, 'I mean I was there, but not physically. I projected myself.'

Tate was tempted to do a little projecting of his own, but before he could tell Cranmer what he thought his immediate future might be, a uniform entered to tell him someone from Los Angeles was trying to get hold of him. It sounded important.

Tate hadn't taken his eyes off Cranmer. He did so now. 'I'll take it in my office,' he said.

When he reached his office, Tate pushed the door closed with his foot and lifted the receiver. No Iwanowski. Nothing. Just a dead line.

He replaced the receiver, and as he waited for the call to be put through, he took stock of the situation. He still wasn't sure whether or not Cranmer was actually worth worrying about. He hoped it would turn out that he just happened to get a kick out of tracking people who, in the ordinary way of things, were more difficult to find than the average person owing to the degree of security that normally surrounded their activities. If so, then the act of successfully tracking a senior copper and coming out of the dark at him might have been an end in itself. He hoped so.

His eyes strayed from the telephone to the papers on his desk. Among them was a file relating to Ginny Mulholland, a girl of eighteen who had worked at Lyndle Hall for part of the summer. He pulled the file towards him and opened it. In it were the usual statements and reports. There was also yet another message relating to Cranmer. It stated that, at 11.17 a.m. that morning, Cranmer walked into the station asking to be allowed to speak to him. The desk sergeant explained that Tate wasn't available, and offered to let him speak to somebody else. Cranmer declined, and left.

None of the previous messages had worried Tate as such, but this was different, because at 11.17 a.m. Tate had been on his way to Durham to talk to Ginny's father. If Cranmer walked into the station when he was on his way to Durham, it meant he couldn't have followed him. And that just didn't make sense.

The phone rang out and he snatched the receiver from the hook. 'Tate,' he said.

Iwanowski answered with: 'You left a message on my voice mail.'

'Thanks for returning my call.'

'What's the problem?'

'John Cranmer,' said Tate. 'Does the name mean anything to you?'

Iwanowski confirmed that he knew Cranmer.

'Tell me about him,' said Tate.

'Where you want me to start?'

'How do you know him?'

Iwanowski replied, 'Some years ago, he walked into the station claiming to have information about a woman who'd been missing for several months. He told us she was dead. Then he studied a map in my office, drew a circle around a particular area, and told us we'd find her body in that vicinity. We looked. We found it. What can I say?'

After a moment, Tate replied, 'If someone walked up to me with a yarn like that, I'd have been inclined to suspect they had something to do with how the body came to be there.'

'The thought occurred to us, believe me.'

'Where was it?'

'In a canyon,' said Iwanowski. 'Turned out her car had spun off the road.'

'How come it hadn't been found?'

'It was hidden by trees. Invisible from the air. And it couldn't be seen from the road. If not for Cranmer . . . well, I doubt we'd have found her.'

Tate had no way of knowing whether or not his picture of Iwanowski was accurate, but he saw him as big, straight talking, and not at all the kind of man who was likely to have much time for people who claimed to be psychic. Which only went to prove how wrong you could be, because Iwanowski was full of it:

'Look,' he said, 'there are plenty of people prepared to vouch for Cranmer. I could give you names – but what would be the point? You have to experience the guy for yourself, and make up your own mind. What do you have to lose?'

Tate could think of any number of things he might have to lose, like credibility, like the respect of his peers, like his chances of future promotion. 'I didn't call to find out whether or not you think Cranmer is genuinely psychic,' said Tate. 'I'm more concerned with whether or not he's ever been known to pose a threat to anyone.'

'A *threat*—' Iwanowski sounded incredulous. 'What's he done to make you think he's a threat?'

Tate wasn't about to tell him what had happened earlier, and when Iwanowski sensed his reluctance, he added:

'What's it all about? I mean, what's your interest in Cranmer?'

As far as Tate was concerned, it was more a question of what Cranmer's interest was in *him*. Or more to the point, what his interest was in the missing Ginny Mulholland.

Prior to stopping off to take a look at Lyndle Hall, Tate had spent the morning at a small brick cottage in Durham. It was within walking distance of the university, where Ginny's father had lectured for the best part of thirty years. He invited Tate into a small, book-cluttered room, and told him what he'd told the less senior police officers who had come before him. 'Ginny is missing.'

By the time Mr Mulholland reported his daughter missing, Ginny had been gone for three weeks.

'What took you so long?'

'I didn't want to be seen to be making a fuss. And Mrs Herrol kept telling me that was what I would be doing if I involved the police.'

Tate decided to take it from the top and find out how Ginny came to be at Lyndle in the first place. She was eighteen. She'd left sixth-form college the previous June, and she'd gone to an open day at Durham University, where she hoped to read politics. Her father said:

'Mrs Herrol's son, Nicholas, is also reading politics apparently. He was given the job of showing a group of prospective students round the campus. Ginny was one of the group. She mentioned she needed a summer job, and he had a word with his mother.'

At that point, Tate had yet to see Lyndle for himself, otherwise he would undoubtedly have asked what could have possessed a girl like Ginny to accept a job in a place described by Bischel as 'an obscenity'. As it was, he merely wondered what made her opt for Durham. It was, of course, one of the top five universities, but it was also on her doorstep, and in his experience most young people couldn't wait to put as much distance between them and their parents as they could possibly manage. Nothing personal. Not usually, at any rate. It was more to do with the psychology of making the break from home, of striking out as a young adult in their own right.

'Why Durham?' he said, and Mr Mulholland replied:

'There were certain practical considerations. We live quite close to the campus, and it was essential for her to keep her expenses down.'

Nothing unusual there. Since grants had been abolished, more and more people were opting to live at home for the duration of their course. It struck Tate as a fairly sensible option, and then he looked around him. This small brick cottage with its scholarly artefacts and academic reference works was hardly the kind of place a girl of eighteen would want to bring her friends to. No television, he noticed. Just an unobtrusive radio.

'I didn't pressure her to carry on living at home,' said her father. 'It was what she wanted.'

Tate wondered about that. When daughters had sensitive, elderly fathers, they sometimes found it difficult to tell them they wanted to leave home and live their own, preferably sexual, lives. And Ginny and her father were very close. So close, in fact, that they phoned one another on an almost daily basis, so when, at the beginning of September, three days went by without him hearing from his daughter, Ginny's father started to grow concerned. 'What did you do?' said Tate.

'Initially, I phoned Mrs Herrol and asked if she could let Ginny know I'd called. She said she'd be delighted to, if only she knew where she was. But she hadn't seen her for the past three days, and nor did she expect to, because she appeared to have taken off with her husband.'

In the light of what he'd been told, Ginny's father hadn't known what to do. He couldn't imagine his daughter running off with a married man. And then he reminded himself that Ginny was no longer a child. 'It was perfectly possible that she and this woman's husband were having an affair. I couldn't condone it, but there it was. I had to face the facts.'

'And how long did it take before you did anything further?'

'I gave it a couple of weeks. She was, after all, due to start at Durham on September the fifteenth. I thought she was *bound* to come home.'

'And when the fifteenth came and went and there was no sign of her, what then?' said Tate.

'I was upset. I felt she'd let me down, not only in the moral sense, you understand, but academically. I couldn't believe she was so besotted with this man that she was prepared to throw away her entire future.'

26

At that point, he explained, he placed an ad in the local paper asking Ginny to get in touch. It was a mistake. A journalist phoned, offering to help. 'With hindsight, I realise he simply scented a story, and I, like a fool, unwittingly gave him one.'

Tate made a note of the journalist's name.

'He asked if I could let him have a photograph of Ginny, so I let him pick one out from the family album.'

Tate knew the photo he was referring to. He'd seen it plastered all over the tabloid press.

'At the time, I couldn't understand what made him choose that particular photograph. It's never been a favourite of mine. It was so *unlike* her, if you understand me.'

Tate understood perfectly. The journalist chose a photo in which Ginny was wearing skin-tight jeans and too much make-up. It had been taken a few years earlier when she and some friends were fooling around. Everything about it was completely over the top, from the ultra-glossy lipstick to the provocative, buttock-thrusting pose. It was the perfect photo for a headline that ran 'Local Toff Runs Off with Girl Half his Age'.

'I complained to the editor,' said Mr Mulholland. 'But nothing was done.'

No surprises there. 'What did Mrs Herrol have to say?'

'She was angry. She asked whether I intended to make a habit of dragging her family name through the mud. I hardly knew what to say. I could only apologise.'

Tate felt desperately sorry for him. He was old, and he was worried, and some reporter had taken complete advantage.

'The worst of it was that Ginny didn't respond, yet she must have read the article. She couldn't have missed it. Surely?'

Maybe. Maybe not. It was surprising what people could miss, just as it was surprising what they could pick up.

'It was then that I started to feel that something might have happened to her, so I phoned Mrs Herrol again. Not that it did much good. She told me I was making a fuss about nothing. After all, her husband was also missing. Surely it was *obvious* they were together.'

Tate was beginning to see why he hadn't automatically called the police.

'She told me Ginny left some of her clothes. I asked her to send them on. They arrived in a cardboard box, and I put it in Ginny's room. But I didn't open it. Not at first. I didn't want to invade her privacy, you see. But as the weeks went by, I started to feel that I really must do something, so I looked through her things – I don't know why. Perhaps I was hoping to find some clue as to where she might be.'

The box contained a couple of pairs of jeans, an old pair of trainers, a novel that looked as though it had been read and discarded. It was likely, even probable, that Ginny left these things because she no longer wanted them. But she also left a bag that was a mass of zips and pockets, and in it he found a letter. It was this that finally prompted him to contact the police, though the letter was hardly new to him as such. It was written by his wife, who died some days after writing it. Mr Mulholland broke down as he handed it to Tate.

Dear Ginny, By the time you are old enough to read this, I will have been dead for many years . . .

'I can imagine that she might have left a few old clothes behind, but she wouldn't have left the only letter her mother ever wrote to her—'

Tate now had a different photograph of Ginny. It was one her father had given him, saying, 'This was the one I tried to persuade the journalist to take. Now, of course, I realise why he preferred the other.'

In it, Ginny was wearing a summer dress, her legs brown, her arms wrapped round the neck of the family dog. She looked like a little girl. Her hair very long. Her smile innocent . . .

Iwanowski brought him back to the present. 'I guess Cranmer must have been in touch with you, otherwise you wouldn't have contacted me.'

'You could say that,' said Tate.

'Where is he?'

Tate replied that he was currently at the station.

28

Iwanowski picked up on something in his tone. Sensing a problem, he said, 'What's he doing there?'

Tate's response was fairly non-committal. 'He seems to think he can help me with a case.'

'What kind of case?'

'I've got a missing person—'

Iwanowski replied, 'If Cranmer is showing an interest, you don't have a missing person.'

Tate waited for it.

'What you have is a homicide,' he said.

4

The carpet was coming away from the floor. Not only the floor, but the wall, as if it were a stale piece of bread, its corners curling inward, to make the bread concave.

The minute Nicholas noticed what was happening to it, he knew it was only a matter of time before the carpet would roll in on itself. It would be like a spring that has expanded and must contract the minute it is released. When it sprang in on itself, such was its size and weight it would act upon him much as the coils of a python might act on its prey. The life would be squeezed out of him. That was the plan of the thing.

When she heard this, Claudia soothed his hair as if he were still a child.

'What makes you think a carpet can possibly kill you?'

'Look at it,' he said.

She offered to nail it down, and then had a better idea. 'Why don't we just get rid of it?' After all, almost every other item that could be removed from the room had been disposed of over the past few weeks; the vast walnut wardrobe, the table, which was ruined now, its surface clawed beyond all hope of repair, the wall lights that had so offended her eyes. The only source of light was the bulb above their heads, the shade dispensed with in case a use could be found for the wire. Even the curtains were gone, for only a matter of days ago she found them torn to shreds. Strips of them were wound around his throat as he lay sleeping.

All that remained was the bed, and between them they dismantled it, then dragged the headboard and frame out on to the landing. Something had fallen out as it was dismantled. A Roman coin. Immediately, the years rolled back, and Claudia remembered the fuss that was made when it was lost.

Nicholas came running in here to show his father the coin, but Francis said, 'I'm afraid you're not allowed that, old chap. It's rather valuable.'

There were a number of similar coins in a display case in the study. He kept it locked as a rule. 'I thought Daddy told you not to touch the things in the glass-topped box.'

'But it wasn't in the box. It was in my room.'

Francis said, 'No fibs, young man. People who fib grow long wooden noses.' And then, as was so typical of him, he relented and let him play with it, intending to put it back later. But the coin was never returned, because Nicholas dropped it. She and Francis searched the entire room, but couldn't find it.

'Perhaps your friend borrowed it?' said Claudia, for this was in the days when they treated the subject of his imaginary friend quite lightly. After all, it wasn't uncommon for children who had no siblings to invent an imaginary friend. Nor was it uncommon for the child to chat away to them. But something about this particular friend . . .

She spoke to her doctor about it, and borrowed books from the library. There was quite a lot of literature relating to the subject, and that in itself was reassuring. It meant that it was *normal*.

According to books devoted to the subject of raising children, imaginary friends were usually much the same age as the child, and this in itself performed a recognised function in that child's development. If asked, the child could often describe their friend in detail, and not only could this prove amusing, but it could give an insight into whether or not the child was developing normally. Parents were therefore advised to ask their child to describe this imaginary being.

'What's his name?' said Claudia.

'It isn't a *he*,' said Nicholas.

'*Her* name, then.'

'It isn't a *she*, either.'

'What is it, then?'

'Don't know.'

Claudia took an even greater interest. 'What does it look like?'

'Which part of it?'

'Its face.'

'It doesn't have a face.'

She grew uneasy. 'Does it wear clothes?'

'Of course it wears clothes.'

'And what are they like, these clothes?'

'Like cobweb, only they're dirty.'

Initially, Francis said she was making a fuss about nothing, but after he spoke to Nicholas himself, he shared her concern. 'What do you do together?'

'Nothing.'

'You must do *something*, Nicholas. Friends don't just sit around doing nothing all day, not unless they're very, very old, and very, very boring.'

'We talk.'

'What about?'

'Nothing.'

Francis was getting sick of this. 'Now look here, Nicholas – you must talk about something.'

Nicholas capitulated. 'All right, then,' he said. 'It tells me things.'

'What kind of things?' said Francis.

Nicholas had turned to him, all of six years old. *It tells me things I never wanted to know—*

5

When he realised Nicholas Herrol was instrumental in bringing Ginny to Lyndle, Tate tried to contact him. There was a phone at the house, but it was never answered. However, if he couldn't get to Nicholas, he could at least question someone who knew him, and he went back to Durham to talk to one of his tutors, Graham Lush.

Lush had given directions to an apartment in a former warehouse, the brick and cast-iron columns a feature of the open-plan design. Consequently, Tate was now sitting on a sofa shaped like a wave. It was carved from solid wood, and appeared to be the only piece of furniture in a room that measured roughly sixty by forty feet. The bed, he decided, was probably a mat on a sheet of glass suspended from the ceiling. 'Lived here long?' he said.

Lush replied, 'Three months.'

'Must be quite a novelty.'

'My wife seems to think so. She left me.'

'Before or after the move?'

Lush smiled. 'I think it was on the cards before I suggested we sell the boring little house and move somewhere a little more . . . challenging.'

He looked like a man who might enjoy explaining, at length, that the apartment wasn't so much a living space as a political statement. Tate wasn't there to talk political statements. 'Nicholas Herrol is one of your students.'

'What about him?'

'What can you tell me about him?'

'What do you want to know?'

There were plenty of things Tate wanted to know, such as

whether Nicholas got on all right with the other students. Was he a bit of a loner? Did he have a girlfriend? Was he gay? Nicholas was reading politics. Presumably the subject interested him, so what political groups did he belong to? Did he ever talk about Lyndle or his parents? What was he like to deal with? *Dozens* of questions – all designed to enable Tate to build a picture of him. For the moment, however, he settled for asking what had made him take a year out of college.

'I'm not sure I can answer that.'

Tate didn't know whether Lush was implying that he couldn't be expected to break some rule relating to confidentiality, or whether he meant he didn't actually know.

'Whose decision was it – his, or the university's?'

'As I said a moment ago, I'm not sure I can answer that.'

Tate had had enough of the wooden sofa. He went to the window and watched workmen positioning a girder in the warehouse opposite. A canal divided the two buildings, a restored coal barge moored by a lock, the words 'Long Boat Café' picked out in enamel on its side. 'I've got a missing girl,' said Tate. 'I think she's dead. So I'll ask you again, Mr Lush. What can you tell me about Nicholas Herrol?'

The press was full of Ginny's disappearance, and Lush must have known the police suspected she was dead, but to have it put to him bluntly produced the desired result. He struggled with his conscience for a moment, and lost: 'I tried to get him off the course altogether. Unfortunately, the best I could do was force him to take a year off. Needless to say, I'm rather hoping he won't come back.'

Tate still had his back to Lush. 'There must be official reports, some record of the problems—'

Maybe Lush hadn't lived in the apartment long enough to have grown accustomed to losing the clutter of small round tables. Whatever the case, he looked for somewhere to put his empty mug, and when he failed to find a suitable surface, he put it on the floor. Then he walked behind a sheet of frosted glass that was hanging from the ceiling and served as a room divider.

A steel filing cabinet stood behind it, its outlines blurred by the glass.

It occurred to Tate that this must be what it was like for those whose view of the world was distorted by cataracts. He blinked, as if expecting the image to clear as Lush opened the filing cabinet, pulled out a file, and drew a report from it.

After he came out from behind the glass, he handed it to Tate. It was marked 'confidential'. 'Nicholas was obsessed with one of the female students – Sylvie Straker. I think you should have a word with her.'

'Where is she?'

'Manchester.'

Term had started over a month ago. 'What's she doing there?'

'Recovering,' said Lush. 'I'll give you her address.'

Four hours later, Tate was standing on a patio at the back of a small, neat bungalow in Manchester. Mrs Straker stood next to him, lighting a cigarette. 'Gave up, once,' she said. 'But since all this business with Sylvie—'

The garden was unkempt, a square of threadbare lawn surrounded by overgrown borders. She flicked a match on to the lawn and added, 'I always knew we'd hear something more about Lyndle.'

Tate assumed she was referring to recent media coverage of the investigation into Ginny's disappearance. He let her go on:

'We were expecting Sylvie to come home for the Easter holidays. But she phoned us to say she'd been invited to spend the weekend with some boy she'd met at college. We'd never heard her mention him before. But when she said his family had a manor house, well, to be honest, I thought she'd dropped lucky. He sounded . . . .' She hesitated over the words, then spat them out. 'Well off.' She smiled. 'Good luck to her, I thought. God knows, I've worked hard enough all my life. Wish I'd met a wealthy feller at her age.'

She went indoors for a moment, leaving Tate on the patio. A short time later, she returned with a photograph of a girl in khaki shorts, her hands thrust into the pockets, her smile broad and casual. 'Whenever I show people this, they say, "Your daughter looks so full of life, so full of confidence."' She suddenly looked dangerously close to tears. 'Looking at her now, you wouldn't know her for the same girl.'

Tate had yet to meet her. He said, 'Something obviously happened that weekend.'

Mrs Straker replied, 'First night she was there, we got a phone call. Hysterical. *Come and get me.*' She took another pull at the cigarette, blew out the smoke and added, 'Middle of the night, but Peter jumped in the car. Took him hours to get there. Sylvie had got away from the house. She was waiting for her dad at the top of the drive.' Mrs Straker extinguished the cigarette by pinching it in her fingers, then threw it on to the patio. 'She was . . . *terrified*.'

'What frightened her?'

Mrs Straker laughed to herself as a breeze snatched the stub and sent it skittering into the bushes. 'If we knew that, we'd be halfway to knowing how to help her. That's what the doctor says. Not sure I believe it.'

'I'd like to talk to her, if that's okay.'

She nodded in the direction of Sylvie's bedroom. 'Can't guarantee you'll get much out of her.'

'I'd like to try,' said Tate.

She led the way to Sylvie's room. It was north facing and cold, the heating inadequate, and Sylvie sat on the edge of her bed, a blanket across her knees. She bore no resemblance whatever to the girl in the photo. Her skin had lost that sun-kissed look and her eyes were dull in a way that suggested she was taking tranquillisers.

She knew why he was there. She'd been told that a girl who worked at Lyndle over the summer was missing, but within minutes of starting to talk to her, Tate realised she had no intention of answering his questions. He also realised she wasn't being difficult for the sake of it. She was frightened. 'I want you to go.'

Tate asked why.

'It might find out you're here.'

'What might find out?'

'And it isn't a good thing to talk about it.'

'Talk about what?' said Tate.

Sylvie Straker looked at Tate properly for the first time since he'd walked into the room. 'It bites him,' she said. And then she began to cry.

6

The last time Marion Thomas dialled Tessa's number, the phone was answered instantly, just as if Tessa were standing there, waiting for it to ring.

Tonight would be no different. Perhaps, earlier in the evening, Tessa spoke to Alex and said, *I'll bet you any money Marion phones tonight*, and perhaps the family held a meeting to decide whose turn it was to try to get rid of her.

If so, Sasha might have argued that, as she was the person Marion wanted to speak to, she ought to be the one to take the call, but since the entire family was united in their determination to protect her, it seemed unlikely they would allow Sasha to martyr herself, which only left Alex or Tessa.

They probably pictured her meandering round that cold little house in Bristol like some lost, demented soul, or perhaps they would draw a comparison with the demon they felt she had become. Whatever the case, at some stage Tessa might well announce that if anyone should answer the phone, it ought to be her. *After all, we used to be friends, though when I think of it now—*

Best not to ring. Better by far to occupy herself by painting the bathroom. The end result would be an improvement on the green-and-cream confection bestowed by a previous owner, but a combination of lack of funds plus its own meagre proportions would ensure that, despite her best efforts, it would still be a far cry from the bathroom at Tessa's, its walls the colour of ice, the wooden floor a highly polished maple. Its cupboard was stacked with towels, oils and soap. Oatmeal to cleanse the skin. Barley to give it moisture. And wheat for skin that was tired, and dull, and in need of exfoliation.

One of the soaps reminded Marion of a bowl her daughter had given her when a child. Small and delicate, it too was made translucent by tiny grains of rice. And there had been a willow pattern on the paper it was wrapped in. Marion had stolen it. Tessa would never miss it, would never know. She had it still, wrapped in tissue and kept in a drawer in the room that Tessa once accused her of turning into a shrine.

After painting the wall, she washed the brushes, then went to the shrine and sat on her daughter's bed. It was now, at this late hour, that the urge to contact Sasha invariably overwhelmed her, and as she gave in to it she told herself what those addicted to illegal substances as well as to inadvisable patterns of behaviour convince themselves is the truth: *Once more can't hurt. Just this once. Then never again, I swear.*

Even as she dialled the number, she could picture what the family would be doing at this time of night: dinner would be over, and they would be settling down to watch the news in the smallest of three reception rooms in that vast old house of theirs. Alex and Tessa would be sitting on one of two baggy old sofas; and Sasha and Dominic would no doubt be slumped on the other. The fire would be lit, its tongues of orange flame reflected by a solid cherry bookcase, and the curtains would be open, pinned back from Georgian windows that gave a seven-figure view across the Avon. It was worth the money, according to Tessa, for whom the Clifton suspension bridge brought San Francisco to mind.

Anyone happening to glance in on them from outside could have been forgiven for assuming that Tessa, Alex and their offspring epitomised a wealthy, middle-class English family at the turn of the millennium. They would probably scarcely believe that such families could still exist, with their marriages intact, their well-adjusted children – a son for her, a daughter for him, it was all so sickeningly perfect. But what they wouldn't see, and what they wouldn't sense, was that this particular family was afraid to answer the phone, though if they happened to be peering in at the moment it rang they would wonder about the look that passed between them. Marion imagined Sasha mouthing the words, *God – not again*, and could just see Tessa saying, *Let me handle it*.

Tessa lifted the receiver the instant the phone rang out, and when she heard Marion's voice she said, 'Marion, it's late.'

'I know, but I was wondering – could I speak to Sasha?'

She sounded like a jilted lover rather than a woman twice Sasha's age, and not only that but the mother of the girl who, in life, had been Sasha's closest friend.

'I'm afraid she isn't in,' said Tessa.

'I'll call back later.'

'She won't be back tonight.'

It was a lie. It was *always* a lie. 'Tessa – please – I know she's there.'

'Marion—'

'I won't keep her long. I just want to ask her something.'

There was a pause, a gathering of some internal strength, a quiet determination to be rid of her. 'Marion, Alex and I have talked this over, and we feel it's time you left Sasha in peace. I'm sorry if that sounds harsh. We sympathise with you – of course we do – but Sasha has her life to lead, and—'

She stopped right there, appalled by the slip of the tongue, but Marion said nothing. Not a word. She stared straight ahead at a photograph of her daughter. Gordon took it two years ago on Kathryn's sixteenth birthday. Sasha was present when it was taken, but off camera, according to Kathryn, who was lounging against a tree.

Gordon posted the photograph to Kathryn, but no cheque, and Marion got on the phone to him, demanding to know on what grounds he thought it fair to expect her to shoulder the full financial burden of raising their daughter.

His response was to tell her she was a damn sight better off than him – he hadn't come out of the divorce with a mortgage-free house, so what was her problem? And then he'd hung up on her, which was what she suspected Tessa would like to do, but didn't dare. She was still apologising for the dreadful slip of the tongue that resulted in her saying that Sasha had her life to lead, but suddenly – or so it seemed to Marion – the phone was snatched away from her and Alex took over. Desperation had stripped his voice of sympathy, and he came across as business-like, almost severe:

'Marion – Sasha can't cope with you phoning her all the time. She wants it to stop.'

Marion pictured Sasha hovering behind him. At eighteen, she was almost as tall as her father, a slender, leggy girl who was similar in colouring to Kathryn but completely different in physical type. 'She doesn't want to hurt your feelings. But the fact is—'

He stopped, then blurted it out:

'She can't help you, Marion. None of us can. None of us can help you any more. We've done as much as we are able to do. That's it.'

His sudden loss of composure left her speechless.

'Marion – are you there?'

'Yes.' It came out in a whisper.

'We do *feel* for you, you know.'

'Yes.' Another whisper.

'We loved Kathryn too – she was like a daughter to us.'

'Yes.'

And now his tone hardened again as he realised he was losing what little ground had been gained in the past few moments. '*But this has to stop!*'

A plane flew low overhead, its landing gear down, the sound of the engine deafening.

Marion fixed her eyes on the photograph of her daughter, and watched the frame, the glass, the image vibrate. She had been about to tell him that it couldn't stop, that she had to know what, if anything, Kathryn had said to Sasha before she died. But Alex Barclay hung up, which was something he had *never* done before.

She stood by the phone, the line dead, and wondered what was going through his mind. Knowing him as she did, she decided he probably hated himself for what he'd just done, but that he was justifying the action by telling himself that drastic measures were needed if he and his family were to have any hope of clawing some semblance of normality back into their lives.

And what will claw some semblance of normality back into mine? she wondered.

She fought the urge to phone again, but lost, and the phone rang into the small hours without being answered. They had, as she well knew, unplugged it from the wall. She knew because they had done it before, and would no doubt do it again.

She kept on phoning.

7

The manager of the bank led Marion into an office, his attitude echoing Alex's determination to be rid of her as he said, 'Here again, Mrs Thomas? I thought we'd made an agreement that this was to stop.'

'I have to speak to Sasha.'

'She'd rather you didn't bother her at work.'

'What choice do I have? Her parents won't let me talk to her any more.'

'That's a matter for you, and Sasha's parents.'

'I'm not leaving until I've spoken to her.'

'Then it may be the case that I have to call the police.'

'Go ahead,' said Marion.

There was a phone on the desk, but he didn't reach for it.

'What's wrong? Forgotten the number?'

The manager said nothing.

'Shall I dial it for you?' Marion reached out, but before she could lift the receiver, he caved in, as she knew he would: the last thing he wanted to do was risk granting her an opportunity to gain publicity by forcing the police to arrest her. For all he knew, she might have alerted the media to the potential of a scene, in which case his superiors would want to know why he couldn't have found a more diplomatic way to resolve the problem. 'Wait there,' he said, and then he left the office.

A short while later, he reappeared with Sasha trailing behind him like a frightened child. She wouldn't look at Marion. 'Five minutes,' he said before leaving them together. 'You've got five minutes.'

The sombre, navy clothes suited Sasha. Marion told her so, adding, 'You look so grown up these days.'

It was a stupid thing to say to a girl of eighteen, she knew that, but when you had known someone from the day they were born, it was hard to grasp that they were now a young adult. And it was equally difficult for them to lose the childhood habit of referring to you by the name they had always called you by, which was why Sasha said, 'Hello, Mrs Thomas,' rather than 'Hello, Marion'.

She looked tired, and Marion said, 'You look as though you haven't been sleeping properly.' Again, old habits died hard. There was once a time when Marion and Tessa discussed the health and welfare of their respective daughters with an ease born of long friendship. 'Why don't you sit down?'

'I've only got a moment,' said Sasha, who then added something unnecessary, something obvious: 'I'm at work.'

Marion pulled a newspaper clipping out of her bag. 'I tried to phone you last night.'

'I know. Mummy told me.'

The middle-class use of the word *mummy*. How it could grate when used by a girl of eighteen. 'She wouldn't let me speak to you.'

'I had things to do.'

Sasha sat down, pulling out the manager's chair, but looking as though she felt guilty for daring to sit in it. She looked very young, very tired, and Marion suddenly felt for her. What had it been like for her to have spent the past two years trying to tell the mother of her best friend what that best friend's last movements, last words, were? And how very difficult when the mother of that friend kept insisting there had to be more, something significant, something to make the loss a little easier to bear. *She didn't even mention you, Mrs Thomas. I'm sorry – but that's the truth. I'm sure that if she knew she was going to die she would have said something meaningful, but she didn't.*

Marion held out the clipping. 'Take a look at this.'

Sasha's immediate response was, 'If it's about Michael Reeve, I don't want to—'

The minute she mentioned Reeve's name, Sasha seemed to

regret it. She bit her lip like a child, and waited for a reaction, because whenever Reeve's name had been mentioned in the past, Marion had, at best, burst into tears. At worst she ranted and screamed, sometimes publicly, and always to the acute embarrassment of those around her. She could just imagine what was going through Sasha's mind: *I shouldn't have mentioned Reeve. What if she gets hysterical and we have to call the police? What will my manager say if the branch is suddenly filled with paramedics?*

'Please,' said Sasha, 'I didn't mean to bring up . . . anyone's name.'

Am I really as bad as that? Am I so unpredictable, so terrifying, so utterly out of control that people are even frightened to mention his name? 'It's nothing to do with Reeve,' she said, and when she sounded calm the look of relief on Sasha's face was almost pitiful. Marion added: 'It's something else entirely.' Once again, she held out the newspaper clipping. 'It won't bite you,' she said. 'It's only a piece of paper.'

But it wasn't merely a piece of paper, was it? There were words on it, and the words might relate to something Sasha didn't want to read, though God knew there couldn't have been anything, over the years, that she hadn't already read about the events leading up to Kathryn's death. 'Go on. Read it. I can't say why I've come until you do, and I'm not going anywhere until I've said what I came to say.'

There was a subtext to that final comment, an underlying threat. *If you don't read it, I'm not going away.*

When Sasha still wouldn't take it, Marion withdrew it and put it on the desk. Then she broke the silence that followed by saying, 'Have you ever wondered whether it's possible to contact the dead?'

Immediately, she realised how strange it must have sounded, put like that. It wasn't the sort of thing you asked straight out of the blue.

There was something fearful about the way Sasha shook her head. Marion was reminded of a stumbling, terrified cow being

45

prodded through a chute. It was as though she expected, at any moment, Marion to stun her, then cut her throat.

'I realise that must have sounded a bit odd,' admitted Marion. 'It's just that, when I came across this article, I wanted to ask your opinion. That's why I phoned.' She pushed the clipping towards her again, adding, 'It relates to a place in Northumberland – a place called Lyndle Hall.'

Sasha tried to take the 'kind but firm' approach that Tessa and Alex had no doubt recommended, but her voice began to shake as she said: 'I don't know Northumberland, and I've never heard of Lyndle.' Standing up, she added: 'I ought to be getting back—' But Marion cut across her:

'There's been some sort of problem there. The police are investigating the disappearance of a girl who used to work there. A psychic called Cranmer is helping them.'

Sasha said nothing to this, and Marion continued cautiously now. 'They say he can communicate with the dead.'

She hardly dared look at Sasha in case what she saw on her face was amusement, or, even worse, pity. She needn't have worried. What she saw was misery.

'I'm going to Lyndle to ask him to contact Kathryn. Maybe she can tell us something . . . something to help us bring Michael Reeve to justice. That's why I phoned. I was hoping you might . . . come.'

She stole a glance at Sasha, and saw that the look of misery had deepened. It ought to have made her stop, but instead she began to gabble, knowing she was doing it, yet utterly unable to control herself:

'You owe it to Kathryn to come. You were friends from the day you were born.' And then, pathetically: 'She might not speak to me, but she'll speak to you.'

Sasha was weeping now, and Marion was ashamed. The family friend Sasha had trusted as a child was gone for ever. And in her place was a ranting obsessive who phoned her, and followed her, and invaded her place of work. Suddenly, she was disgusted with herself. 'Oh, Sasha,' she said. 'Forgive me.'

Sasha stood up sharply, the chair swivelling away from her and crashing into the wall as she fled from the office. And almost immediately the manager entered, bringing with him two male members of staff. 'I think you'd better leave,' he said, and as Marion picked up her bag, he extended his arm in the direction of the exit. 'And I think it would be best if, in future, you used a different branch when operating your account.'

Two days later, Marion was served with a restraining order drawn up by a solicitor acting on Sasha's behalf. She remembered him as the solicitor that Alex and Tessa first engaged two years ago. Then, however, he was representing Sasha at a time when everyone, including the police, thought it might be possible to obtain sufficient evidence against Reeve to convict him.

The restraining order was intended to prevent her from having any further contact with Sasha – whether in person or by phone.

She tore it up.

8

The concept of writing letters to the dead was nothing new. It gave people an opportunity to say things they felt had been left unsaid and helped them come to terms with their loss. Some might have said that writing such letters contradicted everything Audrah claimed to believe in, but she saw it as therapy, an exercise that served the same function as prayer might serve for those who believe in God.

What she did with the letters tended to vary. Sometimes she buried them. Mostly she burned them and scattered the ashes in places that held some special meaning for her. That morning, she burned the letter, and sealed the ash in an envelope which she folded and put in the pocket of her skiing jacket. Then she left her rooms for the station, where she boarded a train that took her out of Edinburgh.

Less than two hours later, the train pulled in fifteen miles from Furlough, and she was surrounded by some of the most beautiful countryside in Scotland. She, however, was less interested in the landscape than in what it concealed from her. It held a secret, one she had come to accept it intended to keep, for it was now eight years since her husband went missing from here.

His parents lived in a house constructed almost entirely of wood and glass. It should have been filled with light, but what light there was entered by default because, since she lost her son, Eva Sidow had kept the blinds drawn. She hated the view of the mountains and all that they represented, yet she refused to move. Lars had designed the house. To leave would be a betrayal.

It was an effort for her to appear pleased to see Audrah, and she didn't try, but Jochen did what his wife was not prepared to do, and set about trying to make Audrah feel welcome. He offered her tea, and made small talk until Eva lost patience with the whole charade:

'What is she *doing* here?'

'Eva—' said Jochen, wearily.

It was fewer than ten minutes since Audrah had arrived, yet already she was looking for a chance to escape, and she took herself off to the ground-floor cloakroom, leaving them to argue.

Once safely inside, she splashed cold water on her face, then held a towel against it. It smelled of Lars. Impossible, she knew that. But there was no mistaking it. Sometimes, she woke in the night with the scent of him on the sheets. It lingered for a moment, then dissipated as she emerged fully from sleep. It was just a trick played by the subconscious. Coming here had sparked the memory of his smell, along with the recollection that she had stood on this spot when there was nothing more than a few bits of string to mark where the foundations were to be laid. And Lars had stood there with her. *One day, I'll design a house for us.*

She didn't want to return to the room in which Eva was haranguing Jochen in low, bitter tones.

'You did *what*?'

'I suggested she stay for lunch.'

'Have you *no* consideration for my feelings?'

'She's come a long way.'

'That's entirely beside the point.'

It might have been better to write rather than have to go through this, but what Audrah wanted to say was something she felt should be said in person. Besides, she wasn't about to allow Eva to make a coward of her.

The argument stopped when they heard her returning, but when she reached the doorway Eva pushed past her abruptly and left the room.

Once she'd gone, Jochen tried to defend her. 'She doesn't mean it, you know.'

'Doesn't she?'

Jochen didn't answer.

Meals were taken within the confines of a glass-walled balcony. Often, the food was as spectacular as the view. But today, the selection of cold meats and indifferent salad indicated that Eva saw no reason to make an effort. As they seated themselves, she said: 'I don't know whether Jochen mentioned it to you, but Detective Inspector Stafford called on us recently. I dare say you remember him.'

It would be hard to forget a man who suspected she'd murdered her husband.

Eva helped herself to a small piece of ham. She placed it on her plate, and arranged a slice of apple beside it. 'He said you'd been in touch with him.'

'I told him I'm leaving Edinburgh.'

Eva moved the slice of apple a fraction. 'Is that why you're here – to tell us you're moving away?'

'Partly, yes.'

Eva lifted her knife away from the apple. 'I shouldn't have thought it would be necessary for you to come all this way just to tell us you're moving. You could have phoned.'

Jochen spoke quietly, but the anger in his voice was evident. 'Eva,' he said. 'Give Audrah a chance to say what she came to say.'

Eva made a point of putting down her cutlery, then resting her elbows on the table. She linked her fingers under her chin. 'I'm listening,' she said.

Audrah hadn't imagined this would be easy. But neither had she realised just how hostile Eva had become. Perhaps the visit from Stafford reopened old wounds. She glanced at Jochen quickly. He didn't look hostile. Embarrassed, and tired perhaps. But that was all. 'My solicitor thinks it's time we faced the facts.'

'And what facts might those be?'

'There are certain legalities I . . . . . *we* . . . . need to attend to, and in order to do that, we need to have Lars . . .'

Eva's fingers locked together like wire cables. 'Need to have Lars . . . what, exactly?'

'Declared . . . . dead . . .'

She expected an outburst. What she got was sarcasm. 'And how do you propose we do that, when we don't have a body?'

It wasn't necessary to have a body. Eva knew that, just as she knew her son was almost certainly dead. It was of course *possible* he was alive, but it was unlikely. So far as anyone could tell, he had had no reason to disappear. He wasn't in any trouble. He wasn't in debt. And his home and professional life seemed to be in order.

Now came the outburst Audrah had expected. 'This is to do with the house, isn't it! I suppose you think everything he owned automatically becomes yours once my son has officially been declared dead. But I'll fight you, Audrah – every inch of the way for every last item of furniture, and every last penny he owned!'

'Eva—' said Jochen, but his wife had stormed from the table, and Audrah bowed her head, hating her for the fact that she never failed to reduce her to tears.

She looked up, and saw that Jochen was close to tears himself. He reached out and covered her hand with his own. 'Maybe you and I should go for a walk.'

A flight of wooden steps connected the house to a footpath that cut through the copse below. The ground was thick with leaves, the light film of snow a portent of harder weather to come.

She and Jochen walked in silence at first, Audrah barely trusting herself to speak, and Jochen trying to accustom himself to the idea of what she'd proposed. But finally, he said, 'Is it necessary this . . . legal business?'

'Eva's partly right,' said Audrah. 'It is to do with the house, but not the way she thinks.'

The house she and Lars had bought together was currently rented out. Audrah wanted to sell it and buy another. She couldn't do that without a death certificate. There were also issues relating to the policy covering the mortgage, and her lawyer had told her to expect the insurance company to fight her all the way. They might even get dirty about it. It had been known for people to disappear, only to reappear with a different identity once their partner had claimed on the insurance. Even if they didn't fight dirty, they were bound to make life difficult, because the longer they could hang on to the money, the longer they could carry on earning interest on the capital.

After hearing her out, Jochen said: 'I'm not standing in judgment – I just want to know. Have you met someone? Is that what it's about?'

'No, but I hope to one day.' And then: 'How would you feel?'

'Lars has been gone eight years. Dead or not, what right would I, or anyone else, have to disapprove?'

Half an hour later, they stood on a rise of ground, a small stone cairn at their backs. Below them was a sweep of land with a copse, a brook and very little else. In summer, people came here with their children, and the children were allowed to wander where they pleased. No cliffs to fall off. No crevices to fall down. No old mine workings or geological faults to swallow a grown man whole. That Lars could have disappeared from such a place was inconceivable really. It was one of the reasons why Stafford kept asking her whether she was sure she'd remembered the events of that day accurately:

'When he left you, where did he say he was going?'

'Back to the car.'

'What for?'

'Gloves. He'd forgotten his gloves.'

'You're only twenty minutes from the house on foot. Why did you bring the car?'

'We hadn't come from the house, we'd come from Lumsdon.'

'And Lumsdon is . . .'

'About twenty miles away.'

'Why had you gone to Lumsdon?'

'Eva invited a few friends over for dinner. She cooks – really well, I mean. But she'd run out of something essential, and Lumsdon is the only place for miles with a delicatessen.'

'I take it you bought what she needed?'

Audrah couldn't remember, but Eva could. There was a shopping list with the items ticked off. Anchovies, capers and olives.

'And on the way back, you stopped off for a walk. You left the car. And the car was parked . . . where?'

'On the other side of the trees.'

'Could you see it from where you were standing?'

'No.'

Stafford stood where Audrah claimed to have been standing, and he couldn't see a vehicle through the trees either.

'You say Lars disappeared into the trees. Did he come out the other side?'

'I assume so.'

'You don't sound sure.'

'He could have walked around the base of the hill opposite, and gone in another direction.'

'Where might he have gone?'

Audrah and Stafford looked in the direction of the Furlough Mountains. Sombre, grey and perpetually capped with snow. It would have been madness to venture into those mountains unprepared. Lars was aware of that. And in any case, if that was what he intended to do, why pretend otherwise? Why say, *I'm just going back to the car – you go on ahead, I'll catch you up* . . .

'What did you do when he didn't come back?' said Stafford.

'I waited a while.'

'How long for?'

'Ten, maybe fifteen minutes.'

'And then?'

'And then I went down to the car to see what was keeping him.'

Impossible to explain what went through her mind when she saw his gloves lying on the seat. Wherever he was, he hadn't gone back to the car, or if he had, he hadn't got what he'd gone for, because they were there, just as he had left them, the gloves so old the leather had taken on the shape of his hands, right down to the life-line that formed a crease at the base of his thumb. The way those gloves were positioned she'd almost imagined his hands in them, reaching out to her.

She felt for the envelope in the pocket of her skiing jacket, and wrapped her fingers around it. 'What are you thinking?' said Jochen.

'I'm thinking I'd like to be alone for a while.'

He hesitated, and she realised he was worried she might be about to do something stupid. Some people would have said that what she was about to do was perhaps a little odd for someone who claimed not to believe in an afterlife, but it wasn't stupid – not to her.

'I'll join you shortly,' she promised.

Jochen didn't have much choice, so headed back to the house. And once she was alone, Audrah drew the envelope out of her pocket.

She stood beneath a Turner sky, the snow reflecting its pink and yellow hues, and scattered the ashes of the letter at the spot where she'd last seen Lars. He had loved it here. If something of him *had* survived, this was where his spirit would choose to rest.

Letters were very much a part of her life at the moment. The day after Audrah returned to Edinburgh, Wober dropped one on to her desk. 'This came in today. The usual thing, but I'd welcome your opinion.'

Letters came in to the Institute on a fairly regular basis, entrepreneurs being quick to realise that a ghost could be good for trade. Often, people tried to entice a parapsychologist into studying alleged paranormal phenomena, then used the fact as some sort of endorsement to attract custom. Consequently, it was usual to turn them down, so Audrah wondered what it was about this particular request that appealed to Wober.

'Northumbria Police are investigating the disappearance of a young girl.'

Audrah didn't see what that had to do with them until he handed her a clipping taken from a newspaper. 'Cranmer appears to be helping them.'

The realisation that Cranmer was involved got Audrah's immediate attention, as did the fact that Nicholas Herrol was being attacked by something that couldn't be seen. His mother had written, 'The injuries frequently result in him being hospitalised,' and although Audrah automatically rejected the possibility that someone could be at the mercy of a malign entity, the fact that the injuries were severe enough to warrant him being admitted to a hospital concerned her deeply. It pointed to a scenario that implied he might be a danger to himself. Either that, or he was almost certainly at the mercy of someone who was psychotic and in a position to take whatever opportunity came their way to injure him.

'I take it you're going to investigate?'

'John Cranmer is your province rather than mine.'

'I've got lectures to give.'

'I want you to go to Lyndle,' said Wober. 'I want you to help this woman. And I want you to have one last crack at Cranmer.'

Cranmer had already caused her more than enough grief. It was time to let someone else try to prove what she was beginning to believe was unprovable. 'I'd rather you asked someone else.'

'Audrah,' said Wober, 'don't allow this opportunity to slip through your fingers. Cranmer is regarded as one of the greatest psychics the world has ever known. If you can succeed where every other parapsychologist has so far failed, *if* you can prove he's a fraud, it will be quite a note to end on, wouldn't you say?'

As Audrah read the last few lines of the letter, it occurred to her that in normal circumstances the fact that someone appeared to be at the mercy of a psychotic individual would, in itself, have been sufficient to prompt her to investigate. But even if there had been no mention of Nicholas Herrol, she doubted she would have been able to turn her back on Claudia's plea:

'Please help us,' she had written. And then she had written again: '*Please, for God's sake, help us.*'

9

Guy Harvey supposed it was his own crumbling ego that was making him reluctant to accept what was staring him in the face – that his marriage of six brief months was already over – but that was the way it looked from where he was standing.

He walked into the house that he and Rachel shared with six other students, then entered the room they'd been living in ever since they were married.

Rachel was lying on the bed, her long dark hair tangled, as if she couldn't be bothered brushing it that morning. Over the past few weeks, she had lost all interest in her appearance. Not that it made much difference. At eighteen, she was beautiful. She could have worn a sack and it wouldn't have mattered.

What did matter was the fact that, when she saw him, she turned away. At that point, Guy lost hope. Until she turned away like that, he had thought that maybe, somehow, they'd be able to work things out. Now, he knew that wasn't going to happen. 'Rachel,' he said, and when he got no reaction he reached out, but as he touched her he felt the muscles of her shoulder tense against him. 'We have to talk.'

The rigidity of her muscles increased, and he withdrew his hand. 'Okay,' he said. 'You listen, and I'll do the talking.' And he told her that walking into the house had become something he dreaded doing; that presumably she felt the marriage had been a mistake, but that she didn't know how to tell him it was over.

That was okay. He understood. People had their different ways of dealing with these things. He was trying to handle it, and trying to work out the best way forward from here. But he was finding it very difficult.

'Right now,' he said, 'I think the best thing would be for me to go and stay with my father for a while.'

She didn't try to argue him out of it. She just lay there, trying not to look at him.

'I love you,' he said. 'This isn't what I want. But I don't know how else to deal with what's happening between us.'

He stood there for a moment, willing her to say something to stop him from walking away.

Not a word. Not so much as a gesture.

He stood up, and left.

If ever he had tried to imagine what it would be like to walk out on a marriage, he would have envisaged a scene followed by him storming out of the house, jumping into a car, and feeling the engine burst into life so that he could screech down the road in a way that suited his mood. The reality was a quiet and dignified exit. He closed the door almost silently, and because the car had failed its MOT, he had no choice but to get a bus into town.

The only thing that equated in any way with what he might have imagined were the feelings of loss – of being ripped apart. That he, at twenty-two, should be sitting on a bus and walking out on a marriage that took place less than six months ago made him feel a failure. But that was nothing to the failure he felt when, after getting off the bus, he did the only thing he could think of: he phoned his father.

He didn't want to do it. If there was anyone else he could have turned to, he would have done it, but most of the people he'd graduated with had either drifted away or settled into relationships. Women weren't known for their generosity when it came to letting their partner's mate from college crash for a while. A night or two, maybe – but this was going to take more than a night or two to sort out. He was going to have to find somewhere to stay for longer than that, and because he had no money, turning to one of his parents seemed like his only option. That meant going to his father, because the last thing he felt he could cope with right now was the kind of emotional reaction he knew he would get from his mother. She would want him to go over every detail of the split, not because she thought she might be able to help him get his relationship back together, but because she would want to see how it equated with her own situation. Women did that. They talked things through until nothing they said meant anything any more. And for all his father's faults, he had his good points. Foremost among these was disinclination to say *I told you so*. Not that he had anything against the exotic, dark-haired Rachel. It was just that when he heard about the marriage, he made it plain that he thought they were too young. That said, he was the last person likely to stand in judgment. After all, his own marriage had gone down the tubes, so who was he to talk? If anything, it was this that gave Guy the guts to phone him and admit what was going on.

'Listen, Dad – bad news. Rachel and I have . . .' He couldn't get the words out. But he didn't have much money, which meant he couldn't afford to fumble around trying to find a prosaic way to say it. '. . . split,' he finished. 'I can't afford to rent anywhere and I need . . . I need to come home. What I mean is . . . I need to stay. I don't know how long for . . .'

His father reacted to the news as if Guy had asked if he could just drop by. 'Sure,' he said. 'When are you coming down?'

'Today, if that's okay? The train gets into Christchurch at around six.'

'I'll pick you up,' said his father, adding, 'What about the fare?'

Guy admitted he didn't have it.

'Go to one of the ticket booths and ask a clerk to phone me. I'll get them to put it through on my credit card.'

Guy hated himself, but what choice did he have? He was grateful when a mechanical voice informed him that he needed to insert more money in order to continue with the call. 'Dad – I've got to go.'

'I'll pick you up at six.'

*   *   *

The beachfront apartment was roughly one-eighth the size of the house Guy's parents had owned towards the end of their marriage. Even so, it wasn't exactly cramped.

He sat on a cream leather sofa in a room that had a view of the Isle of Wight. The weather had a bearing on the colour of the walls. At times, they were almost a Mediterranean blue. At others, they picked up the charcoal hues that were currently all too evident.

His father ripped the tab off a can of Grolsch and handed it to him:

'Have you eaten?'

'On the train,' said Guy. 'Spent my last few quid on a burger.'

Somehow – and Guy couldn't imagine how – his father managed to wear surfing gear without looking a complete dick. At forty-seven, that took some doing, but so did pulling the kind of woman who was currently padding around the apartment. She was blonde, and she was Australian. Wendy, or Wanda, or something.

'Where did you meet her?'

'She did my back.'

She was studying at some chiropractic college in Bournemouth. His father kept insisting she was his student lodger. 'Look,' said Guy, 'it's cool. I'm not about to tell my mother, okay?'

The Wendy-Wanda person disappeared into the bedroom with a book on diseases of the spine. Once she was out of earshot, his father sat on the couch and said, 'Want to talk about it?'

Guy didn't particularly want to try to analyse what had gone wrong, mostly because he didn't have a clue, but he knew he wasn't going to get away with sitting there looking decorative. 'I don't really see what good it will do.'

'Up to you,' said his father. 'Sometimes, it helps.' When Guy made no comment, he added, 'I used to think I didn't know the point when things first started to fall apart between your

60

mother and me. It seemed to me that we'd been tearing each other's throats out for so long we didn't even know why we were fighting any more. Looking back, I realise I was wrong – I knew when the rot set in. I even knew why. I just couldn't be arsed doing anything about it. And you know why?'

It wasn't like his father to open up like this. Normally, he hid his feelings behind a series of wisecracks. You had to peel the joke away to see the pain. 'Why?'

'Because it was gone. Finished. Time to call it a wrap. I didn't love her any more, so it wasn't worth the effort of dissecting what went wrong with a view to trying to put it back together.'

It was a shock to hear him coming out with things like that. At the end of the day, he was talking about his mother. But also, at the end of the day, maybe he wasn't treating him like a child any more. Maybe he was trying to tell him something useful.

'Are you still in love with Rachel? Is she worth the effort of trying to find out where you both went wrong, or do you let it go?'

Good question. His father had once said that one of the things that kept him in the marriage long after he knew it was over was the knowledge that he had so much to lose financially. 'If it's over,' his father said now, 'better to let it go than to hang in there, buy a house, try to make it work, then lose it all in five, maybe ten years. You don't have any kids. That could change. That complicates things.'

He made it sound as though he was willing him to walk away from the marriage. But maybe that was what divorce did to people. Maybe they viewed other people's relationships with a mixture of envy and cynicism.

'I don't particularly want to walk away. I just don't see what choice I have,' said Guy.

'So now you have to ask yourself – when did it start to go wrong?'

Again, good question. Maybe if he scrolled through the mental records to find the point at which he felt Rachel had last behaved normally, he would also find the point at which the relationship had started to disintegrate.

His father suddenly said, 'Tell me something – how much do you really *know* about her?'

The question took him by surprise. 'What kind of question is that?'

'How much?' said his father.

He thought about it for a moment. 'Not a lot,' he admitted. It was quite an admission, because several months ago, if anyone had asked him what he knew about Rachel, he would have replied that he knew as much as most people knew about the person they were marrying. With hindsight, he realised he only knew as much as she told him, largely because she had no family to speak of; there was nothing tangible to corroborate that she never knew her father, that her mother was killed in a hit-and-run when she was three, or that it had fallen to her mother's sister, Ruth, to take responsibility for her.

That being so, Ruth was the only person he could have talked to. But Ruth was no longer alive. She had died a couple of months before he and Rachel met, and the sale of her house had just about paid off debts to a nursing home. She had left a small sum of money, but Rachel wouldn't get it until probate was sorted. Once it came through, they hoped to use it as a deposit on a flat. Right now, they were sharing a house in Leeds with several students, though it was almost a year since Guy graduated from the Northern School of Film.

In addition to the money, Ruth left a cottage. When she heard about it, Rachel claimed not to have known it existed, but Guy found it hard to believe Ruth never mentioned it to her.

'I'm hardly likely to have forgotten something like that,' said Rachel.

He supposed not, but in that case Ruth must have had her reasons for keeping quiet about it.

Rachel found that amusing. 'Surely you're not accusing her of having a guilty secret?'

'No, but people don't usually keep quiet about something like that unless they have good reason.'

They visualised it as thatched and picturesque, and even before they saw it, Rachel was suggesting that maybe they should keep it as a holiday home.

It was a dream, and he told her so. They were living in one room. They needed a deposit for a flat. They had no choice but to sell it.

Reluctantly, Rachel agreed, and Guy got in touch with an agent in the area.

The agent knew the cottage. It was derelict, he told them. He doubted they would get more than the value of the ground it stood on, but he was willing to see what he could do.

They were unwilling to put it on the market at the price the agent advised without at least seeing it for themselves, so they went to take a look at it, and as he remembered these things something suddenly clicked into place for Guy. He wondered why he hadn't realised it before. 'Ruth's cottage,' he said.

'What about it?'

Guy replied, 'The problems started the day we went to see it.'

His father was aware that Ruth had left Rachel a cottage. But Guy had hardly mentioned it other than to confirm that, as yet, they'd had no luck selling it. He lifted the can to his lips. 'Remind me where it was.'

Guy saw himself in the cottage, and in his hand a wooden peg that someone had carved for a child. Rachel wasn't there. She'd gone for a walk out the back. But when she'd returned, the look on her face . . .

'Lyndle,' he replied.

IO

In the two appalling years since Kathryn's death, Marion's experience of the police, of the judicial system, of all forms of authority, had wiped away the respect that she previously held for these things and replaced it with mistrust. So when WPC Fripp turned up on the doorstep, Marion didn't feel inclined to invite her in. She stood there, the rain splashing off her uniform, and she noticed a suitcase dumped at the foot of the stairs.

'Going somewhere, Marion?'

'What's it to you?'

'Just asking.'

Once, she was part of the team that investigated Kathryn's death, and she called on her now and again. Just a friendly visit, according to Fripp, but these occasions invariably ended up in shouting matches:

You're protecting Reeve!

Of course we're not protecting him – be rational.

How could she be expected to be rational when the police were protecting the man who murdered her child? And it wasn't just the police. Authorities that came in every shape and form were just as obliging. The education authority found him another job. The housing authority provided him with accommodation. The judicial authorities were doing what they could to prevent her from causing him further distress. And as a journalist recently pointed out, Reeve lost his job and home as a result of being branded a killer by the mother of one of his pupils, but he'd never been charged with any offence relating to Kathryn's death. The public was reminded that people should be considered innocent until proven guilty.

Marion found the journalist and berated him. As a result, an article appeared depicting her as deranged. She wrote to the paper threatening to sue. The paper printed the letter, so she reported the editor to the relevant press authority. And then she discovered that this was another authority that seemed more inclined to help Reeve than to help her. She was told there was such a thing as freedom of the press. If they wanted to portray Reeve as unjustly vilified and her as the monster responsible for his twice having made an attempt on his own life, they were free to do so. She, however, wasn't free to stop them.

After getting nowhere with the press, she approached radio and television stations, only to discover that they, too, were withdrawing from her now, frightened off by the threat of being sued by Reeve's lawyers. What did you have to do to get it through to people that it was morally wrong to protect men like Reeve purely on the grounds that there was insufficient evidence to support a murder charge? Kathryn was dead. How much more evidence did they need?

Fripp no longer called unless she had to, so Marion wondered why she was there at all. The answer came when she said, 'I hear you've been served with a restraining order.'

'What about it?'

'I came to make sure you realised how serious it would be if you didn't abide by it.'

Marion exploded then. *'Just whose side are you on?'*

'It isn't a matter of taking sides. The fact is, you'd be breaking the law, and believe it or not, I don't want to see you in jail.'

'Michael Reeve was breaking the law, but nobody seems inclined to do anything about it. I, on the other hand, only have to show my face, and every judge in the country starts rubber-stamping injunctions.'

'Marion—'

'How do you know he isn't planning to do to some other young girl what he did to Kathryn?'

Fripp suddenly sounded weary. 'Can I come in a minute?'

And because she asked rather than demanded, and because it was throwing it down, Marion relented.

Once Fripp was inside she said, 'Reeve has made a complaint.'

'Another one?'

'He claims you wrote to his brother's family and threatened to expose them for being related to him.'

Marion replied, 'I find the use of the word "expose" a little emotive, don't you?'

'Reeve found the threat emotive. He's seeking his solicitor's advice.'

'To what purpose?'

Marion had her there, and Fripp knew it. Reeve had managed to get her into court twice before – once for demonstrating outside the school currently employing him, and once for appearing on a television show and accusing him outright of her daughter's murder – but on each occasion the judge let her off with a warning: 'The death of your daughter has clearly affected you deeply, Mrs Thomas. Therefore, on this occasion, I am prepared to overlook the distress your behaviour has caused the plaintiff, though I must warn you—'

'Marion,' she said. 'People aren't bottomless pits of sympathy. People get tired. People run out of patience, of understanding.'

'What are you saying?'

'Leave them alone.'

'Leave who alone?'

'Sasha. Reeve. And everyone else on your hit list, including me.' Fripp moved towards the door. 'Next time Reeve gets you into court, he might just get you jailed.'

'He murdered my daughter.'

'Please,' she said. 'See sense—' And Marion screamed at her then. Sense, when Reeve was free, was little more than an obscene luxury. 'You have a daughter,' she said. 'She's sixteen.'

'Marion—'

'What would you do if a pervert like Reeve got his hands on her?'

Fripp had no answer to that. She left, and Marion ran into the street, shouting after her car as it pulled away: '*What would you do!*'

She returned to the house and stepped over the suitcase as she made her way upstairs. In a very short while she would sling it in the car, and drive through the night. With luck she would reach Northumberland by morning.

I I

Audrah was half out of the door, an overnight bag in her hand, when the phone rang, and she let the answer service kick in in order to decide whether or not to take the call.

When she heard Jochen begin a message with the words *Felt I should warn you*, she dropped the bag and lifted the receiver.

'Jochen,' she said.

He sounded relieved. '. . . tried to talk her out of it . . . but you know what she can be like.'

He could only be referring to Eva. 'What's she done?' said Audrah.

'Consulted our solicitor.'

Audrah assumed he was going to tell her that Eva intended to try to prevent her from having Lars declared dead. But she was wrong about that. What Eva wanted was a walnut desk that once belonged to Lars. It was beautiful, and valuable, a potential family heirloom. Lars was an only child, but Eva had a sister in Sweden. She felt that the desk should go to her sister's children.

As Jochen was speaking, Audrah thought about all the things Eva had demanded over the years. There was a watch that had been given to Lars for his twenty-first birthday, and an Ansel Adams print brought from the States. Audrah hadn't particularly wanted to part with them, but they were gifts to Lars from his parents and she could understand why they might want them back, so she surrendered them. She also returned a wall clock bequeathed to Lars by Jochen's mother, and a large glass bowl that had been in Eva's family for years. His collection of classical records and CDs was somewhat diminished after Eva presented her with a list of those she felt Lars would have wanted her to have. *After all, you're not terribly musical, Audrah. What good would they be to you?* And finally, there were skis, a tennis racquet and fencing gear that Eva felt should be set aside for her nephew.

Audrah relinquished these things without comment, but she wasn't about to relinquish the desk. It was something she had found, and bought, and given to Lars as a wedding present. In its drawers were letters they'd written to one another when Lars was working in Sweden and she was still an undergraduate in London. There were photographs, mementos of their wedding, and the wedding certificate. Soon there would also be a death certificate. She wanted a special place to keep these things. That place was this desk.

'Audrah—'

'I'm sorry, Jochen, but you can tell Eva to . . .' Somehow she managed to moderate her tone. '. . . the answer's no.'

'She won't give up,' said Jochen. 'It might be better to let her have it for the sake of peace.'

The Evas of this world evolved because the people around them gave in to them for the sake of peace. Audrah wished that, just for once, Jochen would stand up to her, and something Lars once said came back to her now: *My mother can be difficult, I'm afraid. If you marry me, you may find yourself having to bite your tongue rather a lot.*

'I bought that desk.'

'Don't take this the wrong way,' said Jochen, 'but do you have a receipt?'

Possibly. Maybe. Somewhere. She didn't know where. 'Why do you ask?'

'That's what the solicitor will argue. If you don't have a receipt, you can't prove you bought it, which means Lars may have bought it prior to marrying you. That would make it something that, in exceptional circumstances, may not necessarily be deemed to have been held in community of property.'

He made it sound as though she and Lars had divorced! 'For God's sake, Jochen – I was his *wife*.'

'He died intestate. That muddies the water, especially where valuable personal possessions are concerned. Close blood relations can sometimes persuade a court to award them property left by their parents, or children.'

If she didn't end the call right now, the relationship she and Jochen had somehow managed to maintain despite Eva's constant assault upon it was finally going to crash. 'I can't talk,' she said. 'I'm about to go away for a couple of days.'

'Where are you going?'

'Northumberland.'

'Holiday?' said Jochen.

'Work,' Audrah replied.

During the drive down to Lyndle, Audrah did her best to take her mind off Eva by concentrating on Cranmer. As Wober had so adroitly pointed out, if she could succeed where every other parapsychologist had failed, it would be quite a note to end on. But one of the difficulties facing her was the fact that Cranmer's background was unimpeachable. Good family. Private education. A mixture of charisma and credibility. Not so the majority of pseudo psychics, a large percentage of whom started out as magicians. Most went on to the club circuit, where they earned a living as entertainers. Others quickly realised they were earning peanuts in comparison with the sums they could earn by convincing people they had access to the spirit world.

One thing they all had in common was an ability to manipulate the media. Cranmer was no different. Within a matter of days, he'd secured himself a deal with a national newspaper. The man heading up the investigation into Ginny's disappearance was asked to comment on Cranmer's claim that he was helping them, but all the press could get out of him was a terse 'No comment'.

Was it true that Ginny was dead?

No comment.

Could Tate confirm that Cranmer had advised them to search for a body?

No comment.

Then could he confirm that Cranmer had said the police should drag the moat?

No comment.

Traditionally, the British police paid scant regard to psychics. Consequently, if someone like Cranmer could be seen to be taken seriously by them, they had a lot to gain. He might not earn anything from the police investigation, but the business that came on its heels would be worth the investment. Even now, people would be writing to him begging him to put them in touch with some lover, husband or child. Cranmer would sort through the letters. He wouldn't even have to read half of them to know they weren't worth his while. A quick glance at the quality of the notepaper, the style of handwriting, the way the very first sentence was phrased would be enough to determine the social and financial status of the writer. The letters written in ballpoint pen on lined notepaper were binned. Cranmer tended to read only those letters that were written in an educated hand. She knew him so well. She had once written just such a letter to him herself.

She turned off the motorway and, within the hour, was deep into Northumbria's National Park. Hard weather had come to the moors some days ago, but she left the worst of the snow behind as she entered Lyndle Wood. The way the trees were closing in registered, but only peripherally, because her thoughts were almost entirely focused on Cranmer. He had probably been waiting for a case like this for some time – one that had all the ingredients he looked for. It would involve a missing person – preferably a good-looking female. Failing that, a celebrity. And there must be a backdrop. Cranmer knew the value of arena.

These past two days, she had read a great deal about this investigation, but she didn't yet know what had attracted Cranmer to it. Ginny was a pretty kid, but the world was full of pretty kids who were missing. There had to be something else – something that had grabbed his attention. So far, she hadn't been able to put her finger on what it was. But the minute she saw the house, she had the answer.

12

This was what had brought him, this place of sheer black walls that hugged the ground like an animal its den. Girls went missing every day of the week. But they didn't go missing from places like Lyndle Hall.

England was once full of medieval houses. Cromwell destroyed most of them. Lyndle had survived. But unless something was done to restore it, time would succeed where Cromwell had failed, because it was slowly being consumed by its surroundings. The masonry was pocked, as if the wind were a worm that had burrowed into the stone, and its elegant latticed windows were, for the most part, broken.

The sight of it made Audrah uneasy, but because she understood the way the subconscious interpreted visual information, she was able to rationalise her unease by analysing what caused it. She didn't have to analyse too deeply: Lyndle was vile.

Places that oozed menace had always existed. Some were made by man. Others occurred in nature. And since the dawn of time, man had responded by developing tools with which he attempted to control or placate the imagined evil. Catholics had their haunted houses exorcised, whilst pagans made offerings to the spirits. The Chinese employed the art of Feng Shui to ensure that the flow of a building's energy was as it should be, whilst geomancers did their best to detect lines of electromagnetic stress.

Six years of studying alleged paranormal activity had convinced her there were no such things as ghosts, energy flows or ley lines. But there was primal instinct, and no matter how sophisticated man liked to think he had become, the fact was certain visual images triggered those primal instincts. Put someone in a wood in the middle of England and leave them there for the night, and instinctively they wanted to climb into the trees when darkness fell. On a conscious level, they could accept that they weren't in any danger from predators. But their subconscious argued that, just to be on the safe side, it couldn't do any harm to sleep in a tree.

In much the same way, houses like Lyndle invoked a primal fear of the unknown. The creeping vines, the smell of stagnant water, the pervading air of gloom. It was repulsive, but then it was *designed* to repel, and it did so on two levels: the first was physical, in that penetrating such properties without the help of modern equipment would be difficult even today; the second was psychological – for all that the house had stood there for upward of six hundred years, it looked as though it belonged to another world.

Audrah could think of a number of parapsychologists who would have liked the chance to study it more closely. One of them was working for a film company in Los Angeles, his speciality being a knowledge of what was required in order to make people afraid of their surroundings. The producer expected designs for the company's latest horror movie. What he got was a series of mathematical equations relating to light, shade and proportion.

Culture and ethos played a part in what frightened people. Tell some kid who lived on a council estate that he'd just had a curse put on him, and provided it didn't interfere with United's chances in the Cup Final, he wouldn't lose any sleep over it. Different things frightened different people. But one thing that was almost guaranteed to frighten anyone was a house that sank its great black walls into water, a house with a bloody history, wretched and depraved. What kind of mind, what kind of people, conceived of such houses? Minds like ours, thought Audrah. And people like our forebears, whose blood still pumps through our veins.

A Range Rover came into view, the logo emblazoned on the bodywork informing her that it belonged to Northumbria

Police. There were three men standing close to it. One of them was trying to deal with a tirade of abuse from a woman Audrah suspected was Claudia Herrol. Her refined features were an odd match for the overlong grey hair and an overcoat that looked as though it might once have been expensive. The buttons were gone, and she held it closed with a belt. She might almost have been living on the street, her clothes orchestrated to conceal the fact. But those who were observant would know that here was a woman who slept in doorways. It was just that the doorways she slept in were her own.

Audrah got out of the car and walked towards them. 'Mrs Herrol?' she said. She held out her hand. 'I'm Audrah Sidow.'

Her name meant nothing to Claudia. 'From the Institute,' said Audrah. 'I came in response to your letter.'

Claudia reciprocated, her own hand light boned and delicate. 'My letter?'

'You wrote,' said Audrah. 'Not to me personally, but your letter was passed on to me. I tried to phone. I think your line must be down.'

Claudia withdrew her hand. 'I don't remember writing.'

Audrah pulled the letter out of her skiing jacket. She handed it to Claudia as Tate introduced himself:

'Do you have some identification?'

Audrah produced a card. It gave her name, *Dr Audrah Sidow*, and a telephone number, but that was all, because Audrah had learned from experience that it didn't always pay to advertise.

'Why are you here?'

Claudia answered for her: 'Dr Sidow is here to see my son.'

Tate looked at her card more closely. 'What kind of a doctor?'

'Psychologist,' said Audrah.

'Good,' he said. 'You can be present while I question him.' He turned to Claudia. 'I take it he *is* in the house?' Claudia confirmed this, but said:

75

'I'd appreciate it if you could give Dr Sidow a chance to see him first.'

It looked as though Tate might be about to refuse, and Audrah, who suspected she might not get another chance to take a look at Nicholas, said:

'Twenty minutes?'

Tate motioned to the other two men to join them, and they walked as a group towards the courtyard.

If Tate had known she was there in the capacity of paranormal psychologist, Audrah doubted he would have allowed her access to Nicholas. The authorities might pay scant regard to people who claimed to have psychic powers, but she knew from experience that they paid even less to those who, to quote Wober, 'attempted to make respectable the study of a subject generally deemed unworthy of serious consideration by academics the world over'.

Tate stood aside to allow everyone into the Hall ahead of him, and once inside they stood in silence as what they were looking at took shape. The blue-grey light that seeped in from the courtyard lit but a fraction of what was essentially an immense dark space, and despite that Audrah had seen more than her share of period properties, nothing could have prepared her for its austerity.

Rush strewn, squalid and cold, it would once have been at the centre of the household's life. Now the floor was flagged, but over the years seeds had taken root between the stones and were dislodging them in their effort to grow towards the light from an oriel window. One day, the floor of Lyndle Hall would resemble an overgrown churchyard, the stones lying this way and that, some of them upended, others merely lying at dangerous angles.

A door at the far end gave on to a passage. There were rooms leading off it. Most looked disused – a sitting room, a billiard room, a kitchen. Claudia led the way past them and on to the foot of a spiral staircase. Once there, she turned to Tate and said, 'At least give Dr Sidow the opportunity to spend a few

76

uninterrupted moments with my son,' and when the conserted, Audrah followed her up steps worn smooth by centuries of use. They gave out on to a landing where snow had blown through the windows to lie on the timber floors like fine white powder.

There were a number of doors leading off the landing. Claudia opened one to reveal a room that was totally stripped of furnishings. No curtains. No carpet. No bedding. Just Nicholas lying on a mattress half covered by a duvet. He was twenty at most, but he still had the look of an adolescent about him, his face very smooth, his hair bleached almost white. He slept very deeply, as if he might be drugged, but what interested Audrah were the marks on his body – some on his face, and some on his shoulders and arms. There were so many of them, and in such close proximity, that they gave his skin a slightly dappled effect.

Audrah was reminded of a case in which a woman claimed that her daughter was the focus of poltergeist activity. One of the better US magazines ran a feature in which photographs depicted the girl suspended several feet above her bed. It was alleged that unseen hands had raised her, were holding her there.

Ultimately, it was discovered that the unseen hands belonged to the girl's mother, who was trying to sell her story to the press. The girl was taken into care, and the mother was currently serving a jail sentence for drugging her, wounding her, and photographing the result in order to provide proof that her daughter was at the mercy of a malign entity to whichever newspaper was willing to pay for it.

Prior to being rescued, the girl, like Nicholas, had also slept in a room that was stripped to the bone. What were needed in here, were a few cameras.

'How did he get these marks?'

Claudia replied, 'When it finds him, it bites him.'

Now was not the time to enter into a discussion about whether or not such things as malign entities existed, much less whether or not they were capable of injuring people. But something was clearly injuring him.

Ninety per cent of people who exhibited evidence of this kind of injury were being harmed – usually by somebody close to them. The other ten per cent were harming themselves. Audrah didn't know which category Nicholas fell into, but police and social services dealt with cases of abuse, and psychiatrists dealt with self-harmers. Speaking of which . . .

'Mrs Herrol, has Nicholas ever been admitted to a psychiatric hospital?'

It took a moment for Claudia answer, but eventually she said, 'Yes.'

'How many times?'

'Too many.'

Why was she not surprised? 'Where was he taken to?'

'Broughton.'

Audrah didn't know the area, but she'd noticed a sign for Broughton as she drove towards Lyndle. It was roughly sixty miles from here. 'What was the diagnosis?'

'They argue about it – some of the psychiatrists insist he's schizophrenic. But the consultant psychiatrist, Goldman, says he isn't sure.'

'And you?' said Audrah. 'What do *you* think?'

'Would I have written to the Institute if I thought he was schizophrenic?'

Audrah supposed not. But it wasn't unusual for parents to reject the idea that their child might be schizophrenic and to scrabble around for some other explanation for their behaviour – no matter how unpalatable, or unlikely. Some parents even preferred to believe their children were drug users rather than face up to the fact that they were psychotic. After all, kids could be weaned off drugs. It wasn't quite so easy to deal with a child's psychosis. Even so, most parents eventually came to accept the diagnosis, if only because they had no choice. The symptoms didn't simply disappear after a good holiday, a change of job, the recovery from what everyone had thought, had *hoped*, was a breakdown. Claudia might well continue to cling to the belief that Nicholas was at the mercy of a malign entity, if only because she could then continue to hope that by throwing the equivalent of a few religious oils around the room, the 'problem' could be made to go away. It wouldn't go away. Not now. Not ever.

'I want it got rid of,' said Claudia. 'Can you do that? Can you get rid of it?'

Audrah replied, 'Parapsychologists don't perform exorcisms, Mrs Herrol. We leave that sort of thing to the religious community.'

'Then what *do* you do?'

'What we do,' said Audrah, 'is establish what might be causing the alleged phenomena.'

'This thing exists,' said Claudia. 'It took me a long time to realise it, but it does.'

'These days, there's a lot that can be done for people like Nicholas.'

'He thinks it's trying to kill him.' She clamped her hands to her mouth as if to keep the words from being spoken. 'Please tell me it can't kill him.'

'Nothing is trying to kill him.'

'You haven't seen what it's capable of,' she replied.

13

Tate couldn't get the memory of Sylvie Straker's terror out of his mind. He didn't know what she meant when she said 'it bites him', but his guess was that Nicholas Herrol had probably done something to frighten her. Maybe he got his kicks out of frightening young girls. And maybe he went a step too far with Ginny. A little simplistic, maybe – after all, it didn't explain where Francis Herrol was – but he felt he could be forgiven for thinking along these lines.

He also suspected Claudia was trying to protect her son, and this was to have been his last attempt at getting into the house without breaking the doors down. Frankly, he hadn't expected her to come out. Nor had he expected a psychologist to turn up, but the fact that Claudia had asked someone to take a look at Nicholas indicated to Tate that even she must recognise that her son had a problem.

In the circumstances, he would have been within his rights to refuse to allow the psychologist anywhere near Nicholas, but he wanted her on his side. Besides, if he handled her correctly, she might prove useful. She was currently with Nicholas, and Tate hoped that by playing his cards right he would manage to persuade her to tell him what was said. Psychologists were notoriously defensive with regard to their clients, but sometimes it was surprising what you could get out of them. And above all else, he didn't want her painting him black in court. All she'd asked for was twenty minutes. It wasn't going to hurt to let her have them. And while she was talking to Nicholas, he and his men would take a good look round.

What he did after that would very much depend on what he found out today. If it looked as though a full-scale search was in order, he would organise one. In the meantime, he intended to get an idea of the layout of the house.

Its passages and the rooms that led off them were darker, more depressing than he had imagined, and he searched around for some way of lighting the place. The electricity ran off a generator, but judging from the look of the wiring, it was installed at a time when the family was already strapped for cash. The small round Bakelite switches were of the chocolate-brown, art deco variety throughout. It had obviously been either prohibitively expensive or impractical to try to conceal the wiring within the solid granite blocks of stone that were as much a feature of Lyndle's interior walls as were the stones that faced the elements, so the brittle black flex ran from the switches, up the walls and across the ceilings to light fittings. It looked like the kind of wiring you got in a bed-sit – cheap and dodgy.

The light shades, like the fittings, were as varied and eccentric as the wiring. In one of the rooms a glass chandelier had been bastardised so that bulbs lit it from within. In another, a paper contraption that looked as though it might have come from Habitat swung precariously from the ceiling, the shade burnt almost sepia in places. Most of the fittings supported several bulbs, but on average only one out of six worked, and the light they cast on the room below was barely worth the bother.

Other than these, there were no other light fittings to speak of, but that hadn't always been the case. Wires poked out of the walls along the passages, suggesting that once there were wall lights. Tate got one of his men to check the wires out. They were live. The place was a death trap.

By now it was obvious to Tate that there was only one wing that was anything like habitable. It was comprised of two downstairs rooms and a kitchen. Its vast range and wooden work surfaces were redundant, but there was a fridge that didn't work, and a 1960s cooker that ran off calor gas. A 1930s unit was coming away from a wall. Some effort had been made to make it blend in – it was painted the same sickly green as the wall tiles.

The Belfast sink unit standing beneath the window was laced with cracks, and the cupboard beneath it crammed with preparations. The brand names were oddly familiar despite that most belonged to a bygone age. How long had it been since he last saw syrup of figs or Eno's Fruit Salts? A block of Fairy soap the size of a brick nestled beside a roll of Bromo toilet paper. And it suddenly occurred to him that he had assumed Ginny was there to perform the kind of tasks required of a Girl Friday. He had envisaged her doing a little cooking, a little cleaning. But no one had laid a finger on Lyndle in years. What had she been employed to do?

A former utility room led off the kitchen. It was accessed by a flight of steps that took it to basement level, and its only window looked out on to the courtyard level with the feet of anyone who walked by. The bed was stripped to reveal an old flock mattress. A wardrobe stood at the foot of the bed, and a couple of wire hangers jangled as he wrestled with the door. It was empty, which was much as he'd expected.

According to Mr Mulholland, Ginny had said she'd been given a room off the kitchen. She described it as very basic. Tate would have said it was indescribably squalid. *What were you thinking of, Ginny?*

It was almost as though he heard her reply, *When you're young, you put up with things. Besides, it wasn't for long – and I needed the money.*

How many girls had died because they needed money? The jobs in bars from here to Hong Kong that led to lines of work that ended in death. But a job at Lyndle Hall wouldn't have sounded dodgy. And Ginny had said she could always leave if she didn't like it. So what made her stay? The thought that she may have been *made* to stay was slowly taking root, was beginning to grow—

There were two other rooms on the lower floor, both large, and both with a view of the lawns. One was a study, its high ceiling and plain stone walls much in keeping with the near-monastic austerity of Lyndle's Great Hall. Two red leather armchairs were positioned in front of an open fire. Behind them, a table partitioned a corner of the room, one wall of which was taken up by a mirror.

He left it, and entered what had probably once been a drawing room. At some stage it had been turned into a billiard room, the table still in situ. Someone had taken a knife to the felt and had scoured the slate beneath it.

The cues were broken in half and lying in a bundle next to a plain stone fireplace. No billiard balls lying around, but every pane of glass in the window was broken. His guess was that someone had used the billiard balls to smash them. Why do it? Boredom. Frustration. Anger?

He walked out and up the spiral staircase to the landing. When he heard Claudia and the psychologist talking in one of the bedrooms, he passed it by, but checked the others out, finding them sparsely furnished.

One of them contained a wardrobe crammed with women's clothes. They weren't of a kind that a girl of eighteen would wear, so he guessed they must belong to Claudia Herrol. They spoke of a time when she must have led a vastly different life. Evening clothes mostly. Cocktail dresses and shoes. All designer labels. He couldn't equate these things with the woman who was currently walking around in an old tweed coat with half the buttons missing.

No sign of any clothes belonging to her husband. He might have taken them with him, but Tate doubted it. Early on in the investigation, he was prepared to consider the possibility that Francis had murdered Ginny and was currently lying low, but as it became increasingly obvious that Nicholas Herrol's behaviour was abnormal, Tate began to doubt this was likely. The more he got a handle on the situation at Lyndle, the more he was beginning to suspect that Francis never left.

He went to the broken window and looked down at the moat. It would have to be dragged, and they would need divers

83

for that, because according to Bischel it was roughly twelve feet deep. That made it deeper than many of the canals that once linked Newcastle to every major waterway in the country. Some had been restored, but most were still cluttered with bikes, prams, cars, fridges and the hulls of scuppered barges. He wondered what the divers would find at the bottom of the moat. *Let it not be a girl of eighteen, weighted down and quietly disposed of . . .*

Like all moats, it was fed by a natural water source. According to Bischel, excess water was once drained via a series of culverts that fed into the wood. In the late 1800s, the culverts were replaced by pipes that ran beneath what were to become croquet lawns. Looking at it now, nobody would guess that the land dividing the house from the trees could ever have been lawned. It would once have been the venue for elegant social gatherings and family occasions, but he couldn't imagine there ever having been a family occasion at Lyndle. Some houses lent themselves to the idea that they were a family home. Lyndle was a fortress, a place of refuge, but above all else it struck him as an aggressive house, something that would suit the kind of man who attacked first and asked questions later. It was no place for wives and children, yet it must have seen its share of both.

He went back downstairs and crossed the courtyard to the wing opposite. It had formerly been a coach house. Now it was a garage. There were currently three cars parked inside it. Fletcher had already run a check on the plates. One of the cars belonged to Claudia, another to Nicholas, and the third to Francis Herrol. According to Mr Mulholland, Ginny had held a licence, but she couldn't afford a car. How were she and Francis supposed to have left? Somehow, he couldn't imagine either of them hitching, and local taxi firms that covered the area had already confirmed that none of their cars had picked up a fare from Lyndle.

Fletcher walked up to him. 'Bevan wants a word,' he said, and Tate called out to him as he entered the timber wing.

84

'Over here,' said Bevan.

Tate now knew why the house was so sparsely furnished. Everything appeared to be in here.

Bevan was examining every piece of furniture. It was a job he was particularly suited to. Prior to joining the police, he had been an antiques dealer, and because he knew his subject so well, he could spot a fake a mile off. He could also *smell* when something had been nicked. Often, it was because the stolen antique was placed in an inappropriate setting. An Elizabethan commode should *not* be displayed in front of the kind of flock wallpaper that belonged down the local pub. Consequently, the minute he saw what was stored in that wing, he knew he hadn't just stumbled on a stash of stolen goods. He explained to Tate that most of the things he was looking at were as much a part of Lyndle as were the stones it was built from. One of the chests dated back to the early 1400s. It was as solid, as ugly, as *priceless* as the doors to Lyndle Hall.

He pointed various pieces out to Tate. Once they had been valuable. Now they were ruined. Tabletops that hadn't been scratched were torn away from the base that supported them. Fine china and hand-woven curtains were smashed and ripped and bundled into boxes, then discarded.

'Whoever did this had no understanding of what they were worth,' said Bevan. They were irreplaceable. And now they were gone, basically.

As they stood there, the wind outside pressed against the walls and the timbers groaned and creaked against the pressure. It was like being in the belly of a ship. And it didn't feel safe.

Tate decided the psychologist had had more than enough time with Nicholas. He had agreed to let her have twenty minutes. She'd had more like forty. But as he and Bevan stepped outside to join Fletcher in the courtyard, Nicholas came out of the house. Or rather he appeared at the doors to Lyndle Hall. He was naked. He had nothing on his feet. Yet he walked down the steps and stood in the courtyard, ankle deep in snow. His skin had a mottled, bluish tinge to it, but what could you expect when someone was walking around stark bollock naked in this temperature?

As far as Tate was concerned, this was just further confirmation that there was something very wrong with him. Any minute now, the psychologist would come out, take one look at him, and shake her head as if to say, *He's all yours.*

He took a step towards him, then just as quickly stepped back as Nicholas raised a vegetable knife towards him. It wasn't the biggest knife Tate had ever been threatened with, but that wasn't the point. Even a penknife could kill. And he wasn't about to take chances. Therefore, what he did next was very much going to depend on what Nicholas did next. And what he did was spin round the courtyard, slashing at the air and yabbering to himself.

It would have been easy enough to disarm him. Ultimately, that was what Tate intended to do. First, however, he wanted to watch him. 'Leave him,' he said, and Fletcher and Bevan held back.

Strictly speaking, it wasn't necessary to try to keep out of his way. Nicholas was too preoccupied with slashing at the air to bother with anyone around him.

Tate couldn't make up his mind whether this was an act or not, something Nicholas or the psychologist might later point to as evidence of diminished responsibility. He wanted to see how long Nicholas would manage to keep it up, but Claudia put a stop to it by running out of the house, the psychologist behind her.

'Nicholas, oh, Nicholas. Somebody help him – please!'

Tate gave Fletcher the nod, and within a matter of seconds Nicholas Herrol was lying on his stomach in the snow. Fletcher cuffed him, then yanked him to his knees, and it was only then that Tate even noticed the welts that were appearing on his body. Some had come up on his face. Others on his throat, back and legs. They reminded Tate of something. He couldn't think what. And then it came to him. They looked like bite marks. Not animal. Human. Small, and oval, and *vicious*, and Sylvia Straker's comment now made sense.

Nicholas knelt there in the snow, head bowed, hands behind his back, like someone waiting for the executioner's blade. It was less than a matter of seconds since those livid welts first appeared. Yet already they were weeping a blood-flecked fluid.

'Get him up,' said Tate, and Fletcher and Bevan tried to yank him to his feet. He screamed like a stuck pig, and Claudia pleaded with them. 'Don't touch him,' she said. 'Please – it's agony for him.'

Tate had been about to say they couldn't just leave him there when a voice he recognised came from somewhere behind him.

'*Leave him!*'

He turned round to find Cranmer in the courtyard, but what interested him was what he said when he saw the psychologist. The way he looked at her – it was almost proprietorial. 'Hello, Audrah.'

Tate suddenly realised this was not a good situation. If Cranmer was there, it was possible the press might be around. If so, then any minute now, some photographer might get a photo of Nicholas kneeling in the snow, covered in bleeding welts. The story would write itself. At best, he would be portrayed as a man possessed by demons. At worst, the implication would be that maybe he was psychotic and that maybe he'd murdered his father and Ginny Mulholland. What-ever the case, it would pave the way for some barrister to claim that, as a result of the way he'd been portrayed by the media, there was no way his client was going to get a fair trial. 'Get him out of here,' said Tate, and Fletcher and Bevan half pushed, half escorted Cranmer out of the courtyard.

When he was gone, Audrah relaxed a little, but Tate had noted the fact that she and Cranmer obviously knew one another. 'Friend of yours?'

'I've had dealings with him professionally.'

Tate couldn't imagine how a psychologist would know

someone like Cranmer. Maybe he'd been a patient at some point. Right now, however, his priority was Nicholas Herrol. He wanted to question him, but there was no way he was going to be able to do that after what had just happened.

Nicholas was still kneeling there. The snow around him was pink with blood. In all his years of experience, Tate had never seen anything like those welts. 'What's wrong with him?' he said.

Audrah didn't answer that, but she made what sounded to Tate like a sensible suggestion: 'He's been a patient at the psychiatric unit in Broughton. We need to get him back there.'

Tate pulled a mobile from his pocket and called an ambulance.

'I want to go with him,' said Claudia.

'I'll drive you,' said Audrah.

14

The nature of the wounds had changed by the time the ambulance got Nicholas to Broughton. The welts had subsided, and all that was left was a gravelled effect to the skin – something akin to a thousand tiny pricks by a small, sharp needle.

As soon as he could bear to be touched, a nurse bathed the blood away. Now, he was dressed in a gown and he lay on a bed in a ward off the office that belonged, the Consultant Psychiatrist, Goldman.

Goldman entered the ward with two male nurses. They were dressed in short white coats and blue trousers, but Goldman, who liked to dress casually enough to make his patients feel at ease, wore chinos, a Paul Smith shirt and Wilson trainers. He moved across the oak-stripped floor almost noiselessly. 'I'm here to try to help you, Nick. I want you to trust me.'

This was exactly what Goldman had said the first time they met, and his words brought to mind the circumstances surrounding his admission. He was twelve, and he was at boarding school, and the sports master had stood him up in front of the class. 'Take off your vest, Herrol.'

Nicholas took off his vest.

'Turn and show the others your back.'

Nicholas turned and showed his back to the other boys.

The master issued a warning to the entire year. 'I don't know who was responsible for this, but this isn't the Dark Ages, and bullying won't be tolerated at this school. Is that understood?'

It was understood.

Later that afternoon, the headmaster took him to one side.

'The thought of one of our boys being beaten by another is totally unacceptable. It has, however, occurred to me that another boy may not be to blame.'

It was the first time anyone had given the slightest indication that they might know what was doing this to him, and just for a moment Nicholas thought the head was going to tell him he knew how to deal with it. His hopes were blown away when the head went on to say he was sending him home to recover, and that when he came back, he expected him to reveal the name of the person responsible.

It wasn't possible to name something that spread on the wall of the dorm like a dark, damp stain, something that had no face, something that whispered obscenities, clawed at your face in the night, dominated your every waking thought.

One of the nurses was holding a syringe of Zyphol. Nicholas was rolled on to his side, and as the needle was pushed into his thigh muscle, Goldman said, 'Nothing to be afraid of, Nick – we're just going to send you to sleep for a while, to give you a chance to rest.'

Nicholas was more interested in what was happening on the drugs trolley than in anything Goldman had to say. The items on it were being moved around. Liquids were being sucked out of the phials, and needles were bending and straightening as if they were strips of cotton.

He was tempted to draw Goldman's attention to it, but what would be the point? The minute Goldman so much as glanced at that trolley, the interference would stop. And assuming Goldman accepted that things were no longer where they should be, he would probably think he'd mislaid them in the first place.

The Zyphol was sending him under. No point trying to fight it. The sedative was already taking effect.

Goldman shone a light into his pupils, then slipped the torch back into the pocket of his Paul Smith shirt and left, but the nurses stayed behind. They were talking to one another. Football, cricket, an imminent move to a flat on the other side of town. They wouldn't be quite so relaxed if they knew what was standing behind them.

One of the nurses raised his hand to his neck, rubbed his throat gently, then lowered his hand again. And the thing that caused him to do it started to speak:

I am still here, Nicholas.

I know.

You think you have outwitted me, but I can still hurt you.

I know.

You breathe me into bottles that you nail into a box, but I stay free.

I know.

I am your only friend.

15

Audrah had thought herself prepared for the moment when she would see Cranmer again, but it appeared that no amount of preparation was enough. He caught her out, and she berated herself for the fact that Tate was there to witness how his sudden appearance affected her. It was somewhat different to the effect Cranmer had had on her when they first met, and she recalled telling Jochen about him as he and she stood on the balcony of the house. They had looked across the wood as if willing Lars to come walking through the trees, and she had said:

'I've met someone.'

Initially, Jochen thought she meant she had fallen in love with someone and in a sense, that was true. But at the time, she covered her embarrassment by explaining that she meant she had met someone who claimed he could help her to find out what happened to Lars.

'Where did he come from?'

'He phoned me.'

'How did he get your number?'

Her name had been in the papers, along with that of Jochen and Eva Sidow. The Sidows were, after all, an influential family. That fact alone was enough to guarantee that the media would show an interest, though most of the news reports had appeared in the Swedish press. There were very few that had appeared in the English nationals, but those that did explained that Lars Sidow, son of a senior executive with First National Bank, had disappeared in highly unusual circumstances.

Jochen had spent his life in the city. He knew a great deal about money. What Audrah hadn't realised was he also knew a great deal about people. She was the qualified psychologist, and yet it was he who pointed out that women who have recently lost someone they love are exceptionally vulnerable. 'What do you actually know about this man?'

'They say he's one of the greatest psychics the world has ever known.'

'Who says?' said Jochen. 'The people who handle his public relations? Be careful, Audrah – men who contact young attractive women who have recently been bereaved rarely do so for altruistic reasons.'

Too late now to wish she'd heeded his warning. All she could do was try to ensure that others didn't suffer as she had.

She felt she should have realised that Cranmer might show at any moment. Whenever he took an interest in a case, he was never far from the action. Still, the fact that Tate told him to leave was a good sign. It meant he wasn't as gullible as some. But it would be a mistake to underestimate Cranmer. He was more than capable of getting to Tate.

As the ambulance was leaving, Tate had asked her whether she was genuinely comfortable with the idea of driving Claudia to Broughton. 'I can arrange for one of my men to take her.'

She assured him it was no problem, but she didn't tell him she was doing it in the hope that it might result in her getting the chance to talk to the psychiatrist who had treated Nicholas in the past. It was going to be interesting to hear what Goldman had to say.

Now she stood in the waiting room at Broughton. It was housed in an old infirmary, and it had all the comfort and atmosphere of a bus shelter. Two plastic benches ran the length of one wall, and as she sat there, Audrah thought about what she'd just walked into. There were so many questions she wanted to ask Claudia, not only about Nicholas, but about the situation generally, not least because she had yet to hear Claudia mention either Ginny or Francis. No wonder the police were so interested. Audrah could well imagine what was going through Tate's mind, particularly after Nicholas wandered into the courtyard waving a knife. He hadn't been in any fit state for Tate to question him, and in the circumstances Tate hadn't thought it appropriate to question Claudia for the time being. Audrah had felt the same as they were following the ambulance. The opportunity to find out what was going on would present itself at some stage. Until then, she was just going to have to curb her curiosity. In the meantime, she tried to work out how Nicholas produced those welts. There was no doubt in her mind that he'd done it himself, but that was as much as she knew.

Often, even when she couldn't explain *how* a particular effect was being produced, she could at least say with some certainty that what she was seeing was nothing more than a stunt being pulled by someone trying to convince the punters he was psychic. Often the stunts were crude, and the illusions easy to detect, but this time she couldn't even hazard a guess as to how it was being done. The wounds were genuine, that much was obvious. It was too violent for an allergic reaction, and she doubted it could be caused by drugs. It was possible he'd rubbed an irritant on his skin, but what?

Once Nicholas was sedated and Claudia had gone to the ward to look in on him, Audrah spoke to one of the nursing staff, explained that she was a psychologist, and asked them to find out whether Goldman could spare her a moment. A short time later, Goldman walked into the waiting room and she stood up as he introduced himself. 'We'll probably be more comfortable in my office.'

Goldman had done his best to rid the room of its more depressing Victorian characteristics. The furnishings were pale, the lines clean. He invited her to sit in one of two comfortable chairs. He took the other, saying: 'You do realise I have to observe doctor/patient confidentiality? The fact that Mrs Herrol invited you to offer an opinion on her son doesn't alter that. It might be different if I had my patient's permission.'

Audrah replied, 'I appreciate you seeing me at all.' Then she came clean, adding, 'And I feel you should know up front that my speciality is parapsychology. I'm based at the BIPR in Edinburgh.'

Goldman didn't say anything for a moment, and when he did, it was only, 'That's interesting.'

Impossible to tell what he was thinking. She could imagine him giving exactly the same response to someone who'd just admitted that biting the heads off small children was central to their favourite sexual fantasy.

'My motto, my *creed*, if you like, is that there is nothing on earth for which there is no rational explanation – which brings me to my reason for wanting to talk to you, because I can't explain how Nicholas produces those welts.'

Goldman smiled. 'You think he's harming himself?'

'Don't you?'

'I'm not sure.'

It wasn't what she had expected him to say.

Goldman added: 'Over the years, I've run every test known to medical science on Nicholas.'

'And?'

'They've always come back negative.' He smiled. 'You might say he's a fascinating case.'

'If you don't think he's harming himself, what *do* you think?'

Goldman went to a bookshelf that took up most of the wall behind his desk. He indicated the textbooks and said, 'There was a time when I thought I might find the answer in one of these, but I was wrong.'

He allowed his hand to wander along the shelves. It stroked the spines of a few favoured editions, then came to rest on a book bound in finest calf. He pulled it out, and passed it to her almost reverentially. '*This*, however, contains a description of Nicholas Herrol's symptoms.' As an afterthought, he added, 'It ought to appeal to someone of your profession.'

When she realised that what Goldman had placed in her hands was a book on demonology, Audrah said, 'You're supposed to be a psychiatrist.'

'I *am* a psychiatrist,' said Goldman. 'And one thing a good psychiatrist should never do is close his mind to all the possibilities. I would have thought the same was true for any parapsychologist?'

'There are certain possibilities that don't warrant serious consideration,' said Audrah.

'You came in here thinking I'd confirm something you suspected from the moment you set eyes on Nicholas – you came in here thinking I would say he's schizophrenic. But I have to disappoint you, because I'm not prepared to make that diagnosis.'

Doctors were often reluctant to diagnose schizophrenia in the early stages of the illness. But once the symptoms became severe, their reluctance usually evaporated. 'Where there is thought disorder, social withdrawal, a deterioration from a previous level of functioning, the diagnosis of schizophrenia has to be considered. Nicholas has all these symptoms, and more.'

'He isn't a classic case.'

'Who is?'

It was a mistake to challenge his opinion. Goldman replied, 'Nicholas has been my patient for over a decade. You've seen him . . . how often?'

'Once.'

'Once,' said Goldman. 'And for how long?'

When Audrah admitted she hadn't even spoken to him, but had talked to his mother as Nicholas lay sleeping, Goldman smiled. 'I'm sure you have his interests at heart, but perhaps it might be best if you were to leave his care to those who are . . . shall we say *academically* equipped to make the right judgments.'

Audrah rose from the chair and returned to the waiting room to find Claudia sitting on one of the benches, staring at the floor. With her tangle of hair and the old tweed coat, she might have come in off the street.

'How is he?' said Audrah.

'Quieter now,' she replied.

She was sitting with her back to artwork produced by some of Broughton's patients. Every psychosis known to man was represented in those paintings, and as Audrah compared the almost invisible strokes of a delicate if surreal watercolour to a riotous cry for help that spoke of a slide into total madness, she wondered what kind of artwork Nicholas would ultimately add to the collection.

Tate stood in the courtyard with Fletcher and Bevan. Between them, they'd got a fair idea of the layout of the house, and that would come in useful, because when Nicholas came out of the house naked and armed with a knife, the decision as to whether or not to undertake a full-scale search rather made itself.

A powdery snow was falling lightly all around them. Soon it would obliterate all trace of their having been there. Time to call it a day, to close those great oak doors and leave the house secure – not that there was anything left worth stealing. Everything of value appeared to have been ruined. Tate was more concerned about the press turning up, taking liberties, and corrupting a potential crime scene in the process.

Bevan stared at the house as if mesmerised by it. 'Beautiful, isn't she.'

It would take a man like Bevan to find a place like Lyndle beautiful. It was too bleak, too plain for Tate. He would have preferred there to have been some simple feature carved into the stone, something to alleviate the relentless black of those endless granite walls.

' "Some old things are lovely . . . warm still with the life of forgotten men who made them." ' Bevan turned to Tate. 'D. H. Lawrence, sir.'

' "Time for bed, said Zebadee." ' Fletcher turned to Bevan. '*Magic Roundabout.*'

Tate smiled, but only briefly. He found it less amusing when Bevan added:

'I feel sorry for her.'

'We don't know for sure she's dead.'

'I meant the house.'

'Save your sympathy for Ginny Mulholland,' said Tate. 'And possibly Francis Herrol.'

His mobile phone rang, as quiet as a whisper. He answered it.

'Don't hang up,' said Cranmer.

Fletcher caught the look on Tate's face. 'What's wrong?'

It occurred to Tate that Cranmer might be in the trees, watching him take the call. If so, he might be amused if he let his anger show. And Tate *was* angry. Cranmer had accessed the number of his mobile phone. The number wasn't listed because Tate was a senior police officer. Therefore, Cranmer could only have done it illegally.

Tate said, 'You've just made a very big mistake, Cranmer,' but whatever he'd been about to say next was lost when Cranmer replied:

'You came across a room off the kitchen . . . green tiles, single bed and a wardrobe. The metal hangers jangled as you opened the wardrobe door. It was Ginny's room. Tell me I'm wrong. *Tell me!*'

Tate was too taken aback to say anything.

'Let me try to help you,' said Cranmer. 'Let me into the house – and if, after that, you want me to stay away, I'll go. No press. No further hassle. Next plane back to the States. I swear. *I swear!*'

A few hours later, Tate and Cranmer were standing in Ginny's room. Tate hadn't told him which it was or where to find it, but then he hadn't had to. Once they were in the house, Cranmer led him straight to it, and Tate could only follow, could only stand there and watch as he absorbed things about it that not even the most experienced of forensics experts could garner with all the technology at their disposal.

Cranmer stood there, eyes closed, his voice filled with emotion. 'She didn't die here,' he said, and Tate felt a coldness creep through him.

'Such rage,' said Cranmer. 'I sense such rage.' And then, 'Where are you buried?'

Tate heard him muttering something about *not buried, but concealed*, and when he heard water mentioned, it brought to mind the moat. 'What are you trying to tell me?' said Tate. 'She's in the moat – is that it?'

Cranmer opened his eyes, and what Tate saw in them frightened him. Those eyes of his . . . there was nothing, nothing *there*!

'Where are you?' said Cranmer, softly. 'Try to tell me . . . *try* . . .'

He nodded as if acknowledging a voice that was audible only to him, then he spoke to Tate.

'I see it now,' he said. 'She's in the wood.'

16

It was now twenty-four hours since Guy walked out, and he hadn't heard from Rachel. He'd expected to, though God knows why. She was probably waiting for him to contact her. Well, she could wait.

He wanted to be alone and was irritated when his father joined him for a walk along the spit. From here, it was possible to see the Purbecks, and memories of a childhood filled with summer walks along the cliffs came flooding back. They should have been happy times, but they were clouded by an awareness that something wasn't right between his parents.

When he was older he realised that what he had detected was a constant air of mistrust, the unspoken acknowledgment that the relationship would only survive provided it was never challenged. Financial hardship, illness, a personal crisis of some sort might send it tumbling off the cliffs and on to the rocks below, and this, of course, was what happened in the end. It might have come by way of an affair. In the event, it came by way of contempt. The occasional sarcastic comment turned into a relentless bickering until neither could stand to be in the presence of the other. It left him hoping for something more with the woman he happened to marry, but he currently felt that he hadn't even made first base. It wasn't a good feeling.

'This cottage,' said his father. 'Tell me more about it.'

There wasn't much to tell other than that it was hugely disappointing to discover it was practically worthless.

In the second week of August, they drove up to see it, arriving to find the village almost deserted. It wasn't the kind of place that was likely to attract tourists, and their hope of finding a guest-house for the night evaporated. They did, however, find a petrol station, its office a chipboard shack, the pumps antique and guarded by someone who seemed rather more suspicious of them than grateful for passing trade. He filled their car without comment, and made no reply when Rachel asked where they could buy food.

There was a store, that was all, and this they found for themselves, but most of what it stocked was very basic. The boy behind the counter looked subnormal. A sliver of saliva hung from his thick, slack lips as he watched them search the shelves for bread and cheese. They were the only people in the store. For some reason, that made Guy uneasy. People had drifted away from this place, leaving a row of cottages to fall into decay. He wondered what had driven them away.

On entering Ruth's cottage, they stood ankle deep in rubble that had fallen from above, looked straight up at the gap-toothed tiles and breathed the smell of rotting wood from eaves that were being consumed by death watch beetle.

It was hopeless. Even if they could afford to renovate it, there was no point spending a fortune doing up a cottage that was attached to a row of twenty others, each just as neglected, each on the brink of almost total collapse. The village was dead, and the silence of a primary school now devoid of children was its epitaph. Not even the ground the cottage stood on was worth much, for who would want to live here, amid the bleeding rocks, and a wind that swept in from the north to gnaw at the brick and stone like a hungry dog?

His discomfiture increased, yet he stayed to check that there was nothing of interest to be had. There might be an implement used by someone who lived here at a time when all the cooking was done on the hearth. There might be the porcelain fragment from a tea service that spent most of its life in a pawnshop and only saw the light of day on very special occasions. The death of the old queen. The coronation of the new. VE Day. The people who lived in these cottages would have been poor, but they would have had their treasures, and their treasures might be lying in the rubble.

Rachel left him to it and wandered out through the yard, and while she was gone he found a wooden clothes-peg. It was the old-fashioned type with long slender shanks and a rounded head. Some father had whittled and painted it into a doll, had presented it to a child who would treasure it all the more for the fact that it was produced from love and effort.

When Rachel returned, he held it out to her, but she showed little interest. She almost pushed his hand away. 'I'll look at it later,' she said.

'Rachel?'

'I'm all right – just tired.'

He pocketed the peg and said, 'Let's find somewhere to eat,' and later they drove into Otterburn and found a guest-house.

Rachel ran a bath and sank into it as if it were amniotic fluid, relishing the warmth, the soothing, protective qualities of the water. He poured her a glass of wine, but she refused it. She felt unwell, she said. All she wanted to do was go to bed.

The following day they drove home. She hardly spoke a word the entire journey, and although, logically, he found it difficult to imagine how going to see the cottage could have had any bearing on her subsequent behaviour, it seemed to mark the beginning of her gradually pulling away from him.

'What do you think?' said Guy.

So far, his father had said very little. Now he said something Guy didn't want to hear. It wasn't that it hadn't already occurred to him – it was more that he couldn't stand the thought of it.

'When she left you alone at the cottage, and went for a walk out the back, you don't think she could have been . . . raped, do you?'

'I don't know,' said Guy. 'But I'm sure I'd know if she had.'

'Are you?'

No, he wasn't. That was the trouble. He'd heard that when women were raped, they sometimes didn't tell a living soul. They were too afraid the police wouldn't believe them, or their partner would reject them, or that they and their entire sexual history would be put on trial. Maybe men who had known their partner longer than he'd known Rachel would have a better idea of how they might react if they were raped. Guy hadn't a clue.

The weather was turning now. Rolling banks of cloud were appearing over the Purbecks, and waders had been driven from the spit by the rising tide.

'We'd better get back,' said his father.

He and Guy returned to a message on the answerphone. Someone called DC Wilcox, West Yorkshire Police, wanted Guy to call him.

Guy couldn't think of anyone who knew where he was other than Rachel. Maybe he was being done for parking the car outside the house when the tax had run out.

He phoned and spoke to Wilcox, who said, 'Before I say anything further, I'm afraid I have to check – you *are* the husband of Rachel Harvey of 14 Rippon Gardens?'

Guy's composure evaporated. 'Has something happened?'

'Mr Harvey, I'm afraid your wife is in Leeds Infirmary.'

Guy's brain was attempting to convince him that the polished parquet flooring was rolling under his feet. He had to put a hand against the wall to steady himself.

'Mr Harvey?'

'I'm . . . I'm listening,' Guy stammered.

'How quickly can you get here?'

17

By the time Audrah returned to Lyndle with Claudia, it was early evening. Tate and his men were gone, but the lights had been left on, the bulbs casting a dull yellow glow on the walls.

It was as cold inside the house as out, and Claudia offered to light a fire in the study. In the meantime, she showed Audrah into a sparsely furnished bedroom. The bed was damp, and the bedding looked as though it could do with changing. 'You might find yourself more comfortable at an hotel.'

Audrah had done enough driving for one day. 'I'll take my chances, thanks.'

A large, ugly radiator jutted away from the wall, and she didn't have to be told that nothing she could do would succeed in coaxing heat from it.

'There's a bathroom on the landing,' said Claudia. She showed her to it. No shower, and no hope of filling the enormous bath with anything but a couple of inches of luke-warm water.

'If you want me, I'll be downstairs,' Claudia said, and then she left her to it.

After she had gone, Audrah lifted her overnight bag on to the bed and pulled out the warmest clothing she could find. But by the time she'd decided to sleep in the clothes she was wearing, Claudia was back.

'Can you come?' she said.

She sounded frightened.

'What's wrong?'

'Come,' she said, and moments later Audrah was in the study. The first thing she saw when she entered it was a suitcase. It was empty, but as she looked around her its former contents stared back at her from every available surface. They were newspaper clippings mostly, all of them dropped behind simple Perspex frames, the headlines highlighted with fluorescent markers. They made an immediate impression, a mosaic in which the words *Bristol* and *Death* and *Arrest* assaulted the eye.

Surfaces that hadn't been covered by clippings were covered by photographs, some of a man who kept his back to the camera, or used his hands to shield his face from the lens. One of the photos had been taken as he was leaving a police station. Another as he was entering a court. But what interested Audrah was the woman who stood up as she entered the room. Everything about her suggested she was up for confrontation. The first thing she said as Audrah walked in was, 'I'm not leaving.'

It would probably be best to try to keep things calm, find out who she was and what she wanted. 'I'm Audrah,' she said, amiably. 'And you must be . . .?'

It looked as though the woman was trying to work out whether or not to tell her. After a moment, she seemed to come to the conclusion than it was safe enough. 'Marion.'

'You're not with the police?' said Audrah, who didn't think she could be but thought it worth checking.

'No,' said Marion.

'How did you get in?'

Marion nodded at Claudia, who was standing in the doorway. 'She left the door open.'

'Why are you here?' said Claudia. 'What do you want?'

'I'm here to see someone called Cranmer,' she replied.

Marion didn't know until she actually got there precisely how she was going to inveigle her way into Lyndle. As in all things, luck played a part. Usually, when she wanted people to let her into a place they might not otherwise allow her access to, she pretended to be ill. It was surprising how easy it was to gain access to even relatively secure buildings – government offices, television studios – by pretending to be ill. The important thing was not to appear to be *mentally* ill. Mental illness frightened people. They called security and had you removed. The trick was to appear well dressed, calm, reasonable, and in need of a little help. Nothing too demanding. Nothing disconcerting. Then people took you inside, let you sit down, offered you a drink. And once you got your foot in the door, they couldn't get you out until you'd got what you came for. But without knowing what to expect when you got to a place, it wasn't easy to plan, and she had no definite plan for what she was going to do when she reached Lyndle. Much depended on what she found when she got there, and what she found was a house that looked malign.

Could an inanimate object be malign? It was a house, no more, no less. She hid her car in the trees, and forced herself to walk across the lawns.

The bridge across the moat gave on to a plain stone arch. Beyond it, Claudia Herrol was dragging a small round table across the courtyard. Marion recognised her from a picture in the paper. Those rather striking features. That greying hair worn long and loose and wild.

When she saw her, Claudia left the table, walked back into the house, and shut the door. It was such a bizarre reaction and so unexpected that Marion simply stood there, gawping after her. For once, she didn't know what to do. It was the first time in a long time that anyone had managed to get the better of her, but when she thought about it she realised that what usually gave her the advantage was the fact that people normally reacted by trying to reason with her. It wasn't *possible* to reason with her. Even she knew that. But it was of course possible to ignore her. Not that it made any difference. There would come a point when Claudia would have to leave the house, and when she did . . .

The doorway to the timber wing was wide enough for livestock. There was no door, just two wooden props taking the weight of a lintel that had bowed. Inside was a row of stalls.

It must have been years since horses were stabled there, yet saddles still sat on the racks, the panels the texture of cardboard, the doe-skin seats like velvet to the touch.

The stalls were crammed with furniture, none of the items large. There were endless dressers and tables, a coarse Dutch marquetry cupboard, a Chippendale stool, and the casing to a grandfather clock minus its mechanism.

Boxes of curtains and bedding lay beside boxes of cutlery and crockery – all bent, all broken. Also, boxes of books, a reminder that she once inhabited a world in which reading comprised a major part of her life. These days she didn't much look like an avid reader, or a person who might once have attended concerts, held dinner parties, entertained friends, and conversed knowledgeably about subjects she no longer even thought about unless they in some way connected with her present situation. Once, she had *lived*. She missed the person she used to be. But that person died when Kathryn was murdered by Reeve.

Some of the books were spoiled, the covers ripped from the text but then carefully replaced, as if by someone who hoped one day to have them rebound. She picked one out and sat with it in an armchair. This, too, was spoiled, the upholstery ripped, the stuffing showing through. Curtains lay in a loosely folded pile beside it. She opened them out. They'd been torn into long wide strips.

The more she looked at what was around her, the more she realised *everything* was ruined. The furnishings were scratched. The crockery was broken. The cutlery was bent. The curtains, bedding and linen were all torn. Why keep these things? Why not throw them away?

She arranged what was left of the curtains on what was left of a chair, and settled down to wait. Sooner or later Claudia would come out of the house, and when she did, it might provide an opportunity for her to creep in.

She didn't have long to wait. A short time later she heard a car, and she eased herself out of the chair and went to the door.

A police Range Rover was slewing across the area of land dividing the house from the trees.

When she saw it, she stepped back into the darkness. She didn't have a right to be there, and what she was doing might be considered trespassing. Or maybe she would be deemed to have broken the terms of the restraining order. She didn't see how she could have, but that meant nothing. Her experience of the law had destroyed her faith in it. Lawyers and judges could claim what they liked and get away with it.

Someone got out of the passenger seat and walked across the courtyard to the Hall. The only way he could make his presence known was by hammering on the door, and when he got no answer he stood back and shouted up at the windows. 'I know you're in there, Mrs Herrol. Do I have to break the door down? I will, if that's what it takes.'

The wind was singing softly through the stones. It caught a handful of powdery snow and whipped it around his face as he waited for a response. When he didn't get one, he left the courtyard and went back to the vehicle, and only then did Claudia leave the house. She strode across the courtyard, leaving the door wide open.

Moments later, Marion stood in front of Lyndles Great Hall. Walking into a place like that would require an act of courage, but what was one act of courage among so many? Her life was made up of such acts, some large, some small. Just getting up in the morning and forcing herself to live another day required courage.

She went inside.

The realisation that someone had broken in demanding to be allowed to speak to Cranmer was no surprise to Audrah. Mediums who put themselves in the public eye often attracted people who were desperate for help. She suggested it might be best if Claudia were to leave them alone for a while, and after she was gone Audrah walked over to the photograph of an adolescent girl. It was propped on the centre of the plain stone mantelpiece. 'That was my daughter,' said Marion, and when Audrah didn't comment, she added: 'She died.'

Audrah had rather gathered that.

'Aren't you going to ask how?'

'How?' said Audrah, softly.

'She was murdered.'

Audrah picked up the photograph, too saddened to know what to say, and when she didn't comment Marion added: 'Most people want the details. The *when*, and *how*, and *why*.'

'I think there are times when people should curb their curiosity.'

'Don't you even want to know who murdered her?' Marion was obviously going to tell her. 'One of her teachers.'

The word 'teacher' came as a shock to Audrah. When murders were committed by people who were placed in a position of trust, it was always particularly disturbing.

'Michael Reeve.'

Audrah had never heard of him. She looked once again at the clippings and realised that most were from newspapers that covered the Bristol area. How could a crime as serious as that not make the nationals?

'What was her name?'

'Kathryn.'

More because she felt it was expected of her than because she felt it was true, Audrah said, 'She was pretty.'

'Thanks, but I know she wasn't. She knew it too. It's a terrible thing to be sixteen, and to wake up one morning and suddenly realise you're not going to be one of the world's great beauties. I know. I remember.'

'She wasn't exactly ugly.'

'She was plain,' said Marion, bluntly. 'But she was mine, and I loved her.'

Audrah put the photograph back on the mantelpiece. 'What are you hoping to achieve by seeing Cranmer?'

She expected Marion to reply that she just needed to know that Kathryn was happy, because that was what most people wanted. *Once I know she's in paradise, I can rest easy.* But Marion wanted something else entirely:

'The night she was murdered, Kathryn was with a friend called Sasha. Sasha is holding something back from the police – something that might help them bring Reeve to justice. I want Cranmer to tell me what she's hiding.'

It sounded vindictive, and dangerous.

'Would you listen if I tried to offer you some advice?'

'No, but if it makes you feel useful, go ahead.'

Audrah was tempted to say that the endless reaching out in the hope of making contact with the dead inhibited a person's ability to come to terms with their loss, that the bereaved were vulnerable, that the mind played tricks on the vulnerable, and that pseudo psychics took advantage of it. But as she realised the magnitude of what had happened to this woman, she realised also that nothing she said was likely to get through to her.

Something caught her eye – something she'd noticed when she first came into the room. At the time, it hadn't really registered. Her attention was taken more by the vitriolic headlines positioned on every conceivable surface. Now her eyes returned to rest on the contents of a large glass case, its sole occupant a beetle mounted in an attitude of threat. *Dorcus Titanus.* Immense and black. His mandibles like the pincers of a crab.

As she studied him, part of the analogy that she used when introducing the course in parapsychology sprang to mind: *We are in the business of finding out whether there is a world, an existence, beyond that which we know.* Surely an insect such as this was proof enough that some other world did indeed exist, not beyond or parallel to ours, but within it; as a fundamental and functioning part of it.

To her, that fact alone was as mysterious and strange as any that might be concocted in the mind of a pseudo psychic.

Claudia was in the kitchen, rooting around in a cupboard filled with cleaning equipment. When Audrah walked in, she stopped what she was doing. 'Where is she?'

'I left her in the study.'

Before Audrah could ask what she wanted her to do about Marion, Claudia said, 'She mentioned someone called Cranmer.' And then, 'Who is he?'

Surely she knew. 'You must have read the papers.'

'Francis used to buy one sometimes. I never bother.'

It was possible she'd never heard of him. His name had only been in the papers in the last few days. Whatever the case, Audrah felt it might not be a good idea to let her know than Cranmer claimed to be psychic. Someone who believed their son was at the mercy of a malign entity might jump at the offer of help from someone like Cranmer, and that could be a disaster. 'Cranmer is someone who tends to latch on to high-profile police investigations.'

'Is that what this is becoming?' said Claudia, softly.

If she hadn't read the papers, she wouldn't know the degree of interest being shown in what was happening at Lyndle. Even so, she must surely realise that the police weren't simply going to go away. Maybe now was the time to try to get that through to her. 'Mrs Herrol,' Audrah said, 'have you any idea at all what might have happened to Ginny and your husband?'

Claudia found a bottle of cleaning fluid in the cupboard. She seemed more interested in unscrewing the cap than in anything Audrah had to say.

'Mrs Herrol?'

Claudia wrapped a cloth round the cap and unscrewed it. Then she poured the contents down the sink, screwed the cap back on, and returned the bottle to the cupboard.

It was difficult to tell whether the evasion was deliberate, or the action of someone whose mind was on other things. Either way, it was obvious there was no point asking her again, just as it was obvious that whatever else she might think, she certainly didn't think her husband had left her for Ginny. Women who had only recently been deserted by their husbands were usually devastated. Even if they didn't feel like talking about it, they found it hard to hide what they were going through. Claudia wasn't behaving like a woman whose husband had left her. But then it was possible she simply couldn't cope with what was happening. People sometimes blocked out the things they couldn't cope with. Sometimes they went on to automatic pilot. They didn't realise they were pouring cleaning fluid down the sink, nor did they notice that they'd been watching water gushing out of a tap for the past two minutes.

Audrah turned the tap off, and led her to a chair. Her mind was still very much on how to get her talking about the situation at Lyndle, but Claudia was thinking about Cranmer.

'Why would he want to latch on to police investigations?'

'He uses them to raise his profile.'

'His profile as what?'

This was getting tricky, but before she could find a way of explaining what Cranmer did without it leading to roads she didn't want Claudia to go down, Marion appeared in the doorway.

'His profile as a psychic,' she said.

It was the last thing Audrah had wanted Claudia to hear. 'I thought I asked you to stay in the study.'

'I wanted to know whether you were planning to get the police to throw me out.'

Claudia turned to Audrah. 'What's she talking about?'

Audrah reconsidered. After all, Claudia was bound to find out in the end. Maybe it was better to tell her who Cranmer was, then warn her off having anything to do with him.

'Cranmer claims to be psychic,' said Audrah. 'He offered to help the police find Ginny. They turned him down, so he went to the press.'

Marion said, 'I thought he might be staying here.'

There was no mistaking Claudia's sudden interest. 'What kind of psychic?'

Marion replied, 'He talks to the dead.'

'Is that true?' said Claudia.

Audrah replied, 'Cranmer is a con man. Not only that, but he's a *dangerous* con man.'

Marion said, 'The papers don't seem to think so.'

'People like Cranmer sell papers,' said Audrah.

Claudia crossed the kitchen and stood in the doorway with Marion. Between them, they presented a united front. Two women, each now determined to meet John Cranmer, each, in Audrah's view, heading for their own, very personal disaster. But she had enough experience not to bother trying to convince them not to have anything to do with him. They hadn't even met him, yet already they were sold on the idea that he could help them. Was it any wonder people like Cranmer found it easy to persuade people they were psychic? The people they were dealing with *wanted* to believe it. And therein lay the pseudo psychic's power – the fact that they even existed fulfilled a certain psychological need.

Claudia said, 'If he's helping the police, that must mean they know where we can find him.'

Audrah replied, 'I doubt the police will tell you. But I shouldn't worry – if I know Cranmer, he'll find you.'

18

Prior to meeting Cranmer, what Tate knew about psychics could have been written on the back of a stamp. Now he was a little better informed, because over the past few days various papers had run articles about him. As a result, he now knew that Cranmer's services were sought by the US military, the FBI and the CIA.

It all looked very impressive, very convincing, but a deep vein of scepticism ran through Tate. Maybe Cranmer was genuinely psychic, in which case that would explain how he knew as much as he did about Ginny's room, but Tate thought it more likely that he somehow managed to get hold of a description of where it was, and what was in it. He therefore began to think about how Cranmer might have accessed this information, and he started by examining what he actually knew.

What he knew was that Cranmer drove up to the courtyard at the moment Nicholas Herrol came out of the house. He also knew that Bevan and Fletcher escorted him back to his car, and watched him drive away.

From that point on, the rest was guesswork. What if Cranmer didn't drive away? What if he hid his car in the trees, then doubled back to the house, broke in, and located the room most likely to have been allocated to Ginny? Alternatively, it was possible he saw the ambulance arrive, followed it to Broughton, found Nicholas and persuaded him to describe Ginny's room.

The more Tate thought about it, the more likely it seemed that Cranmer would have preferred the risk of accessing Nicholas Herrol to the risk of being caught breaking into Lyndle. It wouldn't have been worth his reputation. Besides,

Broughton would have been the easier option. People went in and out of there every day – visitors, patients, nursing and clerical staff, people delivering food, medicines, linen. Hospitals were notoriously difficult to monitor. And Cranmer was well dressed, well spoken, and polite. He wasn't the kind of person who looked as though he should be questioned about what he was doing there. There was only one way to find out. After leaving Lyndle Hall, Tate went to Broughton.

He wasn't sure what kind of reception he could expect. If the psychiatrist treating Nicholas thought he was there in the hope that he might help him prove his patient was a killer, he would be within his rights to be obstructive. Therefore the first thing Tate did after he met Goldman was assure him he was there because he suspected Cranmer had managed to access Nicholas after he was admitted.

Goldman was well aware of everything that had recently happened at Lyndle, and he knew who Cranmer was. He was concerned when Tate told him it was possible Cranmer had tried to access Nicholas, and he showed him into his office where he pulled blinds against windows designed to carry extravagant drapes. The effect, at this time of night, was to make the room seem a little clinical.

Tate said, 'How likely is it that Cranmer could have wandered into the ward?'

Goldman replied, 'I wish I could say it was unlikely. But like every other hospital in the country, our resources are stretched. We don't have enough staff – it's possible he might have wandered through without anybody questioning what he was doing here. And Nicholas isn't in a locked ward.'

'Is Cranmer likely to have been able to get any sense out of him?'

'What kind of sense?'

'Could he have held a conversation with him?'

'No,' said Goldman. 'Nicholas is heavily sedated.'

It looked as though he was going to have to reconsider how Cranmer came by a description of Ginny's room. 'If you don't mind me asking,' said Tate, 'what's Nicholas Herrol's problem?'

Goldman replied, 'You can't expect me to betray my patient's confidence.'

'I've got two missing people,' said Tate. 'I was hoping you'd be as anxious as I am to prevent it from becoming three, or maybe more.'

Goldman appeared to be torn between his duty to his patient, and his duty to the public. His duty to the public won. 'This is off the record,' he said, quietly. And then: 'Nicholas was referred to me by a doctor at a boarding school he attended as a child. One of the masters suspected he was being bullied. He asked the doctor to take a look at him, expecting him to confirm it.'

'And did he?'

Goldman replied: 'Doctors attached to boarding schools learn to identify which children are being bullied, just as they learn to identify which are being abused, and which are engaging in homosexual activity. This particular doctor had never seen anything like the injuries he saw on Nicholas Herrol.'

'What did he think caused them?'

'He suspected they were self-inflicted.'

Tate thought back to the way those welts had just appeared. There was no way they could have been self-inflicted, surely? Yet what other explanation could there be?

'How old was he?'

'Eleven.'

As Tate began to work it out for himself, Goldman added, 'I had to consider the possibility that what Nicholas was doing was part of an auto-erotic ritual.'

'Eleven. It's so young.'

'You'd be surprised,' said Goldman. 'I don't see it often, but I do see it. And some of them are younger than eleven.'

'Surely their parents—'

'Mostly, their parents never know. But sometimes . . . a boy is found dead. The parents are blamed for not noticing how unhappy he was. The picture is given of an isolated boy who hanged himself in a fit of deep depression and everybody accepts it because the verdict of suicide is preferable to the truth. Believe me, Mr Tate, a great many child suicides are in fact cases of accidental death, the auto-erotic experiment gone wrong.'

'Eleven,' said Tate again, incredulously.

Goldman smiled. 'By the time we reach puberty, our sexual identity is already established. All we can do for such children is offer therapy in the hope of encouraging them to modify their behaviour.'

'And what did therapy tell you about Nicholas?'

Goldman said nothing for a moment. And then he replied: 'It told me he was dancing with the uninvited guest.'

Tate had never heard the expression before.

'Some myths are universal. No matter what the country or the culture, there is always the myth relating to the uninvited guest.'

'Go on,' said Tate.

'According to the myth, whenever a child is born, it is essential to have a religious ceremony, not for the family so much as for the spirits. Gifts are offered to good and bad spirits alike. Naturally, it is important to beg the good spirits to watch over the child, but it is equally important to appease the bad, to make them feel as important, as *wanted*, as the good. The worst mistake a family can make is to forget to invite one of those bad spirits. If a bad spirit discovers it hasn't been invited, you might say it invites itself to mingle, unseen, unnoticed, among the other guests. Sometimes it merely places a curse on the child then leaves. But sometimes, it enters the child, only to emerge when the child is older. Then it takes revenge by dancing the child to its death.'

Tate could hardly believe he was hearing this from a professional. 'You're telling me Nicholas woke up one morning to find himself at the mercy of some demon?'

117

'I'm merely telling you primitive people had no other way to explain what mental illness was, or why it should affect some and not others.'

'And you?' said Tate. 'What do you believe?'

Goldman took a moment to reply, and when he did, he was fairly non-committal. 'Most of my colleagues agree that Nicholas is suffering from a schizophrenic illness.' It sounded as though Goldman didn't share their view. 'An early symptom of his illness manifested in the form of an imaginary friend.'

It wasn't abnormal for children to create an imaginary friend, but the nature of this fantasy worried Goldman apparently. 'At one point,' he said, 'I used hypnotherapy to regress him to the age he was at when he first became aware of the existence of this . . . thing.'

When Tate remained silent, Goldman went on, 'Such fantasies don't simply come into being. As a rule, they take shape over a period of time, and the way in which they develop is influenced by many factors.'

'What were you hoping to achieve?'

'I was hoping to find out whether this "friend" resembled his parents in any way. I thought that perhaps it was providing something they were failing to give him.'

'And was it?'

Nothing Nicholas said gave Goldman the impression that his friend was some kind of substitute for parental affection. What child would conjure up something that tormented him, whispered obscenities at him, clawed at his back? 'And the one thing I could never understand . . . right from the start, he could *see* the thing in detail. No period of development. It was *there*.'

As Goldman described what happened in those hypnotherapy sessions, Tate found himself building the picture he had tried to get when talking to Nicholas's tutor, Graham Lush:

'I'd regressed him to the age of four,' said Goldman. 'He told me he was playing in the garden. After a moment, he slid off the couch, and he started to scrape at the carpet with his fingers.

I asked him what he was doing. He told me he was burying things. And when I asked him what he was burying . . .'

Goldman paused, as if the memory of his patient's response disturbed him still. After a moment, he added, 'Nicholas was too young for the word "sacrifice" to have entered his vocabulary. But that was what it amounted to. His friend could have his chocolate, his bear, the ears and tail that were docked from a terrier given to his father.'

The idea of a child burying anything by way of sacrifice rang alarm bells for Tate. 'Is that normal?'

Goldman replied, 'Generally speaking, the imaginary friend tends to take the more subservient role.'

The implications hardly needed stating: what if this thing still existed, albeit only in Nicholas Herrol's head – and what if it was still demanding sacrifices? Tate said, 'What do you call someone who suffers from this kind of . . .'

'Psychosis?' said Goldman. He smiled. 'As I said a moment ago, certain of my colleagues believe he's schizophrenic.'

Tate's line of work brought him into contact with schizophrenics now and again. A lot of them lived on the street. A fair percentage wandered into police stations, libraries – anywhere they could get out of the cold and into the warm, anywhere they could shelter from the rain. He'd got to know a few of them. Not well, but enough to know what their problems were. These problems were many and varied. But none, to his knowledge, developed livid bleeding welts that appeared in a matter of minutes, and went in a matter of hours.

'And what about you?' said Tate. 'What's *your* diagnosis?'

When Goldman made no reply, Tate added, 'You don't agree with your colleagues' diagnosis. Why not?'

Goldman replied, 'Schizophrenia can't be cured, but it can be treated, and generally speaking Schizophrenics respond to medication. Treating them is largely a matter of finding out which drugs work best for them. But *nothing* has ever worked for Nicholas, and it makes me wonder—'

He glanced at some of the books lining the shelves behind

him. 'A century or so ago, psychiatry had about as much credibility as reflexology. We think we know so much. But I ask myself – what do we really know? Has our smattering of knowledge made us so arrogant we can no longer accept what's staring us in the face?'

'You can't mean that.'

'Why? Because of what I am, what I do? Suddenly, psychiatrists aren't allowed to believe in anything other than the great god science? I don't know what to believe, Mr Tate. Nicholas Herrol has been my patient for almost a decade. I'm no closer to understanding his condition now than I was when he was first referred to me – I only know I can't help him.'

'What makes your colleagues so certain he's schizophrenic?'

'He sees things, hears things – for them, that's enough to warrant the diagnosis.'

Tate cast his mind back to when he'd been standing in Ginny's room with Cranmer. What was Cranmer doing if not seeing and hearing things? 'What about Cranmer?' said Tate. 'What do you call someone who claims they hear the voices of the dead?'

Goldman read the papers. He knew who Cranmer was. He replied:

'Those same colleagues of mine would take the view that Cranmer is probably every bit as schizophrenic as Nicholas.'

'Can someone be schizophrenic and still function relatively normally?'

Goldman replied, 'The majority of us meet schizophrenics every day of our lives. We work with them, interact with them, never even suspecting they have a problem, either because their symptoms are well controlled by medication, or because their illness manifests in its mildest form. It's only when people start claiming they've been abducted by aliens, or that God keeps telling them to rid the world of prostitutes that we start to notice there's something wrong with them. And then there are people who realise that it mightn't be a great idea to admit they've been talking to fairies for the best part of thirty years.

They're not so out of touch with reality that they don't know what the reaction will be if they admit what's going on inside their heads, so their intimate relationship with fairies becomes their little secret. These are the milder cases. There are hundreds of thousands of people like that. Assuming he actually "hears" these voices, Cranmer could be someone who manages, somehow, to hold it all together.'

'What do you think of Cranmer?'

Goldman replied, 'Pretty much what I think of Nicholas Herrol. He might be schizophrenic, he might not – we just don't know.'

Tate still didn't know what to make of Cranmer, but one thing was for sure – his involvement guaranteed constant media coverage, and that was a double-edged sword. On the one hand, it prompted people to phone in with information. On the other, most of the information turned out to be irrelevant. All he could do was trust other people to sift through and decide what he should look at.

After leaving Goldman, he returned to the station to find two messages from Fletcher. One related to Dr Audrah Sidow. The other related to a man called Williams. He'd read about what was happening at Lyndle, and the name Francis Herrol meant something to him. Could Tate call him?

Tate decided Audrah Sidow could wait. He would see her tomorrow and confront her with what Fletcher had found out. Then she could explain what she was *really* doing at Lyndle. But he would respond to the message from Williams straight away.

He'd given a London telephone number. Tate dialled it. Williams answered. There was a background noise of teenage kids fighting over the Play Station. It reminded him that he hadn't seen much of June and the kids for a week. It also reassured him that Williams was a family man. He sounded fairly sensible – not the type to fabricate a story.

'What do you want to know?' he said.

'Just tell me what you told Fletcher,' Tate replied.

Williams told him that in 1985, he was a security guard at one of the most prestigious modelling agencies in the country. 'A place called Margo's,' said Williams.

The premises were off Bond Street, and good security was essential because some of the models were obvious targets for paparazzi. They were also obvious targets for unwelcome attention from members of the public. Speaking of which . . .

On several occasions, Williams was told to escort Francis Herrol off the premises. 'He was mad about one of the girls. Wouldn't leave her alone. I was told to get him out, and keep him out.'

'How do you know it's the same Francis Herrol?'

'Saw his photo in the press,' said Williams. 'It was taken when he was older – but it's him.'

'How can you be sure?'

'I'm a security guard,' said Williams. 'You show me a photo of someone, and I remember their face. My job depends on me being able to pick them out in a crowd, not just the day you show me their photo, but weeks, months, maybe even years down the road. It was him.'

Tate brought the call to a close, then considered the information. By 1985, Francis and Claudia would have been married a good five years. He wondered what Claudia thought of her husband chasing after some young model. He also wondered whether Francis had chased after Ginny. If so, maybe Nicholas took exception, and killed him. It was thin, but it was at least a motive. And up until that moment, Tate hadn't been able to imagine why Nicholas might kill his father. Not that a reason was necessary. When someone was as sick as Nicholas Herrol, God only knew what went on in their mind. Goldman said he wasn't schizophrenic. Maybe he wasn't. But there was something very wrong with him. It didn't much matter what you called it.

He shouted goodnight as he left the station and stood on the steps a moment. Not a cloud in the sky. Just stars and the certainty that there wouldn't be further snow before morning.

He welcomed it on the grounds that snow would have made tomorrow's job more difficult, for tomorrow, they were scheduled to start a thorough search of the moat and woodland. It might take days to find her, but Ginny was out there somewhere. He didn't need John Cranmer to tell him that.

19

Guy and his father had arrived at Leeds Infirmary half an hour ago. Now they were sitting in an office with a junior doctor. He consulted notes that were made at the time of Rachel's admission, and said:

'Your wife was brought in earlier this afternoon after someone heard her crying in her room.'

That would be one of the people they shared the house with. Guy wondered who.

'When she refused to open the door to them, they forced it.' The doctor dispensed with his notes. 'Mr Harvey,' he said, and just for a moment Guy thought he must be talking to his father. Nobody ever called him Mr Harvey. 'Have you any idea why your wife might take an overdose?'

The doctor made it sound as though it were his fault, but what else could he do but leave after Rachel had made it so obvious she didn't want him around? 'No,' he said. 'None.'

'You're saying your wife gave no indication there was anything wrong?'

'I didn't say that,' said Guy. 'For the past few months she—'

His father butted in. 'Never mind what happened in the last few months – the question is, what happens *now*?'

The doctor replied: 'That very much depends on Mr Harvey. I'm assuming he will want to see his wife, then—'

'I didn't mean that. I meant . . . what happens after somebody tries to top themselves? I assume you don't just kick them out on the street?'

The doctor caught his drift. 'Attempted suicides are assessed by a psychiatrist. It's up to the psychiatrist to decide whether or not they should be discharged. Rachel has already been seen by . . .' He checked his notes again. '. . . Dr Elizabeth Rossiter. Dr Rossiter said your wife can go home tomorrow, provided there's somebody around to keep an eye on her, but she'd like a word with you first.'

When Guy made no response, the doctor added: 'I take it you *are* prepared to keep an eye on her?'

'Yes,' said Guy, and the word came out like cardboard.

'Then I'll ask one of the nurses to take you up to the ward.'

His father had barely spoken during the journey, but as he and Guy made their way to the ward, he more than made up for it:

Attempted suicide was a big deal. Rachel was clearly unstable. She was probably going to spend the rest of her life needing psychiatric care. If Guy stayed with her, he could forget about having any kind of normal existence. Kids would be out of the question. Whatever was wrong with Rachel might be genetic. He should start divorce proceedings. She wasn't his problem.

Right now, Guy pointed out, Rachel *was* his problem because the hospital authorities wanted to discharge her – they needed the bed. They had pumped her stomach, biopsied her liver and done a battery of tests, if only to cover themselves after she was safely off their hands. They didn't want her dying on the street owing to organ failure, but nor did they want to have to keep her in longer than was necessary. She had a home to go to. And he was expected to care for her. He didn't really see what choice he had.

His father said, 'You have to make them *give* you a choice.'

'And how do I do that?'

'By walking away.'

'I can't.'

His father was losing patience. 'Give it twenty years and you'll be looking at one of those middle-aged women with greying hair and vacant eyes. And you won't get away with shoving her in an attic, Guy. One way or another, the way things are going in this country, either you'll end up looking after her at home – and what kind of a life do you think *that's* going to be for you – or you'll find yourself paying through the nose for her to be looked after.'

Guy still had the feeling that the ground was rolling, a feeling made worse when he and his father climbed into a lift. It opened on to the third floor and they stepped out into a corridor that led to a number of wards, each divided into four-bed units.

The bed that Rachel lay in was concealed by curtains. A nurse drew them back, then left Guy to it, his father having said he would prefer to sit in the corridor and wait.

Guy, who was having a hard time understanding his feelings right now, almost wished he could stay in the corridor with him. He was monumentally relieved that Rachel was all right, but he was also angry – and something else, something he couldn't identify at first: he was frightened. What Rachel had done was way beyond anything he had ever experienced, and he didn't know how to deal with it. What were the implications for the future? Even if he divorced her, maybe the courts would see to it that he maintained her for the rest of her life.

He was ashamed of how afraid that made him feel. A few days ago, he would have said that nothing could destroy what he felt for her. Was love so fragile that it melted away at the first sign of serious trouble? Right now, he didn't feel love. He didn't feel anything but fear. He wanted this whole thing not to have happened. And when he realised that he didn't want to have to take responsibility for his wife, he saw a slice of his father poking through the skin of his own psyche. It wasn't a welcome revelation, but it was there.

Rachel was sitting in bed, a sickly yellow hospital gown draining her skin of colour, making her look sallow and – he hated himself for this – unattractive. As if it mattered what she looked like! And yet, it did. It mattered that in the instant he saw her he was reminded of what his father had warned him she would become: middle aged, vacant eyed and dependent.

He felt he should say something, but didn't know what.

126

Besides, he was afraid that once he started he might end up admitting how tempted he was to follow his father's advice. *Do yourself a favour, Guy – start divorce proceedings, right now!*

There was a window by the bed. He walked over to it and flicked the latches to find that it was of a kind that rotated to make for easier cleaning. How stupid to put someone who had just tried to kill themselves next to a window like this. If she wanted to, Rachel could open it wide and jump out. *Maybe it would be better for everyone if she did.*

He hated himself for that, too. How could he even think it? He pushed at the glass with his fingertips. It slid away from his hand with the ease of something attached to a mechanism that was kept extraordinarily well oiled.

'Do I get to hear why?' he said.

'Do you *want* to know why?'

It was the most rational response he'd had from her in as long as he could remember. Maybe there was something to be said for trying to kill yourself. Maybe it cleared your mind. 'What's it been about?' he said. 'I don't just mean the overdose – I mean the past few months.'

'It wasn't you,' she said. 'It was never anything to do with you.'

'Then what was it?'

It seemed she'd done some thinking in the past few hours. It was going to take guts to tell him this, but she was going to try. All she asked was that he *tried* to believe her.

'Remember the day we went to see the cottage?'

So it *did* have something to do with the cottage. 'What about it?'

'I went for a walk out the back. The garden was overgrown. I had to wade through nettles and out between two posts where a gate used to be.'

She smiled as if the memory of walking through that shambles of a garden had been pleasant. 'There was a lane.'

He knew the lane she meant. It divided the row of cottages from a wood.

'It was beautiful, Guy. The leaves had started to turn, and I found a sort of sunken road cutting through the wood.'

Surely she hadn't wandered down a lonely sunken road? Women didn't *do* that – not if they had any sense.

Outside, it was dark. The window became a mirror. In it, he could see Rachel's reflection as she lay on the bed. 'Are you trying to tell me you were raped? Is that what this is about?'

The image began to shatter. His wife had once been whole. Now she was shaking, fragmenting in front of his eyes.

'Guy,' she said, 'I think I saw a ghost.'

The hospital carpark was floodlit. Guy noticed a closed-circuit television camera fixed to a nearby wall. It rotated, then focused on them as if operated by someone who couldn't make up their mind whether he and his father were the owners of the vehicle they were standing next to, or thieves just weighing it up. Dressed as they were in jeans and leather bomber jackets, they could well be thieves. They didn't look wealthy enough to own a Jag like that, and thieves were attracted to Jags, or so it was said.

His father leaned against the passenger door of the neighbouring vehicle. 'Guy, you're my son. I don't want to see you screw up the rest of your life.'

'She's ill.'

'I'm glad you realise that. Now realise this. It's not your problem.'

But it *was* his problem. 'I can't just walk away from her. Where will she go?'

'Let the hospital find somewhere for her.'

'Like where?'

'A hostel or something – who knows? Nobody can *force* you to take her on.'

'Nobody's forcing me. You don't understand.'

'You'll regret it,' said his father.

Maybe he was right. But he couldn't just walk away. 'First thing tomorrow,' he said, 'I'm taking her home.'

20

The following morning, Guy arrived at the hospital to find Rachel sitting on a chair by her bed. He handed her a plastic laundry bag. It was all he could find for the clothes that the hospital asked him to bring when he collected her. The clothes she'd been wearing when admitted were soiled, he was told. He looked for them in her locker. They weren't there, and the minute he asked her where she thought they might be, he recalled a warning issued by his father: *You'll end up washing her, feeding her, and watching her every move in case she takes off down the street in her nightdress.*

'Don't know,' she said. 'Ask a nurse.'

Guy pulled jeans, jumper, knickers, bra, socks and shoes out of the bag. 'I've probably forgotten something,' he admitted.

She'd showered, or been washed. He didn't know which. Her hair was damp. 'Better get it dry before we go – it's bitter out.'

The city was very lightly dusted with snow. Some of it had stuck on roofs that could be seen from that lethal revolving window by her bed. He hadn't thought to bring her a coat. He would give her his before they left the building.

He wondered whether he could kick a little more life out of the three-bar electric fire in their room. 'Fuck,' he said, softly.

'What's wrong?'

How could he tell her that the past few days at his father's place had reminded him of what it was like to live in a civilised manner, with furnishings that weren't decorated with cigarette burns, and rooms that were centrally heated. He shouldn't have to take her back to Rippon Gardens.

'We're going to have to stop off somewhere for another heater.'

The minute he said it, it struck him as the world's most banal comment. That was what she would turn him into – a person referred to by Social Services as a *carer*. It was a label sewn on to the soul of every person who sacrificed their life in the name of love, or duty. No social life. No holidays. No pension. No chance whatsoever of leading a life of your own. Every ounce of his being wanted to leave her there, to let someone else handle it, to relinquish responsibility. But he just couldn't do it. Maybe walking out on the sick took practice. It was certainly a fuck sight more difficult than walking out on people who were well.

'What are you thinking?' said Rachel.

Such a lucid question. He suddenly felt that, somehow, she could read every thought in his head, and he was ashamed. 'The psychiatrist who spoke to you yesterday morning wants a word with me before we go.'

He left her to dress and went in search of Dr Elizabeth Rossiter, finding her on the other side of the building.

She took him into an office which she 'borrowed' now and again, and told him she was satisfied that Rachel's suicide attempt was a cry for help. 'A reaction to the death of her aunt,' she said.

'Why would the death of her aunt make her want to kill herself?'

Rossiter replied: 'When somebody close to us dies, it brings us face to face with our own mortality. Breakdown is common. The pattern of Rachel's behaviour would support a diagnosis of bereavement-related depression.'

Guy didn't know many people who had lost someone they were close to. There was someone at college whose father had died. She had been devastated, but she didn't start seeing things.

Rossiter wasn't finished with him yet:

'In addition to losing her aunt, Rachel has had to redetermine her identity over the past few months, and I suspect that's had a bearing on the nature of her breakdown.'

'How do you mean – redetermine?'

'I understand the authorities forced the sale of her aunt's house to pay for nursing-home fees.'

Guy confirmed it, and Rossiter added, 'It's bad enough losing our home when we ourselves make the decision to move, but in cases where losing our home is something beyond our control, it's doubly traumatic.'

When he looked at it that way, he supposed it made sense.

'In addition,' said Rossiter, 'Rachel married you six months ago having met you only three months earlier.'

'Did she say she wished she hadn't?'

Rossiter hastened to reassure him that nothing of what Rachel had told her indicated that she felt the marriage was a mistake. 'But marriage requires that we make certain fairly fundamental adjustments to the way we live. That takes some getting used to.'

'What you mean is that a combination of these things tipped her over the edge?'

'That's exactly what I mean.'

'So she'll get over it?'

'Most people do. I'd advise that she takes a course of antidepressants, and I'll give you the name of a good bereavement counsellor.'

He should have felt the anxiety lifting from his shoulders, but it stayed there like a cold, dead weight, pressing him down.

'You seem concerned about something—'

Why was he such a coward? Why couldn't he admit that what Rachel told him was vastly different to what she'd told Rossiter? Yesterday, when he stood by her bed, she hadn't even mentioned the death of her aunt. She said she'd seen a ghost, and what could he do but ask her what made her think so.

'Remember I said I'd found a sunken road?'

The way she described it enabled him to visualise it vividly.

'I followed it,' said Rachel. 'Right up to the grounds of some old house.'

He knew the house she meant. Lyndle Hall was marked on the map that he'd used when they drove to the cottage.

'There was some sort of field dividing the house from the trees. A man was walking across it, carrying flowers. He laid them next to a pipe that was jutting out of the embankment. The way he put them down . . . I can't describe it. . . . And then he saw me and he sort of stumbled away. It was as though the sight of me came as an enormous shock to him . . .'

If she hadn't been raped. . . . if nothing had happened . . . then what was all this about?

'And then I looked behind me and . . . I saw a woman crawling through the undergrowth . . . just dragging herself along. She was covered in blood – just *smothered* in it.'

At this point, Rachel was sobbing.

'She was looking for somewhere to hide, and all she could see was the pipe. She . . . she crawled inside . . .'

Lyndle Hall had been in the news over the past few weeks, and initially he wondered whether Rachel had witnessed the murder of the girl the police were looking for. Then he realised she couldn't have done. He and Rachel went to Lyndle towards the end of August. According to what he had read in the press, Ginny's father had still been in contact with his daughter in September.

'Why didn't you tell me?'

Rachel replied, 'How could I? She wasn't *there*.'

What would have been the point in trying to make sense of a statement like that. 'Why don't you try to get some sleep,' said Guy, and she knew then that he was humouring her.

'You think I'm losing my mind.'

For five, maybe ten seconds, Guy was tempted to tell Rossiter what Rachel had told him. And then he wondered what his motive was. Maybe he was hoping that Rossiter would want to keep her in to evaluate her further. Maybe he just wanted to shove responsibility for Rachel on to somebody else. Then he could go back home and talk himself into believing everything his father said about it not being his problem.

'Mr Harvey?'

Tell her, thought Guy. *Tell her!* He said, 'Are you sure that Rachel is okay? I mean, *really* okay?'

'Nothing she told me yesterday makes me feel it wouldn't be wise to discharge her. She may be depressed and a little confused, but she isn't . . . to put it in layman's terms, *mad*, if that's what you're thinking.'

Forget it, he told himself. The least you can do is give your wife a chance. 'Thanks,' he said, and he took the prescription, then headed back to the ward.

The first thing he saw was a screen around the bed. He pulled it back, expecting to find her sitting behind it. What he found was an auxiliary nurse stripping the bed of sheets. 'Where's Rachel?' he said.

'You've missed her, love. She's gone.'

'Gone where?'

'Home, I should think. There was somebody coming to collect her.'

He fought the urge to yell that the 'somebody' was him. Surely they hadn't let her walk out of there? He was staggered by how calmly he managed to say, 'Roughly what time did she leave?'

'About half an hour ago.'

It had started to snow. The city was losing its icing-sugar look, and he pictured her wandering around out there in nothing more than jeans, a jumper and trainers. He ran, not knowing why, or where he should run to next when he left the building. Common sense was telling him to calm down, to alert the hospital authorities, to tell the police she was missing. But panic sent him running down the corridors, the stairs, and out into the carpark, and it was only then that he realised he still loved her. Don't let anything have happened to her – *please*.

21

Getting a warrant to search a Grade 1 listed building was no easy matter. Tate discovered he first lied to prove that he had at his disposal people who were trained to search historic houses without damaging the fabric of the building. That was going to take a couple of days to organise. In the meantime, he intended to drag the moat and search the wood, and he'd returned with enough men to do both.

The men outside were smashing the ice on the moat in preparation for the divers, who would very shortly slide down into its depths. He, however, was in the study with Claudia.

He saw the room reflected in the mottled gilt-framed mirror that ran the length of one wall. It had the effect of making the study seem twice its actual size. It also had the effect of making it look as though everything in it was drowning in a deep green pool. A trick of the light, something that resulted from the density, the age, the quality of the glass.

Claudia stood at an angle to it, all the better to see what was going on outside. She wasn't amused when, at 6 a.m. that morning, a convoy of vehicles slewed across the lawn. Two 4 × 4s, a Transit van, and a mobile police canteen. Of all these vehicles, it was the canteen she objected to most. It looked like some sort of hot-dog stand. She wanted it 'removed'.

He thought it incredible that she, who walked around dressed like a tramp, could object to 'that vulgar contraption' parked on the lawn. And yet, he could see her point: there was something quite imperious about Lyndle. It frowned down on the vehicles below as if to point out that people had been dying here for centuries, some of them in violent, perhaps even horrific circumstances. What was one young girl among so many? Why the sudden fuss?

This was the first time Tate had had the opportunity to talk to Claudia, and he began by saying it must be a constant battle to keep a place like this from falling apart. He didn't add that it was a battle she'd obviously lost. He wanted to keep it light, to lull her into a feeling that he was there to help her. 'When did you first come here?'

'I lived here as a child.'

It wasn't the answer he had expected. He'd assumed that Francis inherited Lyndle, and that Claudia had lived there since they married.

'Francis and I are cousins,' she said. 'Our parents lived abroad. We went away to school, and spent the holidays here. Grandfather left us Lyndle on condition that we married.'

Tate couldn't think why anyone would impose a condition like that, unless . . .

'You and your husband must have been very close.'

She didn't reply.

He resisted the temptation to ask her what she felt about Francis being escorted off the premises of a modelling agency, because what he did sixteen years ago was hardly likely to have had a bearing on what Nicholas had done in the past few weeks. Besides, even assuming Claudia actually *knew* about him being thrown out of Margo's, raking up some marital infidelity would only make her raise her defences. And Tate didn't want to do that. He wanted to win her trust. He wanted to coax her into confiding in him.

'You must be finding it hard to deal with all this.' He indicated what was going on outside. 'You're alone. No one to turn to. And Nicholas . . . well, he's ill, I realise that . . .'

She sat in one of the red leather armchairs. The heat from the fire lit her face, yet she still hugged her coat around her. Tate suspected she slept in it. She smelled very faintly of damp. And he suddenly realised how thin she was. Not only her face, but her fingers – a mass of elegant bones. She probably hadn't eaten properly for weeks. 'Claudia,' he said. 'I want to help . . . but I can't do that unless you trust me.'

She sat there, her fingers white with cold. 'What you saw yesterday . . . means nothing . . .'

'I spoke to Goldman. I know he's very sick.'

'He isn't sick,' said Claudia.

One of the divers surfaced clutching the face of a grandfather clock – a moon and stars surrounded by the planets. He handed it to Fletcher, who placed it on the bank. 'I know about his friend,' said Tate. 'I know he makes sacrifices to it. And what worries me . . . what worries me is that Ginny . . .'

She suddenly started to weep. It wasn't an opening up. It was more a very private, very internal kind of weeping. And he couldn't help softening towards her. 'Claudia, let me help you.'

'Nobody can help me.'

'Let me try.'

Weeping was a weakness, according to Francis. Not once, in all these years, had she seen him cry. But that wasn't to say he didn't feel things deeply. He did. By God he did. How else could a person swear never to speak to his wife again, and keep it up for sixteen miserable years? Not once, in all that time, had he spoken to her unless it was absolutely necessary, unless it was to say, *I think I shall hate you all the days of my life.*

After Tate had gone, she stayed in the study. The thought of anyone seeing her like this . . . What wouldn't she have given to have been able to tell him . . . But there was Nicholas to consider. He needed her. She couldn't betray his trust.

A fountain pen lay on the desk, the casing black, the trim, like the nib, fourteen-carat gold. She picked it up. It had once belonged to her grandfather. It now belonged to Francis, whose father argued that it should have gone to him.

Nothing had gone to him. And nothing had gone to her father either, because grandfather's sons were a disappointment to him. He therefore left Lyndle to her and to Francis equally, not least because, by the time they reached adolescence, it was obvious that there existed between them a bond that transgressed the boundaries of the kind of affection one might have expected to find between first cousins.

Clearly, this amused him, or perhaps what amused him was the extent to which their relationship appalled his rather dull sons. Whatever the case, he made it a condition that, in order to inherit, they must marry, and whatever misgivings his sons might have had were consumed by greed. They wanted some stake in their birthright, if only by default. Therefore, they voiced no objection to the arrangement. Indeed, their marrying seemed the right, the proper thing, and they were, after all, old enough to challenge the terms of the will. The fact that neither did so spoke volumes, and their relationship became a topic of conversation that was never discussed after they inherited. 'They have married. Let that be an end to it' was the prevailing attitude.

The first, euphoric response to the news that Lyndle was theirs crumbled under the realisation that their inheritance was a decaying, debt-ridden millstone. Francis wanted to sell it. To burn it and grab the insurance. To run away to some hot little country where brown-skinned girls carried seed to the fields in brightly coloured pots. She wanted to keep it, but then how could she have known what the future held?

One of the men outside was resting his foot on a vehicle. He pushed his feet into walking boots, and the way he tied his laces—

Such wonderful light. I thought I might spend the morning on the moors.

You're going to meet her.

I don't have the time, or the patience, for histrionics.

I'll kill her . . . I swear to you, Francis . . . I'll kill her . . . I'll kill her!

22

Audrah awoke to the sound of vehicles pulling up outside. She got out of bed, fully dressed, and went to the window. No curtains, just a film of ice on the delicate panes of glass. She wiped it with her sleeve, looked out, and saw police spilling on to the lawn.

Tate was climbing out of one of the vehicles. There was somebody with him. It took a moment for her to realise who it was. He was wearing mountaineering gear. It wasn't the kind of clothing she was used to seeing him wear. Usually, Cranmer wore a suit.

Yesterday, Tate had thrown him out of the courtyard. Now he was looking in the direction Cranmer was pointing in, nodding, talking, drinking in whatever Cranmer was saying. It reminded her just how good Cranmer was. In less than twenty-four hours, he had managed to come up with something guaranteed to change Tate's attitude towards him. She didn't know what, but she knew him well enough to know that this was what he'd done. Just wait until he got his hands on Nicholas Herrol . . .

She suddenly remembered Marion. Once Claudia realised what she wanted, she let her stay the night. As far as Audrah knew, she was in the room next door. She hoped it was warmer, less sparse, than this . . .

She answered a knock, expecting Claudia, but finding Bevan at the door.

'Tate would like a word.'

He led her downstairs to a room off the kitchen where Tate stood in front of the few slits of glass that passed for a window. He had his back to the room, as if the sight of it offended him.

'Yesterday, you told me you were a psychologist.' He turned away from the window. 'You neglected to mention that you lecture in paranormal psychology at the BIPR.' She wasn't surprised he knew. He would have been failing in his job if he'd neglected to find out who people were, and what they were really doing there. 'What brought you here?'

'Mrs Herrol hoped I could help her son.'

'And can you?'

'No,' said Audrah.

'If you can't help him why are you still here?'

'I don't want to see him exploited by John Cranmer.'

'What have you got against Cranmer?'

'He's a con man.'

Tate said nothing for a moment. And then he said, 'Yesterday, I got a phone call from Cranmer. He'd never seen this room, yet he described it.'

'What's so special about it?'

'It was Ginny's.'

She supposed she should have guessed. It might be the twenty-first century, but some things never changed: who but a girl who was there to perform the most menial of tasks would accept a room off the kitchen? 'I'll be honest with you,' said Tate. 'I'm struggling to explain how he could describe it so accurately.' He opened the wardrobe door. The wire hangers jangled. 'Right down to the sound the hangers make.'

Audrah thought about how easily Marion had slipped into Lyndle without being seen, and how she'd managed to evade being found by Tate, two of his men, Claudia, and herself. If Marion could do that, how much easier must it have been for Cranmer, particularly if he slipped in before the case really took off? And how difficult would it have been for him to pick out the room most likely to have been allotted to someone like Ginny?

'He probably broke in.'

'Not worth his reputation' said Tate.

'He'd have wriggled out of it,' said Audrah. 'Pseudo psychics make a living out of making the implausible sound credible.'

Tate smiled. 'You obviously hold a fairly dim view of psychics.'

'Years of working with them has taught me they're all con men. Cranmer is slicker than most.'

'Why do they do it?'

Such a simple question. Such a complex answer.

Throughout the history of criminology, numerous psychics appeared to have been of inestimable value to the police. Among them were Janos Kele, the Hungarian clairvoyant, who was said to have had the ability to perceive physical objects, situations or events from a distance, and Gerard Croiset, who, in 1964, was said to have helped Mississippi police investigate the murder of three civil rights workers.

These people were assumed to be genuine, if only because they refused payment, but much of what they were said to have achieved was difficult to prove. It was thought there might be evidence to suggest they were genuinely in touch with the spirit world, but all too often the information they came up with was vague, if not completely off the mark. Even when they appeared uncannily accurate, there was always at least one possible explanation as to how they might have managed to come by the information.

'They do it for money, mostly. But not always. Some do it for the kick they get from outwitting the academics who study them. Others are addicted to people thinking they're special in some way.'

'And Cranmer?' said Tate. 'Which category does he fall into?'

'Cranmer craves adulation and respect.'

'Sounds like a man after my own heart,' said Tate.

'Did he tell you where to look for the body?'

'In the wood.'

'I'd say that was a fairly sensible guess. It's a safer bet than telling you to concentrate on the house.'

'He was a bit more specific than that – he said he sensed it was in or near something round.'

'Round is good,' said Audrah. 'You can't go far wrong with "round".'

Tate wasn't sure what she was getting at. 'Tree trunks are round,' said Audrah. 'So are mushrooms, and stones. Some plants are round. *Round* is a shape that occurs in nature. I'd have been more impressed if he told you to look for something octagonal.'

'Even so, I don't see what harm can come from taking a look at anything he advises us to look at.'

'And if you find Ginny, the press will claim Cranmer found her for you. If you don't, Cranmer will argue that you weren't thorough enough. The press will back him up because journalists love a psychic, but they don't much like the police. They'll demolish your reputation long before they demolish his.'

'Have you seen the reports from the FBI?'

'His reputation is based on a few lucky guesses.'

'How could anyone guess that kind of information?'

The thought that Tate was now willing to give Cranmer the benefit of the doubt infuriated her. She dipped into one of her pockets and drew out a rubber ball. 'What if I were to tell you I can stop my heart at will?'

Tate looked nonplussed.

'Take my pulse,' she offered.

Tate felt her wrist and found that her pulse had stopped. 'How's it done?'

She reached into her jacket and pulled the rubber ball out from under her arm. 'I cut off the blood supply by squeezing the ball between an artery and my ribcage.'

'The point being?'

'I created the illusion that I could stop my heartbeat,' said Audrah. 'That's what pseudo psychics do – they create illusions, some with props, others with information that they've somehow managed to access. Cranmer is a master at creating the illusion that he has information he couldn't have got by any normal means.' She tossed him the ball. 'Keep it,' she said. 'And whenever you're tempted to believe Cranmer is genuine, reach for it – let it be a reminder.'

The meeting with Tate left her feeling that she had to get outside, and she stood on the bridge watching the divers pulling equipment out of the back of the vehicles.

They struggled into wet suits, and a short while later waded into the moat, the jagged slabs of ice parting momentarily, then sliding closed as they sank from view, committing them to the depths. *Now you are ours forever . . . and must forget the world of light and air that exists above the surface.*

'Audrah,' said Cranmer.

She turned to find him behind her.

'You were with Tate. How did it go? Or would you rather I didn't ask?'

He knew full well that she had probably tried to talk some sense into Tate, and also knew she had very probably failed. He drew a rubber ball out of his pocket, and tossed it into the air. It was one she once gave to somebody who was every inch as enamoured of Cranmer as Tate appeared to be. He caught it as it fell, then tossed it back into the air as he added:

'Whenever I think of you Audrah – which admittedly, isn't often – I picture you walking into a children's toy shop and ordering small rubber balls by the dozen.' He suddenly threw the ball over the parapet of the bridge. It landed in the water and bobbed between two jagged slabs of ice. 'You must have shares in Fisher Price by now.'

It was an effort not to rise to the bait. 'I must admit – congratulations appear to be in order.'

'In what regard?'

'Tate,' she replied. 'He can't work out how you knew what Ginny's room looked like. But I can, because I know how you do it.'

He shook his head and smiled as she added, 'You read about Ginny Mulholland. You keep an eye on the story because maybe, *just maybe*, she hasn't taken off with the husband. Maybe she's been murdered. Nine times out of ten you're wrong but this time, you strike lucky. So you come over here, and you access the house, and you pick out the room that was Ginny's.'

Cranmer sounded exasperated as much as anything. 'Why can't you accept that there are people who can *do* this, who *have* these gifts, who use them to help others?'

'I know your every trick.'

'There is no trick.'

Audrah replied, 'You know, John, it took me a while to work out why you do it. For a while, I thought it had something to do with money, or a craving for respect – that's what I told Tate – but recently, I've realised I was wrong.'

'Correct me if I'm mistaken, but don't we have this conversation every time we meet?'

She continued as if he hadn't interrupted. 'Parapsychologists tend not to believe in good and evil – it would be like admitting to a belief in the spirit world, and that might invalidate their research. But in your case, I'm willing to make an exception.' She turned to him. 'You're evil, John. You devastate people because it amuses you.'

Cranmer replied, 'I suppose I ought to be flattered that someone has centred their entire life around trying to understand me, but actually, I'm beginning to get a little bit bored with it. Besides, you're inconsistent, and frankly, that worries me Audrah. It indicates that one may have reason to question the integrity of your research.'

'There's nothing inconsistent about any conclusions I might have come to about you.'

'On the contrary,' Cranmer replied. 'On your own admission, there was once a time when you thought I did it for money, or respect. But you obviously changed your mind because you recently had the audacity to publish a paper suggesting I do it because I get an erotic charge from making love to women who have recently been bereaved – something to do with sex and death, I believe. Don't ask me why I didn't sue you – I would have been well within my rights.'

'Why didn't you?'

Cranmer produced a second rubber ball from his pocket, as if he had armed himself with a supply with which to irritate her. As with the first, he tossed it into the air as he replied, 'Whenever I'm in the States, I find myself surrounded by people who are suing one another over issues they would be better advised to ignore.'

'You were afraid of the publicity—'

'I was afraid of the lawyer's bills,' said Cranmer, dryly. 'Besides, there was the possibility that you might have managed to dredge up one or two unfortunates as proof of your claim.'

Audrah had dredged up more than one or two. She had fully expected Cranmer to sue. The fact that he didn't do so had surprised her.

'Though having said that . . .' The rubber ball made a slapping sound as it landed in Cranmer's hand, 'you'll be glad to know I've slept with quite a few women since you first begged me to help you find your husband. None of them wrote to me for help, but then, none of them had husbands who walked out on them quite so completely as Lars walked out on you.'

One of the metal poles used by the men who smashed the ice was close to hand. Just for a moment, she was tempted to pick it up and drive the hook through his skull.

'You should be grateful,' he added. 'If not for me, you'd be scraping a living listening to bored housewives bleating about their unfaithful husbands and their disappointing kids. Instead, you appear to have awarded yourself the fascinating task of trying to prove me a fraud.'

He threw the ball towards her and the action she made to catch it was both involuntary, and regretted. She threw it back, hard, and Cranmer laughed as it hit him. 'Temper temper Audrah,' said Cranmer, softly.

144

23

The previous night, Claudia had shown Marion to a room next to the one in which Nicholas normally slept. It was cold, and there was hardly any furniture. But there was a bed, and Marion, who would have slept in the timber wing if need be, was grateful for it. Before she settled down, she collected the clippings from the study and arranged them around the room. She liked them to be the last thing she saw at night, and the first thing she saw when she woke.

Usually, she opened her eyes to the sight of Michael Reeve shielding his face from a camera, but that morning she'd woken up to the sight of a convoy of vehicles being driven across the lawn. Michael Reeve was forgotten as she got out of bed and went to the window to see what was going on.

Tate had returned and, this time, he'd brought more men. A short while later, one of them knocked on the door to tell her to stay in her room until further notice. He was followed by Claudia, who told her that the police had brought Cranmer with them. He was willing to see her later on that morning.

The fact that the police had put their trust in Cranmer increased her confidence in him. She didn't care how long she had to wait before he saw her, just so long as he saw her. She stayed in her room until Claudia returned to tell her he was ready for her, then, despite the fact that the police had asked her not to leave it, she followed Claudia down to the study where Cranmer stood with his back to the large gilt mirror.

He turned when she walked in, and appeared quite relaxed, but then none of this was new to him, whereas what was about to happen suddenly seemed a frightening prospect to her. The idea of coming here in the hope of meeting someone who might be able to put her in contact with Kathryn was one thing; the reality, she discovered, was another.

During the past few days, there had been too many practicalities to attend to for her to waste energy worrying about whether she would suddenly want to back out. Now that it came to it, she found herself considering the potential implications of being presented with evidence of an afterlife. Proof would call for a re-evaluation of her attitude to life and the way she dealt with people. What if it this was not, after all, the only world in which justice might be meted out? *Vengeance is mine, said the Lord.* What if she was required to forgive Michael Reeve? She didn't *want* to forgive him; and nor did she want to hand responsibility for meting out vengeance to someone she formerly disregarded as a myth.

When he noticed her hovering in the doorway, Cranmer invited her in, and when she continued to hover, he said, 'There's nothing to be afraid of. Nothing is going to happen that you won't be able to deal with.'

He was attractive, and that surprised her – it was a long time since she'd found a man attractive. She would have said that Gordon's behaviour had finished her with men. The realisation that this wasn't true came as a surprise. He took her hand as he talked her through what he was about to do – and the way he did it made her feel there was nothing he would rather do than hold her hand.

'Is there anything in particular that worries you?'

She told him she had heard of mediums going into trances, and of ectoplasm pouring from their mouths. She didn't much like the sound of that.

Cranmer replied that he didn't much like the sound of it either. He assured her that he wasn't about to start producing apparitions out of cheesecloth – such things were best left in the expert hands of Victorian pseudo psychics. He was merely going to talk. How did she feel about that?

'Relieved,' said Marion, and Cranmer smiled, then fell silent.

He closed his eyes, and Marion expected him to start talking straight away. But Cranmer stayed silent for what felt like a lifetime, and she started to lose her nerve. Suddenly the room seemed very small, yet the doors appeared to be an impossible distance away. If she stood up, if she ran to them, they would recede; she could run for the rest of her life and never reach them.

She'd suffered from panic attacks ever since Kathryn was murdered. Most caught her out in the quiet of her home, but some sneaked up on her in public. The battle to maintain the façade of normality when walls were folding in was immense, as was the urge to curl up on the pavement, to roll into a ball and shut out her surroundings; and when people spoke, as Cranmer did now, their words came from another world, one she could no longer cope with, or relate to.

'Marion, sit down – there's something I have to tell you.'

She *was* sitting down. What did he mean? Then she remembered that this was that Gordon had said the day he left.

She had known it was coming. She'd known for months. And when Tessa had asked what it felt like, she told her it was like finding yourself driving the wrong way down a dual carriageway. She hadn't known whether to stop or keep going in the hope that she could somehow dodge the traffic. She opted for dodging traffic, but it hadn't made any difference to the outcome. Eventually, inevitably, there had been the kind of crash that always comes when someone you love informs you they don't want you any more.

For Marion, it was more an internal implosion than a head-on collision. But having told her, having 'broken it to her as best he could', as he put it, Gordon behaved as if he'd just read the minutes of some previous meeting. The issue of his desire to live with another woman having been dealt with, he then moved on to the issue of how he felt they should break the news to Kathryn.

In the very words Gordon had used, Cranmer added, 'She needs to know that she isn't losing me.'

Even now, it amazed her that Gordon hadn't grasped that no

matter what he said, Kathryn would still have felt he was deserting her. 'Tell him,' said Kathryn. 'Tell him he can't just go!'

'She'll get over it,' Gordon said. 'There are loads of kids in Kathryn's situation. So long as she knows we love her, she'll be fine.'

Cranmer said, 'I see a house. No garden. Just a patio, and the sound of heavy traffic in the background.'

Home. That drab little house in one of Bristol's less desirable suburbs – the one purchased with the proceeds of the divorce settlement. The first time she saw it, Kathryn wept. She refused to believe that, from now on, this was where they were going to be living.

Cranmer's description of it was uncannily accurate, right down to the postwar metal frames that had replaced the old sash windows. She intended to restore them if ever she could afford it. In the meantime, there was cellophane fixed to the glass – someone had told her it formed a kind of double glazing.

Kathryn said she'd rather freeze than live in a house with cellophane tacked to the windows, but a house like that was all they could afford. Gordon had planned his defection so well, and so very far in advance, that by the time he left his business appeared to be failing, and the matrimonial home had been remortgaged without her knowledge. After they'd sold it and paid off debts that she didn't know they had, there was nothing left. Yet magically, once the court proceedings were out of the way, and once she had finally accepted the paltry sum awarded her, Gordon bought a house that wasn't that much smaller than the former matrimonial home.

How come Daddy's got a lovely house, and we're living in this!

Somebody had to be to blame, and since Kathryn adored her father that 'somebody' must be her mother. So unfair, but just since when were adolescents fair?

The image of the house had gone, and in its place was a

different type of property altogether. From Cranmer's description, it could only be Darracott Road, where the transient, the addicted, the long-term unemployed passed through with such frequency, and such indifference to what went on around them, that what Tessa so often referred to as 'the criminal class of person' could come and go unnoticed.

One of the houses was a riot of colour, blankets at its windows in place of curtains, the ethnic design of broad gold bands striped through with red and ochre.

Marion knew which house it was the minute Cranmer started to describe it. Two years ago, the police had put a cordon round it. She ran towards the cordon. *Please God, let it not be true—*

'And now I can see you, Marion – you're running down the road. You reach the house, and a cop grabs you, stops you from going in. You struggle, and he tries to calm you down.'

Listen, love, I wouldn't go in – there's nothing you can do, and she wouldn't want you to remember her like that.

She didn't go into the house. Fripp had seen to that. And now she regretted not having seen the room where Kathryn died, for in the absence of facts it was left to imagination to provide a picture of what it looked like, the details culled from press reports and statements. A rug covered the floorboards, and a mattress lay on the floor, and on the mattress, naked, her skin a bright cherry red—

The smell of filth predominated. Who wrote that? One of the tabloid journalists – someone who had interviewed the landlord and sensationalised every word he said. It was the landlord who first grew suspicious, who hammered on the door. He broke it down, then called the police. *Two young girls – both dead.* It was the police who realised that one of the girls was still alive, and the landlord stood by watching as paramedics did what they could to save the girl who was clinging to life by a thread.

She suddenly thought of Tessa, and a carcinogenic resentment that threatened almost daily to consume her rose in her throat. Why me? she wanted to shout. Why me, and not you? You, who have so much, a husband who loves you. Money. Social status. A career. And most important of all, *another child.*

Cranmer's demeanour was changing now. 'Mummy,' he said. 'Tell them they were wrong.'

Marion leaned forward. 'Wrong?' she said. 'Wrong about what?'

'I tried to tell them. But none of them would listen.'

'Tell them what?' said Marion.

Cranmer was growing distressed: 'They made her breathe, but nobody bothered with me. I stood there, and I watched them, and they just didn't bother. How could they do that, Mummy? How could they leave me like that?'

'Kathryn, darling – what do you mean?'

'They left me. They thought I was dead. And I wasn't, Mummy. I *wasn't.*'

Audrah saw Marion come out of the house. She stood in the courtyard, her back to the timber wing. Seconds later, she sank down on to her haunches, her head in her hands, and Tate ran over to her. He got to her seconds before Audrah reached her.

When he spoke to her, and got no response, he turned to Audrah. 'Do you know her?'

'She turned up yesterday, hoping for a sitting with Cranmer.'

'Any idea what's wrong with her?'

'I suspect she got what she came for.'

Tate didn't know what she meant by that. 'Let's get her back inside.'

24

Their reaction to the clippings was quite a little study in human behaviour. The psychologist behaved as if it were perfectly normal to smother the walls of a room with whatever was smothering your ability to function normally, whereas Tate studied them openly.

'I wasn't aware that you'd lost your daughter – I'm sorry.'

That was what people always said, but sorry didn't matter. Not any more. What *mattered* was that Reeve had got away with it. Kathryn was dead, but Reeve was still free. Not that she intended that he should ever enjoy his life. He, like Gordon, had recently moved as far away from her as possible, though unlike Gordon he did it because she discovered where he was living, shoved petrol through his letterbox, lit a match, flicked it through, and stuck around to watch him run from the house. *The death of your daughter has clearly affected you deeply, Mrs Thomas. Therefore, on this occasion . . .*

Tate was studying the photograph of Kathryn, the one that Gordon had taken two years ago. The insolence radiated from it, but so did vulnerability. She was putting on an act for her father, when what she most wanted to do was turn back the clock, to run towards him with arms outstretched and be swept up on to his shoulders.

Kathryn liked that photo, because just for once she was the focus of attention. It didn't happen often. All her life, she seemed to go unnoticed. Some children were like that. They were born just the wrong side of pretty or bright; not plain or stupid exactly, but *ordinary*. Maybe that was why she started to behave so badly when she hit her teens. 'You're such an embarrassment. Look at you! No wonder Dad walked out.'

Tessa couldn't believe she was prepared to tolerate such behaviour, and she tried to make excuses. 'Since Gordon left, she's found it very hard.'

'There's no excuse,' said Tessa. 'Sasha would never *dare* speak to *me* like that!'

Perhaps not. But then Sasha was a mouse. More to the point, Sasha had a father still very much in evidence, whereas Kathryn's father now lived at the other end of the country with the thirtysomething features editor of the kind of women's magazine that Marion never bought. It was all a cry for attention, that was all – a kind of declaration. *When will anyone notice I exist?*

She imagined what the paramedics saw when they entered the room: Kathryn was naked, but Sasha was wearing pyjamas. She ran away from home to keep her best friend company, but not without taking a clean pair of pyjamas, a toothbrush, and her history homework, something she later claimed she intended to post. Such a goody-two-shoes – but more to the point, thought Marion, a *pretty* goody-two-shoes, and the paramedics, faced with a choice, left the duck for the swan.

That was unfair, and she knew it. These people were professional. They would no more have left her daughter to die than they would a urine-soaked drunk who lay in his own vomit on some street corner.

A mistake, then, thought Marion. They thought she was dead, so they left her.

But it didn't detract from the fact that she needn't have died. She didn't know how she was ever going to break the news to Gordon.

The day of Kathryn's funeral, he had stood at the side of the grave, shaking his head like a dog that was shaking off water. 'This time last week, we were sitting in a cinema. And now we're burying her. Somebody tell me it isn't fucking true!'

Well, it *was* fucking true, and she wanted to see him cry – something he'd never done in front of her in all the years they were married. What was the big deal? Why did he stand there fighting the need to cry? He was too fucking proud, that's what it was. He was too proud to cry for his daughter; but he wasn't too proud to steal from her – he stole her home, her security, her trust. Most of all, he stole himself. He took himself from her life. Removed himself without his daughter's permission. Wasn't there some law against that? What did they call it?

Taking Without Consent.

People left them standing at the grave. They distanced themselves politely as if expecting that, at a time like this, she and Gordon would want to be alone together.

The truth of it was they didn't know how to comfort one another. You would think that when two people had raised a child together, had lost her, they would be able to find something more meaningful to say than *You all right*?

What a stupid thing to say. Of course she wasn't all right, and neither was Gordon. He looked like a horse that nobody had the guts to shoot, something in terrible pain. *Please, somebody – kill me.*

Then Tessa walked up to tell them the car was waiting. Good old Tessa. What a pal. *Leave it all to me.* So people went back to Tessa's after the funeral. Friends of Kathryn's accompanied by their parents. Former neighbours. Distant relations. But not Sasha. Too ill. Too fragile. Too traumatised to attend.

She wanted to escape the sympathy and pity, so she crept upstairs to the bathroom with its walls the colour of ice. And she stole the soap with its willow-pattern paper. She was in there so long Alex started hammering on the door. When she didn't reply, he put his shoulder to it, expecting God knows what but finding that, in fact, she was standing at the window, looking out at the bridge and wondering when she could decently leave.

'I'll give you a lift,' said Gordon, whose skill at concealing capital had left her with too little to buy a car, and she accepted with indifference. There was once a time when climbing into a car next to Gordon would have been beyond her. Too painful. Too reminiscent of happier times. Holidays. School plays.

Driving into London to watch that rather wonderful play by Stoppard. That was no longer the case. On the contrary, from the moment Kathryn was murdered the fact of losing Gordon ceased to matter. The loss of her daughter instantly cast an entirely new perspective on what was, and was not, important.

Impossible to imagine that the breakdown of her marriage once occupied her every waking thought. For three solid years she had analysed every aspect of it in an attempt to identify the point at which Gordon came to the realisation that, for him, the marriage was over. Kathryn's death wiped all that away; rendered it unimportant. Gordon no longer loved her. So what? He left her for somebody else. So what? How could it possibly matter beside the greater, more grievous loss?

It was the first time Gordon had seen inside that house, and she made a point of showing him around: *These are the windows that Kathryn felt embarrassed to show her friends, and this is the kitchen she dreaded them ever seeing.*

His response was to imply that her poverty wasn't his problem, his attitude echoing Kathryn's when she made it clear that the mess they were in had to be her fault. So she showed him Kathryn's room, and the sight of it threatened to crush his resolve not to break down in front of her. He tried to get out of there, but she closed the door and trapped him as efficiently as she would later trap anyone who tried not to hear her out. There was something she wanted to tell him – something she felt he should know: Kathryn hated that house. She was afraid of living in the area. Some of her friends had dropped her since she moved. It wasn't so much snobbery as the fact that it was difficult to get to on public transport and none of them could drive. Also, there was the question of personal safety. 'Why couldn't you have left us with enough to make a decent life for ourselves?'

She expected him to argue that the business was his, that he'd built it up while she chose to earn a pittance doing the kind of work that he dismissed as 'worthy', but all he said was, 'People get divorced, Marion. They fall out of love. They move on. I'm sorry there wasn't more money to go around.'

'You stole from us,' said Marion. 'Kathryn adored you, but in the end she knew you for a thief. And you were just as much to blame for her death as Reeve.'

That was more than Gordon was prepared to stand. His words exploded around her. 'And where the fuck were you when she needed someone to talk to?'

'I was right here – where the fuck were you!'

He was too close to breaking down to maintain the attack. Whatever he wanted to say, he couldn't get it out.

'She felt she had no one to turn to. Who could she turn to, Gordon? You'd left us, and she blamed me. She'd lost all trust in us.'

Tate turned away from the photograph. 'Is there someone – a friend – who could come and collect you?'

'I'm okay to drive.'

'I'd rather you didn't,' said Tate. 'Not at the moment.'

'I can't think of anyone,' she said, and it was true. She'd driven her friends away. No one to blame but herself.

'There must be *someone*,' he said, but the only person she could think of was quite possibly the last person on earth who would want to help her. Having said that, she couldn't think of anyone she would like to inconvenience more.

'I suppose you could try giving Sasha Barclay a ring.'

Sasha would be horrified. No way would she come. But if someone like Tate were to contact her, it would get it through to her that no amount of restraining orders were going to set her free to lead a normal life.

Tessa's voice came back to her now as clearly as if she were standing in the room. 'Why are you haunting her, Marion? Why don't you leave her alone?'

'How can I, when I know she's hiding something from me?'

'What on earth makes you think she's hiding something?'

Marion couldn't answer that other than to say that when

you had known someone from the day they were born you knew when they were lying. And when they were *hiding* something – by God you could tell.

'Sasha,' she said again. 'I'll give you the number.'

Tessa Barclay remained perfectly still. Perfectly silent. In front of her, a white-painted banister began its gracious sweep towards a hall that recently featured in an interiors magazine. An article described how Tessa had found 'the most wonderful little vase' for that very hall. It stood on the table that Sasha was staring at now, the one on which the phone was displayed like a minor work of art.

Tessa heard it ringing and caught the conversation between her daughter and someone whom she quickly realised Sasha didn't know. And when Sasha replaced the receiver, Tessa shouted, 'Who was that, darling?'

Sasha replied so quietly it was left to the acoustics of the hall to carry the words up the stairwell to her mother. 'Someone called Tate – Detective Inspector Tate.'

The tone of Tessa's voice changed immediately. She sounded fearful, and she bounded down the stairs. 'Police?'

'I can't think of any other profession that produces detective inspectors.'

'Where from?'

'Northumbria.'

'*Where?*'

'You must have heard of it, Mummy – it's just on the border of England and Scotland. It can't have been *that* long since you were at school.'

'Darling – why are you talking to me like this? You sound like—'

'Like Kathryn?' said Sasha, and suddenly Tessa knew what this person – Tate – had called in connection with.

'It was something to do with Marion, wasn't it? Sasha – tell me. It was, wasn't it?'

Sasha left the hall for the room that had the seven-figure view of the Avon. Tessa walked in behind her. 'What's going on?' she said.

Sasha replied, 'He asked me to go and get her.'

'Go and get who?'

'Marion,' said Sasha.

'Marion!'

'Oh, for God's sake,' said Sasha. 'Stop screaming at me, Mummy.'

'Collect her from where?'

'Lyndle Hall,' said Sasha. 'I told you – she went to see that psychic.'

'I take it you told him you couldn't?'

'She's ill,' said Sasha, quietly. 'What else could I do?'

'But you can't—'

'I don't have a choice.' Tears spilled over. 'I'll never be free of her, Mummy.'

Tessa held the tops of her arms as if she might shake her. 'She's manipulating you, darling – this is just what she wants.'

'Tate said she couldn't think of anyone else to ask.'

'I'm not standing for this,' said Tessa. She released Sasha, marched into the hall and picked up the phone.

'Mummy – don't,' said Sasha, and something in her tone made Tessa stop. Sasha added, 'I'm going—'

Tessa, speechless for a moment, finally found her voice. 'What on earth *for*?'

'I have to. I'll never be free if I don't.'

'The order—'

'The order won't bind her for ever. It doesn't bind her *now*! And I can't spend the rest of my life dreading the sound of the phone or hoping she doesn't manage to get me fired, or looking over my shoulder in supermarkets, or clothes shops, or even in restaurants. Mummy – I can't stand it any more. Besides—'

Tessa just stood there, her hand on the phone, her face a picture of rage.

'I owe it to her.'

'You don't owe her anything.' It came out in a hiss.

'Yes,' said Sasha. 'I do.'

There was something inscrutable about the way she made this particular comment, and Tessa responded to it by saying: 'If I can't persuade you not to go, then I shall come too.'

'I'd rather you didn't.'

'You don't have a choice,' said Tessa. She dialled 1471, and after she got the number Tate had called from, she pressed 3. The phone rang twice. Tate picked up. And Tessa said, 'Detective Inspector Tate? Good. I'm Tessa Barclay, the mother of the person you spoke to a moment ago. No . . . there's no problem . . . my daughter and I will collect her and bring her back. But before we arrive, I think there are a few things you should know.'

25

As Tate walked into the kitchen, Claudia took a handful of spinach and tossed it into a pan of scrambled eggs. The leaves shrivelled as he informed her that the moat had produced a negative result.

A negative result, thought Claudia. What an odd turn of phrase. Where had it come from, and how had it seeped into the contemporary vernacular of a man who had been born and bred in a Newcastle suburb, for that was where he was from; she was certain of it.

She transferred the eggs to a plate from a pan so large and heavy she had to use both hands to lift it. It defeated her efforts to lay it down quietly, and it crashed down altogether as Fletcher walked into the kitchen from the courtyard. 'Have you got a minute?'

Tate followed him out, and Claudia went with them. Nicholas was standing in the courtyard. He was surrounded by police. Audrah was standing next to him, as if to protect him from them. A taxi was disappearing into the trees.

'Don't tell me they've discharged him,' said Tate.

'They wouldn't have to,' said Claudia. 'He went in as a voluntary patient. He's entitled to walk out any time he likes.'

She should have foreseen that this might happen. Once the sedatives wore off, Nicholas either fooled the nurses into thinking he'd taken the morning dose, or he refused it altogether. He hated Broughton. *One day, mother, they'll drill a hole in my skull and suck me out.* And maybe they would. Goldman had said often enough that there was once a time when Nicholas would have been lobotomised. Nowadays a lobotomy was performed with the aid of chemicals. The constant drip of the chemical tap that would eat away at the liver as surely as it ate away at the brain.

'Does Goldman know you're here?'

'He tried to phone you.'

Of course. The phones were down. Nicholas had pulled them from the walls. *It talks to me, Mother. It tells me things I never wanted to know.*

Tate spoke to Fletcher. 'Give Goldman a ring.'

'I'm not going back,' said Nicholas.

Claudia intervened. 'Where's Cranmer?'

Audrah replied, 'What do you want with Cranmer?'

'I want to know what we're dealing with. I want to know what's *harassing* my son.'

'I don't think that's a good idea.'

'I do,' said Claudia. She turned on Audrah. 'Goldman can't help him. You can't help him. Well maybe Cranmer can.'

The light from the Oriel window formed a milky oval on the stones, and Cranmer stood within it as though spotlit.

Audrah had sought him out in the hope that she might somehow persuade him not to grant Nicholas a sitting. Common sense dictated she was wasting her time, but she had to try.

'Do you realise the damage you can do by letting someone like Nicholas believe they're at the mercy of a malign spirit?'

Cranmer replied, 'Do you realise the damage you can do by letting someone like Nicholas believe a handful of drugs and therapy can help them? And in any event, none of the medication prescribed by Goldman has had an effect – what does that tell you?'

Audrah replied, 'It tells me he hasn't yet found the right medication for him.'

'Besides,' said Cranmer, 'Tate is very keen for me to go ahead. He's hoping it will result in Nicholas admitting that he killed Ginny.'

This was a waste of time. She turned to go. Cranmer stopped her by adding, 'Actually, I'm rather glad you came looking for

160

me.' He smiled. 'I have a message for you, Audrah.' She knew that tone of voice so well. 'Something to do with a walnut desk—'

She stood in the shadows, grateful that Cranmer couldn't see her, all too aware that the look on her face would have told him she couldn't imagine how he knew about it.

'You do possess a walnut desk. Don't deny it . . . I know it's true . . .'

Voices filtered in as the men outside prepared to enter the sunken road. They were walking across the land that divided the moat from the trees. Soon the trees would swallow them, and the Hall would be silent again.

'Who told you?'

'Eva's mother.'

Cranmer could only be referring to Lars's maternal grandmother – and she was long dead.

'Why so quiet, Audrah?'

'I'm trying to work out how you found out about it.'

'She told me it would be a wonderful gesture if you were to give the desk to Eva – as a token of your desire to make the peace, perhaps?'

Eva was the last person on earth to whom Audrah felt like making a wonderful gesture. And as for making the peace – she doubted any mother who believed her daughter-in-law had murdered her son would be willing to bury the hatchet as the result of being given a walnut desk. She couldn't imagine how Cranmer had found out about what was going on between her and Eva, but it was obvious he had, and it was his ability to access this kind of information that had made his reputation as a psychic. 'John,' she said. 'That was absolutely brilliant.'

'Audrah, just for once—'

'But assuming Lars is alive, which we all know he can't be – I don't suppose his grandmother happened to tell you where he was living?'

Cranmer replied, 'There are reasons why that information can't be divulged.'

'There always are,' said Audrah. 'Remarkable how visions tend to fade at a crucial moment. People like you can *almost* see the name of the street where somebody is living, and you can *almost* see the first letter of a killer's name, but you're invariably too exhausted to stay in the trance long enough to read the street sign, or the letter, or it's too dangerous, or your spirit guides are called away, or maybe they simply drift off to another realm.'

The milky oval of light lay undisturbed on the stones. Cranmer was no longer spotlit. Cranmer was no longer there. She felt his breath on her neck, and his fingers as they brushed against her breasts.

And then he was gone.

Her mobile phone was lying on the bed. On impulse, she picked it up and dialled Wober's number.

'I'm coming back.'

'Why so soon?'

She replied that Cranmer had excelled himself. It usually took him at least a couple of days to get everyone around him eating out of his hand. This time, it appeared to have taken him less than twenty-four hours. There was no point her staying any longer. Besides, there was nothing she could do for Nicholas Herrol. Claudia was sold on the idea of allowing Cranmer to try to make contact with what she believed was a malign entity, and she didn't want to be around to witness the result.

'What would you say was wrong with him?' said Wober.

Audrah replied that Nicholas was exhibiting all the symptoms of a schizophrenic illness. Unfortunately, as sometimes happened, he was being treated by a psychiatrist who wasn't prepared to commit to a diagnosis. That meant he wasn't getting the right medication.

When he heard that nobody had yet discovered how he produced the welts, Wober said, 'I'd think I'd rather like to know more about his case. What did you say the name of the psychiatrist was?'

'Goldman,' said Audrah.

'Do you think he might be prepared to talk to me?'

Audrah's experience of Goldman was that he didn't have much time for parapsychologists, but Wober was acknowledged as being an expert on religious visionaries. He was also a doctor of medicine. 'It's possible.'

'I'll phone him,' said Wober.

'Assuming he agrees to see you, when will you be here?'

'Tomorrow at the earliest,' said Wober. 'And I'll probably go straight to Broughton. In the meantime, I'd like you to stay at Lyndle.'

Audrah stood at the window, looking down at the moat. The divers had gone. The water was still. And a film of fresh ice was forming on the surface.

Tate and his men were melting into the trees. It would be just Cranmer's luck if Ginny Mulholland's remains were found in there. But luck was all it would be. Guesswork based on sensible deduction.

26

For the first time since setting off from Edinburgh, Steven Harris was having second thoughts about bringing his wife to the Furlough Mountains. It hadn't helped that, when she realised where they were going, Paula had declared herself 'gobsmacked', an expression he particularly hated. 'You want to go where?' she said. 'At this time of year?' And then: 'Why do you want to drag us out there?'

He was tempted to point out that it was an area of outstanding natural beauty. Surely that was reason enough to want to go. But in the end he simply admitted that, in recent years, he'd begun to harbour a quiet ambition to sell up and move to Furlough. 'We could have a different kind of life.'

'What's wrong with the life we've got?' she said. 'I get in the car, and I'm in the centre of Edinburgh in less than twenty minutes. What do you want to change it for?'

He was looking at a landscape that was older than the European Alps. *That* was what he wanted to change it for.

'And what about Marc? Where will he go to school?'

'He can go to school here,' Harris replied. *And every day of his life, he'll enjoy an environment that I was lucky to see once every couple of years when I was a kid.* 'I think it'll be good for him.'

She didn't look convinced, and he sensed that, for once, she probably wished she could argue that it would damage her career prospects if they moved to the country. With no career to damage, she had no excuse; but she would find one, he was sure.

She stared through the electronic windows of the Land Rover Discovery that she'd never forgiven him for buying, and said, 'If I'd known this was your reason for wanting to come—'

You'd have stopped me, like you stop me from doing everything else.

Resentment formed a solid lump in his gut. That was another thing. Left unchecked, that resentment would one day result in him walking away from everything he'd worked for. He would simply leave her to it. And why should he? He was the one who'd bloody well worked for it all while she sat on her tight little arse and moaned about how little they had by comparison with her friends. But if he left, he would come here anyway, and he would live in a caravan parked on one of those fields beyond the copse. There were no caravans there at the moment, just the clearing where people left their vehicles in summer.

'I wanted you to see it, that's all.'

'Well, now I've seen it,' she said. 'So let's go home.'

A comment like this would usually have resulted in him swallowing his anger and conceding for the sake of peace. But they were here now, and if nothing else he wanted to walk up to the cairn before they left. He hadn't seen it in years. Not since his father had been active enough to walk up to it with him. And since his father's death, he hadn't had the heart to tackle the walk alone. It was time to change all that. Time to pay his respects to the old man in a place that had meant a great deal to both of them.

'Why are we here, Daddy?'

'We've come for a walk,' said Harris.

'Nobody's stopping you,' said Paula. 'But we're staying here.' She craned her neck to look at five-year-old Marc in the back. 'Isn't that right, Marc? Daddy can go for a walk – we'll wait in the car.'

Harris replied, 'I'd like us all to go. Just this once.' He was almost pleading now, and he hated himself for that. 'No point coming all this way just to drive straight back. Just up to the cairn. It isn't far. *Please?*'

For a moment, it looked as though she might refuse point

blank to get out of the car. He could see it in the sudden stiffening of her back, the tension in her neck. And then her lips curled in a small, triumphant smile. She pointed to the sling-backed shoes he'd advised her not to wear. 'You can't expect me to walk through the snow in these!'

For a short while after they met, they'd often gone walking together. Nothing too adventurous. Just a few miles across undemanding countryside. He bought her some boots. He doubted she'd worn them more than a couple of times since they were married. 'I put your boots in the back,' he said. 'Along with a pair of jeans.'

She kept her composure. 'What about Marc?'

'I'll carry him.'

She spoke like a ventriloquist, rage freezing her lips so that the words came out without her appearing to move them. 'You appear to have thought of everything.'

He had indeed thought of everything, as she discovered when she got out of the car to look in the boot. He indicated a cardboard box, and she flicked the lid open to reveal the jackets, scarves, gloves, socks and chocolate that he'd packed without her knowing. He'd even thought to pack a torch the size of a pen, and the mobile phone – both items that he usually took only on those long, solitary walks that were something of an escape for him.

The minute she saw the phone, she had a go at him about it:

'You're always saying these walks of yours let you get away from it all – and what's the first thing you pack? A mobile bloody phone!'

But when you were alone in remote areas you never knew when a mobile phone might save your life. In the event of an accident, it could make the difference between the emergency services finding you quickly, or spending hours – perhaps even days – looking for you in an area that extended for thousands of acres.

'Just how far do you intend to drag us?' she added.

He pointed to the cairn. 'Just up there. Not far.'

She looked beyond the copse to the hill that rose up behind it. The cairn was a triangle of rocks stacked on its summit. 'That's miles away.'

'A mile there. A mile back. You can manage that.'

His uncharacteristic stubbornness persuaded her that arguing would be futile, but the look she gave him conveyed exactly what was going through her mind: let him have his little walk. But she'd make him pay in the days and weeks to come. No sex. A monumental phone bill. Items on the credit card for clothes that couldn't be returned because she'd worn them.

They set off down a track that led to the copse. He could have parked in the clearing beneath the trees, but he didn't want to. There was something about the view from here that reminded him of his father. And that was what he had come here to touch base with.

He had first come here as a boy of five, his father carrying him on his shoulders, just as he was now carrying Marc, and the tension between him and Paula reminded him that his father had hated his mother, that walking alone together had been their escape from a woman who was idle, selfish and hostile.

Perhaps there was a pattern to these things. Perhaps it was true what they said about people marrying partners who reflected certain parental characteristics. If so, then he, like his father, would try to find a way of sticking it out until Marc was old enough to choose who he wanted to live with. Hopefully, he would make the same choice he had, and dump his mother.

Marc sat on his shoulders, his frog-eyed wellingtons dripping snow down the front of his jacket. Paula dragged behind, and several times she stopped, sometimes to retie the laces of her boots.

They were too loose.

Now they were too tight.

She thought she had a stone in her sock.

No stone.

And then the drama of adjusting the laces was played out all over again.

He and Marc forged on, Marc now singing a song he'd learned at nursery school, and then they reached the copse. Harris had never seen it like this, with not a soul in sight, but then he had never before seen it in winter.

People had walked there recently. The snow was impacted along the route that he knew the track should take. He followed it with Paula roughly twenty yards behind.

At one point he heard her yell at him to wait, and he turned to see her sitting on a tree stump, scraping at the sole of her boot with a stick. He waited for a moment, but when it looked as though she was having a genuine problem, he went back. 'What now?'

'There's frozen snow in the tread of my boot. It's making it hard to walk.'

It was like dealing with a six-year-old.

He waited while she took off her boots and beat them against a tree. The snow flew out of the tread. In seconds they would be impacted again. Not that it mattered. The ground wasn't difficult to walk on.

Paula put her boots back on, tied the laces, untied them, retied them, then said she'd had enough. 'I'll meet you back at the car.'

The idea of her returning to the car and leaving him with Marc was incredibly appealing, but he was determined to get her to walk as far as the cairn. The going was very easy. If he could do it carrying a child, she could certainly do it. 'Just for once,' he said, 'let's do something together – as a family.'

She dragged herself along the path behind him, dropping farther back with every step. And when he turned to see where she was, he found that she was standing in the trees, watching him.

Everything about her made it abundantly clear that she'd gone as far as she was prepared to go. 'Come on!' he shouted, but she stayed where she was. Intractable.

168

Marc took up the chorus. 'Come on, Mummy – not far now!' But Paula Harris stood there, her arms folded, her weight more on one leg than the other.

If she bends down to do something else with those laces, I'll whip them out of the boots and throttle her with them. 'Pau-la!' he shouted. '*Come on.*'

Nothing. Not the slightest sign that she might relent.

Furious, he retraced his steps, Marc gripping his hair so tightly he was almost wincing by the time he reached her. 'What now?' he said.

She nodded towards the cairn. 'I'm not climbing that.'

'Nobody's asking you to climb the fucking cairn – just the slope that leads to it!'

'Daddy swore, Daddy swore!' Marc, delighted, gripped his hair even tighter.

'I'll wait,' she said. 'You go up. I'll stay here.'

'We're going as a family.'

She jabbed a finger inches from his eyes. 'You want to climb it, so climb it,' she said, and he knew then that, short of dragging her by the throat, he wasn't going to get her up that slope.

He wanted to say something – anything – to convey how very deeply he hated her whining guts, but with Marc on his shoulders he controlled himself. He swallowed, then took the deepest breath he could. It calmed him, but only slightly. 'Here,' he said, and he gave her the keys to the car. 'Go back, and wait. We won't be long.'

She took the keys and stomped off down the track. He watched her go. And when she entered the trees, he turned away.

How many steps had he taken before he heard the muffled shout? A dozen? Maybe more? He'd no sooner started climbing than he heard it.

Ignore it, he told himself, and he visualised what he would find if he went to investigate. Paula would be sitting on the ground, nursing an ankle that she would insist was twisted. He would have to help her back to the car, and there was no way – no way at all – that he would ever get up to that cairn. And that, of course, was precisely what she wanted. The shout, the pretence at a twisted ankle that would miraculously recover the minute they got back to Edinburgh, was designed to prevent him from doing something he very much wanted to do.

'Daddy,' said Marc. 'I heard Mummy shout.'

'Mummy's fine,' said Harris. 'Mummy's just playing a game.'

He carried on walking.

'But what if she's not?'

'She's just playing.'

'But what if Mummy's *hurt*?'

It was no good. It was *never* any good. She would always, *always* win. And what if Marc was right? What if, this time, something had really happened to his mother? If so, Marc would remember it all his life, and he would also remember that his father hadn't gone back to investigate that cry.

He took a last look at the cairn, then turned round and walked back down the track.

He followed it through the trees, but couldn't see any sign of his wife. 'Pau-la,' he shouted.

'Mu-mmee,' yelled Marc.

And from somewhere close by, he heard another muffled cry. Harris couldn't see her, but he could hear her. He scanned the trees and the track that threaded through them, and something caught his attention, something just off the track that didn't look quite right.

He went over to it, crouched down, and lifted Marc from his shoulders. Then he fished in his pocket for a torch so small, so neat, it looked more like a pen. He switched it on, and shone it into a hole concealed between rotting wooden boards. Paula's weight had caused them to give, and what Harris saw shocked him beyond belief.

He stood back, grabbed Marc, and pulled him away from the hole, aware that his mind had gone into overdrive. *You can't just fucking leave her there – she's the mother of your child.*

It was the fact that Marc had heard her cries for help that decided him. If not for that, he didn't doubt he would have made up a game called 'Let's look for mummy'. And by the time they found her, mummy would be dead.

Mummy was currently very much alive. She was now wailing for help, and Harris pulled the mobile out of his pocket. He dialled 999, aware that Marc was crying, aware that some instinct had told him that his mother was in serious trouble. And then he realised something very dreadful, something so absolutely dreadful, and wonderful, and fortuitous, and appalling, that he grabbed his child and started to run through the trees. 'Don't leave her, Daddy – don't leave her—'

Marc was five years old. How could he be expected to understand that he had no choice? If he'd told Paula once he must have told her a thousand times to stick the mobile back on charge after she'd run the battery down yattering to those air-brain friends of hers.

The only thing he could do was get to the car as quickly as possible, drive to the nearest house and raise the alarm. With luck, provided they reached her in time, Paula might just make it.

He reached the car, sweat streaming down his face, and dumped Marc down while he fished for the keys. Then he stopped – dead – as he remembered when he'd last had them. *Here are the keys*, he'd said.

And he'd handed them to his wife.

27

Nicholas sat facing the mirror. In it he could see the moat reflected clearly. One of the divers had drowned. His head had become detached. It bobbed beneath the ice some yards away from the body. The lips were moving. He couldn't make out the words.

'I want you to trust me,' said Cranmer. 'Can you do that, Nicholas? Can you trust me?'

The moat was strewn with centuries of junk. As Cranmer spoke, Nicholas fixed his attention on objects that were lying on the bank. A table leg. A broken lamp. A fragment of frosted glass that had come from a vase.

'I'm going to tell you what I see,' said Cranmer. 'And you're going to tell me what it relates to.'

You breathe me into bottles which you nail into a box, but I stay free.

'I see a girl,' said Cranmer. 'She's running through the wood. She looks frightened.'

It could only be Sylvie.

'Where did you meet her?'

'At college.'

'You're having sex with her.'

He didn't like the thought that Cranmer could see so intimate a thing.

'And you're bleeding,' said Cranmer.

He'd never had a sexual relationship before. Sylvie thought this accounted for his initial reluctance to let her see him naked.

She traced the scars on his back with the tips of her fingers.

'How did you get them?'

'I fell through a door.'

172

'How old were you?'

'Four.'

She kissed the scars. 'All better now?'

'All better.'

The big mistake had been to bring her to Lyndle. But when you loved someone, you wanted to show them off. You wanted your parents to meet them. So you took them home. He should have foreseen that when something had no substance, no physical means to satisfy its own lust, it would be jealous. How could he not have realised it would turn on him with a vengeance?

Sylvie's face when the welts rose up on his skin – he would never forget that moment. She phoned her father and begged him to take her home. Then she ran through the wood and she stood at the top of the drive until he came.

He wrote to her, and never received a reply, and when she returned to college she avoided him. He understood. She was shocked. She needed time. But time passed. *Weeks* passed. And still she wouldn't come near him.

The worst of it was she humoured him at first. She told him she understood. It was just that, right now, she couldn't see him. She had an essay to write. She was visiting a friend. She was working this weekend. She was ill. She had commitments. And finally, inevitably, she 'felt she needed space'.

He knew straight away what had happened: something had taken her over; something that felt like her, smelt like her, fucked like her, but took an exquisite pleasure in telling him it was over. Sylvie was gone, and the thing that was inhabiting her body was fucking people in return for personal favours.

As soon as he found out, he started posting notices all round college. In them, he described what she was doing – right down to the last sexual detail. If she could be explicit with her body, he could be explicit with his pen. She was now quite openly prostituting herself and was raddled with disease. He wrote to people warning them to get themselves checked out. And that was when people started to turn against him. You're a sick bastard, Herrol. Sick.

Men were crossing the lawns, making for the woods.

At night, the trees come to life, and walk across the moors. Hands come out of the ground to catch you by the ankles. Children fall through invisible doors into worlds of terror and pain.

He went in search of these doors until finally, his father told him the woods were haunted by the ghost of someone who died there long ago.

'How long?'

'Long enough.'

Cranmer brought him gently back on track. 'We were talking about Sylvie.'

'Sylvie's dead.'

Cranmer replied that according to Tate, Sylvie was alive and well and living at home with her mother. That wasn't true. The truth was that the thing that was inhabiting her body and was fucking his friends and tutors kept her corpse at home. It never came back to college. Too raddled to deceive. It stayed away. And he knew all this because he'd been told—

'Who by?'

'You know—'

Before Cranmer could say another word, Nicholas leapt in. 'Don't name it. Don't say its name. Don't call it out. Don't bring it.'

'Is it here?'

'Shush,' said Nicholas. Finger to his lips. And whispering now. 'Don't let it see you looking.'

'Where is it?' said Cranmer, gently.

Nicholas, head bowed, pointed to a small irregular shape in the topmost corner of the mirror. 'That's where it lives. In the mirror. Don't tell Tate.'

'I won't tell,' said Cranmer.

After a moment, he added, 'Has it always been there?'

'Always.'

'Even when you were a child?'

'Even then.'

'What did it want from you?'

'Things.'

'What kind of things?' said Cranmer.

'Just things – things that I buried.'

'Offerings,' said Cranmer.

'Offerings,' he confirmed.

'And now that you're older, do you still make offerings?'

Nicholas didn't reply.

'What kind of offerings?' said Cranmer.

'Sometimes I masturbate – and just at the point where I'm about to come, I stop.'

'Why?'

'Because it pisses me off.'

'Why would you want to piss yourself off?'

'It hates me being happy.'

'What makes you think it hates you being happy?'

'That's when it has a go at me.'

'What makes you think it would have a go at you, just because you're happy?'

'It's jealous.'

Cranmer made no comment, and Nicholas added:

'That was my big mistake. I let it see me having sex with her. It hated me for that. Whatever else it can do, it can't do that – that's why it likes me not to come.' There were times when he despaired of his own stupidity. 'My fault,' he said. 'I shouldn't have waved her under its nose. It was like saying "Look what I've got – look what I can *do*". You can't blame it, not really. I brought it on myself.'

There was something about the way Cranmer was looking at him – not accusatory, but sad, and afraid, and the fear was all for him. 'Nicholas,' said Cranmer. 'Remember I asked you to trust me?'

Don't listen to him, Nicholas. I am your only friend.

'Where's Ginny?'

Nicholas looked at the shape in the mirror. The physical manifestation of his own sickness was feeding on him, was consuming him line by line. Other people had substance, had colour, had depth. He, on the other hand, was little more than a few lines scrawled on the page with a soft lead pencil, his nose an oblique, his mouth like the mathematical symbol for an equation.

Let them not erase me.

Let them not delete me letter by letter.

Let there be some watermark as proof that I existed.

'I'm being rubbed out,' he observed. 'Soon there won't be a line of me left on the page.'

28

Tate felt in his pocket for the solid rubber ball. He squeezed it in the palm of his hand, and remembered Audrah's warning. *Whenever you're tempted to believe Cranmer is genuine, reach for it – let it be a reminder.*

The truth was he didn't need reminding. As Goldman had said, Cranmer might be schizophrenic, or psychic, or a fraud, but whatever he was, he needed watching, and Tate's reason for keeping him close had more to do with wanting to control him than with wanting to make use of his alleged supernatural powers. If he was here, at Lyndle, then he couldn't be somewhere else talking to the press. It made it easier to keep an eye on him. It also made it possible to use him in order to get information out of Nicholas. Whatever he learned as a result might not be admissible in court, but at least it would provide some idea of what had happened to Ginny. After that, it would largely be a question of finding the evidence to prove it. In the meantime, there was woodland to be searched, and the sunken road was an obvious place to start.

To either side of him men were pushing foliage aside with lightweight metal poles. Periodically, one of them would squat down to take a closer look at something, then straighten and continue. Not easy to search dense woodland, especially when there was snow on the ground. At least the sunken road was too wet for the snow to settle. It made the going difficult, but it also made the job of seeing what was underfoot a little easier.

Fletcher came up to him and reported that what looked like a bunch of flowers had been found on an embankment. It was unusual, and Tate followed him to the spot where they had been found. All that remained were the stalks, and they were little more than a mass of fibre bound with twine. They weren't the kind of flowers that grew in ancient woodland. These had been bought in a shop. And the way they were positioned suggested they'd been placed rather than thrown there.

As he straightened, his attention was taken by something jutting out from the bank. He scraped at the soil to get a better idea of what it was, and realised fairly quickly it was a pipe.

Bischel had written that excess water had once been drained from the lawns via a series of culverts that fed into the wood. In the late 1800s, the culverts were replaced by pipes that ran beneath what were to become croquet lawns. They fed into a single pipe that gave out on to the sunken road.

At the time this pipe was laid, the sunken road was a public right of way. The Herrols had turned it into a glorified ditch. According to Bischel, the locals objected, but only among themselves. The village and everything in it belonged to the Herrols. People knew better than to jeopardise their jobs, their homes.

He reached out and traced the rim with his fingers. It was brown, enamelled, and cracked. It was also over two and a half feet in circumference. Cranmer had said the body was concealed in or near something round. And those flowers . . . the way they'd been placed there . . . it put him in mind of the way people sometimes laid flowers at a grave.

The pipe was almost completely blocked with debris. 'Give me a hand,' he said.

Between them, he and Fletcher cleared the mouth of the pipe to a depth of a metre, which was just about as far as a man's arm would reach. They would need equipment in order to go deeper, but was there any point? Dead bodies were a dead weight. They were also inclined to do their own thing. They didn't oblige by staying nice and straight, or nice and stiff. Anyone trying to push a body into a pipe that was only just large enough to accommodate the width of the shoulders would find it incredibly difficult. They might get it in so far . . . but no farther. If Ginny's body had been shoved in that pipe, they'd have found it by now. Not only that, but the stench of decomposing flesh would have knocked them clean off their feet. All he could smell was mud and rotting leaves. Speaking of which . . .

When people tried to hide a body by covering it with mud, there was something artificial about the look of it. The debris that he pulled from the pipe looked as though it had accumulated over a long period. It was impacted. Getting it out had been a hell of a job. And yet . . .

He shouted to some of the men who were searching the woodland around him. They came over. 'Go back to the vehicles, get me the following equipment—'

The deeper the road ran into the wood, the higher the embankments became. But here, so close to the lawns, there were only a few feet of soil dividing the higher ground from the pipe below. If they revealed the pipe to a length of ten feet or so, then opened it up, that would settle the matter once and for all.

When the men returned, Tate set to with a spade, partly because he preferred digging to standing around watching the others graft, but mostly because he suspected he had set them a task that would turn out to be pointless.

The air around them was damp and bitterly cold, but it wasn't long before sweat was running down his back. The topsoil was frozen solid. It was almost like trying to shove the spade through ice. Worst of all, this was a waste of time. He had already worked out that there was no way anyone could shove a body into a pipe such as this, so there was certainly no way anyone would have managed to get it ten feet in. Therefore, he took on more than his share of the work because, when they opened the pipe and found nothing there, he wanted his men to feel that he hadn't just left them to it. He wanted them to be able to look at the sweat pouring off him and know that he hadn't done it on a whim.

By the time they were finished, the ditch they had dug looked every inch like a shallow grave. It was nine feet long and eighteen inches deep, and the pipe lay at the bottom like a long brown coffin. The clay that it was made from had darkened over the years. It gleamed a brownish black, the glaze still intact, but cracked, a testament to Victorian craftsmanship.

An angle grinder was used to place two cuts along its length, and as the pipe was opened he told himself there wasn't much he hadn't seen before. But he was wrong about that. He realised almost instantly that nothing could have prepared him for what that pipe contained.

He was no stranger to what happened to a body after death. Death wasn't beautiful. Death left mouths wide open so that the contents of the lungs could froth and bubble around the lips. Death evacuated the bladder and bowels, and stripped the body of dignity. Death also rotted corpses to the bone, some-times extraordinarily quickly, particularly when the remains were lying in wet conditions, as these were.

It wasn't the fact that she was already a mass of bones that horrified him so much as the position she was in, because it indicated something about the manner of her death that he found appalling: she was lying on her front facing away from the road, her arms stretched out before her, as if attempting to hold back the tide of leaves and mud. Nobody could have laid her there like that. She crawled inside.

Somebody was speaking to him. Fletcher. Tate looked up to see two of his men trying to stand in the way of Claudia Herrol. She pushed them aside as if they were children, and stared down into the pipe. For five, maybe ten seconds, she just stood there. Then she raised her face to the heavens, and fell to her knees.

Jochen had left a message on Audrah's mobile. Detective Inspector Stafford was trying to contact her to let her know that someone had gone missing in circumstances similar to those in which Lars disappeared. 'Can you call me back?'

Audrah couldn't get a signal in her room. She went down to the courtyard and tried from there. Her hands were shaking as she dialled the number.

'I think this it,' said Jochen. 'I think we're finally going to find out what happened to Lars.'

'What happens now?'

Jochen replied that it would take the police a few days to get together the men and equipment they would need in order to find out whether Lars had died the same way as Paula Harris. 'Do you want to be present?'

She wasn't sure.

'Take your time,' said Jochen. 'Nobody expects you to be able to make a decision straight away.'

She hadn't known what she would feel if ever this moment came. She supposed it was stupid to hope she would feel relieved. It was just that she hadn't expected to feel afraid.

She cut the call when Tate walked into the courtyard. As he started to tell her that Ginny's remains had been found, the sound of shattering glass sent them both running towards the study.

What they saw when they entered was a scene of total chaos. Nicholas sat like a limp rag doll at the foot of the vast gilt mirror. Shards of glass lay everywhere, and he was looking down at his hands, as if wondering where all the blood had come from.

Cranmer was white with shock.

'What happened?' said Tate.

'He tried to jump through the mirror.'

It had left him relatively unscathed, considering. A few cuts. No more than that. But the fact that he'd tried to jump through it was enough for Audrah. 'We need to get him back to Broughton,' she said. 'With luck, they won't admit him on a voluntary basis. Maybe this time they'll section him.'

29

This time it was Cranmer who drove Claudia to Broughton. Tate had returned to the sunken road, and Audrah went in search of Marion Thomas.

She found her in her room, sitting on the bed. She plucked at the duvet as Audrah explained that Ginny's remains had been found on the sunken road.

'I'm sorry,' Marion said. And then: 'I hate it when people say that. It's what they say whenever they discover I've lost my daughter. Does she have parents?'

'A father,' said Audrah.

'It'll probably kill him,' said Marion. 'I wish something would kill me. I wish something would put an end to what I've been going through ever since Kathryn—'

She stopped, and Audrah said, 'Whatever Cranmer told you, it wasn't true.'

'But he knew so much about me. How can you explain even half the things he knew?'

Audrah replied, 'Marion, where's your car?'

The question threw her. 'On the drive. Why?'

'Would anyone looking at it mistake it for an unmarked police car?'

It wasn't a fair question. Audrah had already seen it. The car was an H registration, which meant it was ten years old. The metallic blue paint was speckled with rust. No one in their right mind could possibly mistake it for a police car.

'People like Cranmer have contacts in public and government offices. They pay them well. They have to. They don't just buy information from them, they buy their loyalty, and their silence.'

'I don't understand what this has to do with my car.'

'The minute someone like Cranmer arrives at a place like this, they access information on the people they might come into contact with. They take a note of the registration number of any car parked near by that clearly doesn't belong to either the press or the police. Cranmer has contacts at DVLC. They'll have given him your name, age and address. Once he knew those things, it would have been easy for him to match your name to news reports going back a decade, if not more. He'll have found out about Kathryn in minutes.'

'I find it hard to believe that anyone would do a thing like that.'

'Really?' said Audrah. 'Then let me tell you something else about pseudo psychics. When the good ones – the *really* good ones – are booked to appear in public, they access news archives local to the area weeks in advance. They scour the columns for accident reports, and memorise details given in the obituary columns. Because when people who have recently lost someone hear that a well-known medium is about to hit town, they often can't resist going along "just to see what happens". Imagine how staggered they are when someone like Cranmer tells them that "a little girl is coming through with a message for her grandma. Is there anyone in the audience who would recognise this child – she tells me her name is Anna, that she's five years old, and that she spent the last eighteen months of her life in a children's hospital?" Nine times out of ten, somebody puts up their hand and says, "Anna was my grandchild."'

Marion plucked at the duvet.

'And it doesn't stop there,' said Audrah. 'Because very soon, people from the audience get in touch with the psychic and ask for a private sitting. It doesn't take much for the psychic to find out how much they're worth and how much they can be bled for.'

Marion didn't react, and Audrah trod warily now, not at all sure how what she was about to say would be received. 'Sasha's mother phoned Tate.'

The edge of the duvet cover was embroidered. Marion found a stray strand of silk and plucked at it as Audrah continued:

'She told him what happened to Kathryn.'

'What did she say?'

'That Kathryn ran away from home after leaving a note accusing her teacher of attempted rape. She said she couldn't face going back to school because she was terrified of Reeve, and she was frightened to tell because she didn't think anyone would believe her.'

Marion said, 'What else did she tell him?' and Audrah realised that she wanted to know whether she, like so many people, would take the view that the authorities had been right not to pursue Reeve. Cautiously, she went on:

'Kathryn persuaded Sasha to go with her. They booked into a guest-house for the night. It was cold. They went to bed and left the gas fire lit. Both were overcome by carbon monoxide poisoning.'

And that was it. Kathryn was killed not by Reeve, but by poison gas. Not the victim of murder. But the victim of a devastating accident.

The only sound was the scratching of Marion's nails on the cotton duvet. One by one, she was unpicking the stitches. Pulling the threads apart. 'Kathryn would still be alive if not for Reeve.'

Audrah wanted to argue that Kathryn would still be alive if not for the fact that the landlord hadn't maintained the flue. But then the landlord hadn't committed the act that prompted Kathryn to run away in the first place.

Referring to a statement that Sasha had made to the police, Marion said, 'The word of a sixteen-year-old girl wasn't enough to get Reeve into court. What does that tell you?'

When Audrah made no reply, she added: 'It tells you that the law considers a girl of sixteen to be old enough for sex, but it doesn't consider her word to be worth a fuck.'

Audrah was tempted to argue that the police had backed off for no other reason than that they knew they had no case. But she was aware that there was probably no point trying to reason with her. Reeve had been forced to move home and job six times since Kathryn's death owing to the extent to which Marion had harassed him. 'All these things were reported in various papers.'

'Cranmer wouldn't have had time to access them.'

'You'd be surprised the archives you can access on the Internet – or maybe he just relies on a few trusted contacts. He gives them your name. They phone him back within the hour giving him the basics of what he needs to know to convince you.'

'You're saying he tricked me – you're saying he's a fraud.'

'Yes,' replied Audrah. 'That's exactly what I'm saying.'

Marion pulled the silken thread. The cotton duvet puckered.

'That's not what you want to hear, is it?'

Marion admitted it.

'Why not?'

'Because—'

'Because what?'

Marion replied, 'Because I can't stand the thought of never seeing her again.'

Audrah knew what it felt like to be desperate for proof that someone you loved still existed somewhere. God knew, she'd wished the same. But Lars was dead. Gone for ever. Never to return. How hard it was to face that simple fact. Small wonder people shied from it. Small wonder they clung to the hope that they and the people they loved would be reunited after death. But they wouldn't be. Death really *was* the end.

30

After leaving Marion, Audrah made her way across the court-yard. Now she saw a glimmer of light forcing its way through the glass in Ginny's room, and she assumed that Tate was back in there. Strange how he was attracted to that room. It was almost as though he hoped it would give him some clue with regard to what had happened to her, as if he believed she might have left an impression on the place, something that might speak to him in quiet moments.

She entered the house via the door to the kitchen. And as she approached Ginny's room, she saw that the door to the ward-robe had been left open. A full-length mirror was fixed to the inside of it, and the angle at which it was open gave her a view of the room.

What she saw reflected in the mirror was something Audrah denied could possibly be there. Ginny's remains were lying in a pipe. Therefore, the girl with her back to that slit of a window couldn't exist. She turned when she saw Audrah in the door-way. There was a waxen quality to her skin, the suggestion that she wasn't quite of this world.

'Somebody's taken my letter,' she said. 'The letter from my mother.'

Tate's reaction to the news that Ginny was alive and well and rummaging around her room was predictable. 'If this is a joke—'

'No joke,' Audrah assured him.

Tate followed her back to Ginny's room, and when he walked in and saw her, Audrah watched his mind go into overdrive. Ginny was dead. Her remains were in a pipe by the sunken road. Therefore what he was seeing couldn't be real.

Her own reaction to seeing Ginny had struck her as interesting: logic insisted that what she was looking at couldn't be an apparition – there was no such thing. At the same time, she experienced a strong desire to touch her – just to make sure she was truly flesh and blood. Parapsychologists called this the Doubting Thomas syndrome, and she wasn't surprised when, after telling her who he was, Tate walked over to Ginny and put his hand on her arm.

When he touched her, it made her nervous. Ginny drew away. 'How do I know you're really police?' she said.

Tate showed her his ID and, reassured, she relaxed as he said, 'Where have you been?'

'Glastonbury.'

Tate's voice was slightly hoarse, as though the shock of seeing her had tightened the muscles of the throat to such an extent he could hardly get the words out. His questions, however, struck Audrah as mundane. But what did you say when someone you had good reason to think was dead turned up alive and well. You were glad – of course you were – but you were also shocked. 'How did you support yourself?'

'Bar work, mostly. Why?'

'People have been very worried about you. Don't you read the papers?'

She wouldn't look at him.

'What made you run away? I take it you *did* run away?'

'Because of Durham. Time was running out.'

Tate didn't know what she meant. He invited her to sit on the bed and explain.

'I didn't get in,' said Ginny.

'You mean you failed your exams?' said Tate, and there was neither condemnation nor pity in the remark; he was merely getting his facts straight. She gave a nod. 'I didn't know how to break it to my father.'

'You could have resat them.'

'I didn't want to.' She elaborated. 'I'm not terribly academic,' she admitted, and then, almost immediately, she corrected herself: 'I'm not interested, actually, if I'm honest. I don't *want* to resit my exams. I just want . . . I want people to leave me alone, to let me find out what I'm good at, what I really want to do.'

'What *do* you want to do?'

'I haven't thought that far. I just know I don't want to go to university.'

'Well, why didn't you just say so?'

'You don't understand. My father was a lecturer. I couldn't face admitting it – not to him.'

'You could at least have phoned to let him know you were all right.'

'He'd have wanted to know why I ran away.'

'He'd have found out sooner or later. I'm staggered he doesn't know already.'

'You don't know him – he'd rather think of me as dead than stupid.'

Tate replied gently, 'I think you'll find that dead is the last thing he'd rather you were. In fact, he's going to be so ecstatic to find out you're alive, I doubt he'll care one way or another what you want to do with your life.'

She looked ashamed. 'I *tried* to phone,' she said, and before anyone could say that she couldn't have tried very hard, she added: 'But the longer I was gone, the harder it got. In the end, I just couldn't face it.'

Audrah wondered how many people felt the same. Having been gone so long, it would be impossible to turn up as though nothing had happened. *Everything* had happened. When you walked out on the people who loved you without so much as a word of explanation, they could hardly be expected to take you back without you telling them what made you do it, and maybe you didn't know. Maybe, one day, things just got too much and walking out seemed the only solution. Maybe you didn't intend to be gone for more than a day or so, but your family asked the police to institute a search, and suddenly you had to deal with that on top of all the other problems piling up on you. Maybe there were people who would have come back by now if not for feeling overwhelmed whenever they thought of all the explaining they were going to have to do. How many times had she wondered whether that was what happened to Lars?

There was something Audrah wanted to know. 'Ginny,' she said. 'Nicholas got you the job.'

'He knew I was desperate – it was sweet of him.'

'And you were here how long?'

'Three weeks.'

'What was your job?'

She seemed to have to think about that. 'I'm not sure. I expected to have to do some housework, but nobody actually asked me to do anything. I was just . . . just here.'

'And where was Nicholas?'

'In his room, mostly.'

'Did he bother you?'

'If anything he seemed to want to avoid me. Why?'

Audrah considered the sheer sparsity of the room. 'What did you think when you saw where you were going to be living?'

Ginny replied, 'I thought it was a bit of a dump, if I'm honest.'

'What I meant was – weren't you frightened?'

Ginny looked around as if seeing her surroundings for the first time.

'What was there to be frightened of? A bit of dirt. A few old stones. No big deal.'

It was a fascinating insight for Audrah. Some people were highly sensitive to their surroundings. It was part of what made them think they might be psychic. Ginny stood at the opposite end of the spectrum. Give her a sleeping bag and a packet of digestives and she could probably happily spend the night in a graveyard. Lyndle held no terrors for her. Discomfort, perhaps, but not terror. She'd make a good parapsychologist.

'What brought you back?' said Tate.

'The letter,' said Ginny. 'Where is it?'

'It was returned to your father.'

She started to panic now. 'Will I get prosecuted for not letting people know I was all right? Will my father have to pay for the cost of the search?'

After Tate had reassured her that her father wouldn't be held financially responsible, she added, 'Will you tell him? I can't face it – about Durham, I mean.'

Tate and Audrah exchanged a look of pure exasperation, neither of them voicing what was running through their minds.

If the remains that had been found on the Old Lyndle Road weren't Ginny's, whose were they?

31

Tate dreamed of flowers that grew in a pipe. They took root in a compost of debris, reached out from the darkness, and sought the light and air. But when they found it, they withered, and he, not realising their significance, trod them underfoot.

He was woken by the telephone. The previous day the remains had been examined by the pathologist, who wanted to conduct further tests before they were moved. Darkness was closing in, and a screen had been erected around them to protect them, not only from the elements but also from prying eyes. The press already knew that something had been found.

The sunken road had been sealed off and declared a scene of crime, and after leaving enough men in place to repel an entire army of reporters, Tate went to see Ginny's father. He wept with relief when told that his daughter was alive. 'When can I see her?'

'Right now,' said Tate. 'She's sitting in the car.'

It wasn't often he managed to give people good news for a change. He should have slept well that night, but the stems of those flowers wove through his dreams like so much bindweed.

He read the morning papers as he ate breakfast. Two headlines fought for supremacy. One read, 'Ginny Alive!' The other read 'Human remains found in Lyndle Wood'. In both cases a picture of Ginny hugging her father dominated the front page. Mr Mulholland claimed that words simply failed to express what he had felt when told that Ginny was alive. It was a sentiment Tate could relate to. The urge to touch her, to make sure she was really *there*, had been overwhelming. But Ginny was warm and solid. Nothing whatsoever like the girl they'd found in the pipe.

He arrived at Lyndle to find that the pathologist had been delayed, but somebody wanted to talk to him – somebody who gave her name as Veronica Lundy. She'd heard about the discovery on the news the night before, and had driven from Carlisle to speak to him.

'Where is she?' said Tate.

'Sitting in her car,' Fletcher replied.

Tate walked over to a car parked by the moat. A woman got out of it as he approached, her skin the colour of melted chocolate. 'Inspector Tate?' she said. She offered her hand. He took it. 'Veronica Lundy.'

The melted chocolate was poured into tailored slacks and a linen shirt, both beautifully cut, and he sensed his men's bemusement as he led her towards the Hall.

The fire had gone out in the study. It was cold in there, but it was still an improvement on standing around outside.

'Sit down,' he invited, and she settled herself in one of the red leather armchairs. As she did so, she wrapped one incredibly long leg around the other as if it were rubber. Then she glanced around and added, 'So much has changed.'

'Changed?' said Tate.

'The books are gone. Most of them. I wonder why she sold them.'

'You've been here before?'

'Only briefly. But I remember it. How could one forget a place like Lyndle?'

He asked her why she'd driven from as far away as Carlislé to speak to him, and she replied that in order to give him a proper picture she would have to tell him something about her background.

'I'm listening,' said Tate.

'In 1985,' she said, 'my only ambition in life was to be a successful model. I was lucky. I was signed by one of the most prestigious agencies in Europe. It was called Margo's.'

*   *   *

When Tate emerged from the house, he was told that the pathologist had arrived. He made his way to the pipe and spoke to him briefly. 'What are the chances of establishing a cause of death?'

He was told not to get his hopes up – there wasn't much left of her now. 'Any idea who she is?'

Tate, who now had a very good idea who she *might* be, told the pathologist he had already taken steps to access information that might help them get an ID. The pathologist wasn't listening. He was looking down the length of the sunken road. Tate turned. A woman was standing some distance away, watching from the trees.

She would turn out to be a local, someone who had heard the news and had come to see for herself, not realising that real life wasn't entertainment. He was going to have to talk to her, if only to point out that she may have contaminated the scene of crime – if she didn't know that was an offence, she soon would.

She was dressed in jeans and trainers, and she was dirty in a way that suggested she slept rough. She also looked as though she might have been crying, but then people were often deeply affected by the news that the remains of a murder victim had been found in the vicinity. They came to talk to the uniforms – partly to find things out, and often just to say how sorry they were. They may not have known the victim, but the thought that someone had been murdered, that their body had been dumped in a place where they themselves had played as children, or walked their dogs, or done their courting, appalled them. It brought it home to them.

He would normally have demolished anyone found any-where near the scene of crime, but the closer he got, the more he realised how young, how *frightened*, she looked. He showed his ID and said, 'What's your name?'

'Rachel,' she replied.

'Well, Rachel,' he said, 'I don't know if you realise, but this is currently the focus of a murder investigation. You shouldn't be here.'

She wiped her face with the palm of her hand, streaking it, making herself look slightly savage. 'Tell me,' she said. 'Tell me honestly – the woman in the pipe, did she crawl into it?'

A statement had been released to the media, but that kind of detail hadn't been made public knowledge, and Tate's original plan, which had been to ask the woman to move away from the scene and leave it at that, evaporated.

'Where do you live?'

'Leeds.'

Leeds! She must have come miles. 'What are you doing here?'

'I came back.'

'You've been here before?'

A timid nod confirmed it, and Tate added, 'When?'

'Last August.'

'What did you come back for?'

She pointed at the screen. 'To find out if I would see her again.'

The comment made no sense. 'See who?'

'The woman in the pipe.'

He was beginning to realise what she was trying to tell him. 'Are you trying to say you saw her crawl into it?'

Another timid nod.

Less than a few moments ago, the pathologist had pointed out something that made Tate realise Rachel must be mistaken.

'That isn't possible,' he said.

'Why not?' she replied.

Rachel's reaction, was one he hadn't anticipated. She put her hands to her face, and started to scream.

32

Marion had packed the clippings. Tessa didn't know she had them, and she didn't want her to know. Not that there was any harm in her knowing – it was just that if Tessa discovered just one more reason to pity her, she didn't think she could stand it.

Audrah walked into the study to let her know that Sasha had arrived.

'Tessa's with her,' she said, and it sounded like a warning, as though she'd managed to weigh Tessa up pretty swiftly. Perhaps she had. Here was a woman for whom life had always been sweet. Loving parents had raised her to be married to an adoring husband, someone who could afford to allow her to indulge herself in countless, pointless projects – the foundation course in pottery that she would abandon once she realised she couldn't get her nails clean, the businesses that would never quite get off the ground. Wouldn't it be wonderful if, just once, something were to jolt her out of the world in which everything went her way?

She was ashamed of herself. These were the thoughts of someone who was small and mean and bitter. It was just that Tessa hadn't suffered. Not really. The closest she'd come to suffering was when she discovered that Sasha and Kathryn had run away from home, and even then she was cool about it. Teenage girls *did* that kind of thing. It was rather amusing really. They were sensible, said Tessa. Besides, they were together. Some nice policeman would find them, and bring them home.

She was right about them being found by police. But even when it was broken to her that one of the girls was dead, the words had barely registered before Tessa was assured that the dead girl was Kathryn. In the light of that, what else could possibly matter? Such a shock to Tessa. She banged on about those two seconds of mind-numbing shock as if they'd lasted a lifetime, or as though they gave her an insight into what it must be like for people who had to cope with the fact of their child's death every day for the rest of their lives. Absurd that Tessa could possibly believe they were bonded by Kathryn's death when what they had experienced as a result of it was so different. *We'll always be friends, Marion. People can't go through what we've gone through together and not be friends for ever . . .*

For ever had lasted approximately four months, after which Tessa began to want her out of her life. More specifically, she wanted her out of Sasha's life: *You do understand – you're such a reminder.*

Fuck Sasha. Fuck Tessa. And fuck that they were turning up to take her home like some halfwit who had managed to escape the constraints put upon her by the authorities.

Audrah entered the study ahead of Tessa, who was followed by Sasha. In their quality suits and those rather beautiful flat-heeled calf-leather boots they looked like a matching pair of dolls. Tessa, however, looked the epitome of sophistication, whereas Sasha had the air of a small, frightened deer. It was as if, at any moment, she might leap over the furniture and go crashing out of the room.

She sat in a red leather armchair, folding her slender legs very shyly, and the more Marion observed her, the stranger she found it that Sasha was there at all. She appeared to have no interest in her surroundings, but Tessa looked around as if she couldn't believe that houses like Lyndle Hall could actually exist. She, like everyone else, would have read the papers, so she would know why the police were there. And Sasha would have told her what had happened at the bank. Therefore Tessa would know what had brought her to Lyndle. What she wouldn't know was whether or not she managed to find John Cranmer, or what the outcome was.

There was once a time when Tessa would have pecked her on the cheek. Not any more. She stood as close to the door as possible, grim faced and hating every moment of being there. 'I thought it best that I came,' she said. 'I couldn't expect Sasha to drive hundreds of miles here and hundreds of miles back in two days.'

Marion could imagine that Tessa had done her best to persuade Sasha not to come. She wondered what had made her agree to it. If she were honest with herself, when she gave Sasha's name to Tate she hadn't for one moment expected her to say yes.

'I've had a sitting with Cranmer.'

'You can tell us in the car,' said Tessa.

'I'd rather tell you now.'

'We've such a long drive ahead of us.'

'Kathryn was alive when the ambulance came.'

For a moment – but a moment only – Tessa was stunned into silence. Then she got a grip. 'Don't be ridiculous, Marion. You *know* that can't be true.'

'He described the house she died in. Right down to the curtains at the window.'

'He must have read about it,' said Tessa.

Throughout the exchange, Sasha just stared at the floor. Moments ago, her hair had been swept up in a soft French plait. Now she was working away at some of the strands, twisting them round her fingers, pulling it apart.

'They thought she was dead,' said Marion. And now she spoke to Sasha. 'Kathryn was watching them save you. She begged them not to leave her, but they did. She wasn't like you, Sasha. She wasn't pretty, and privileged. The average man wouldn't have thought her worth saving by comparison with you. And so they left her. That's why she died.'

'For God's sake, Marion!' It was rare for Tessa to shout. 'What are you trying to do to her?'

Audrah stepped in. 'Marion, maybe it would be better if you let me drive you—'

'I don't want you to drive me. I want *her* to drive me. I want her to explain why she refused to admit that Michael Reeve lured her, and my daughter, to that bed-sit.'

She turned on Sasha now. 'What's wrong, Sasha? Were you the one who was screwing him? Was Kathryn covering for you?'

Tessa looked as though she might actually hit her. She appealed to Audrah. 'Do we really have to put up with this?'

'She's ill,' said Audrah. 'Let me arrange for someone else to—'

Tessa made for the door. 'Sasha, we're leaving.' But Sasha stayed where she was. 'In a moment,' she said. 'Not yet. Not until I've said what I came to say.'

She suddenly broke down, and Tessa turned on Marion again. 'Are you satisfied?' she said. 'Is this what you wanted to achieve?' She grabbed Sasha by the arm, as if she could physically lift her out of the chair. 'We're leaving,' she repeated.

'Please,' said Sasha, pulling away from her mother. 'There's something I have to tell her. I owe it to her to—'

'You don't owe her anything!'

'I do – and I owe it to Kathryn too.'

'Darling—'

'For God's sake,' said Marion. 'Let her spit it out!' But now that it had come to it, Sasha lost her nerve. 'Michael Reeve—' she said, and instantly Tessa put her hands to her ears. 'I don't want to hear that name.'

The colour was beginning to drain from Sasha's face. 'Michael Reeve—' she said again, and then she took a breath. She held it for a moment, then added, '—was everything to Kathryn. She adored him.'

She couldn't have made a greater impact if she had claimed to have witnessed Reeve murdering Kathryn. For several seconds, nobody said a word. Then Tessa cut in:

'Are you saying he took advantage of a schoolgirl crush?'

'He didn't take advantage of anything,' said Sasha. 'I'm saying that Kathryn had a *thing* about him. She hung around just to catch a glimpse of him. She followed him home from school. She—'

Marion took a step towards her. Instantly Audrah put herself between them, but Marion forced herself to stay calm: 'Go on, Sasha.'

'Mr Reeve told her it had to stop. And that's when she started threatening him. She accused him of leading her on, but he didn't, Mrs Thomas. Even then, all he did was try to talk some sense into her. He said he didn't want to get her into trouble with the headmaster. He was trying to give her a chance.'

It wasn't true. All she had to do was look at Sasha's face to know she was lying. When you knew a person from childhood, you knew when they were lying.

'Why?' she said, and what she meant was 'why are you lying?' But Sasha thought she was asking why Kathryn would behave in such a way.

'She was so hurt,' she said. 'She couldn't stand the rejection.'

When Marion looked at Tessa, she realised that whatever she'd expected Sasha to say, it wasn't this. 'Sasha, stop it – you don't know what you're saying.' But Sasha continued, her words a torrent, as if for a very long time she had longed to let them out:

'It wasn't true about him trying to rape her. She said it to punish him. She said that if we ran away from home it would teach him a lesson, and we planned what to say when we were found.' She appealed to Marion. 'We knew we'd be found, you see, and Kathryn knew that provided we stuck to our story, Mr Reeve would probably have to resign. That was what she wanted. She wanted him to have to leave his job. She wanted him to have to move away. She wanted to *punish* him.'

She turned to her mother and, despite the fact that two years had turned her into a woman, reverted to the girlhood she had so very recently left. 'I didn't want to go with her. And I didn't want to say those things about Mr Reeve. I don't know how she managed to talk me into it. Mummy – I'm so sorry.'

This was more than Marion could stand. She launched herself at Sasha. 'You lying little bitch!'

Between them, Tessa and Audrah held her back long enough for Sasha to run out of the room. And then Tate's men were there, relieving them of the job of having to restrain her. She was weeping, and she hated to let Tessa see her cry. 'I'll kill her,' she said. 'I promise you, Tessa – if it's the last thing I do.'

'You're mad,' said Tessa, but she, too, was weeping. 'What will it take to get you out of our lives?'

Moments later, Audrah stood in the courtyard with Tessa and Sasha. They were watching Marion climb into the back of a police car.

'What's going to happen to her?' said Sasha.

'The police will make arrangements to get her home,' said Audrah. 'After that I don't know.'

As the car pulled away, Sasha said, 'Now that I've told the truth, she'll have to leave me alone, won't she?'

Audrah only wished she could offer the reassurance that Sasha so touchingly expected her to deliver, like a seal performing a trick at the whim of its keeper. But she could no more assure Sasha that Marion would leave her alone than balance a coloured ball on the tip of her nose. 'Telling the truth is one thing. Getting someone to believe it is another,' she replied.

'She'll have to believe me once I've apologised to Mr Reeve and made a statement to the police.'

Tessa was appalled. 'Sasha – you mustn't! Don't even consider it.'

'What else can I do?'

Audrah could see Tessa working it out. In order for Reeve's name to be cleared, the facts would have to be made very public, and the tabloids were never kind to girls from middle-class backgrounds. They might suggest that Sasha was responsible for everything Reeve had been through in the past two years, for she, even more than Marion, ought to be held to account for his suicide attempts, his move from job to job, from home to home, the loss of his friends, his happiness, his wellbeing. Because Marion didn't know the facts. But Sasha did. There would be no point her trying to argue that she'd done it for Kathryn's sake. The press wouldn't see it that way.

Tessa suddenly said, 'Kathryn was an immensely difficult girl. Something seemed to happen after her father left. She changed. I can't imagine what she could have been thinking to fabricate such lies, and to drag my daughter into it all. To be honest, I'm almost—'

Almost glad she's dead. That was what she had been about to say, but the fact that Kathryn *was* dead stopped her from voicing her thoughts. She no doubt felt the same way about Marion. How convenient it would be if people would just take their pain and depart with it, leaving others to their neat and tidy world, the world in which people never phoned to demand explanations, apologies or consideration.

She stroked the top of Sasha's head. 'Darling, why didn't you tell us?'

Audrah suspected she knew the answer to that: the people who surrounded her after the tragedy were so distraught, so glad that she, at least, had survived, that she couldn't bring herself to admit the truth. To have risked doing so would have been to risk turning their sympathy to venomous condemnation. 'I was frightened,' Sasha said. 'Everyone was so kind. Once they knew the truth, they weren't going to be kind any more. And then there was Mrs Thomas—' She began to weep again as she added: 'I didn't want to hurt her. And although I knew it was wrong to let people think Mr Reeve tried to rape Kathryn, I thought it must be worse for her than for him. I thought he could find a new job, somewhere else to live where people wouldn't know what he'd been accused of. I suppose I thought it would all be forgotten after a few weeks. Stupid, I know, but I honestly thought he'd be able to put it behind him.

Mrs Thomas was never going to put it all behind her. Kathryn was all she had.'

She looked at Audrah. 'You must think we were wicked. But we didn't mean to be. We didn't really know what we were doing.'

It occurred to Audrah that what she meant was that neither she nor Kathryn had any idea of the magnitude of the allegations they were making, much less of the impact they would have on Reeve.

'We thought it would make him miserable for a couple of weeks. We didn't know it would ruin his life. That's what I can't live with – not Mrs Thomas harassing me, or the guilt of knowing we lied, but the fact that two years on I've realised what we did to him. I want to put it right. The only way I can do that is to admit it.'

Audrah replied, 'I expect most people will see the situation for what it was – something a couple of schoolgirls did without true understanding or thought for the consequences.'

Tessa steered her towards the car, a Mercedes convertible, the paintwork as creamy as the snow. As Sasha climbed in to the passenger seat, something she said after making the admission came back to Audrah. 'Now that I've told the truth, she'll have to leave me alone, won't she.'

Audrah wouldn't have liked to stake her life on it. She could be wrong, but Marion didn't strike her as the type who would ever give up.

No sooner had the Mercedes melted into the trees than Tate walked over. Audrah assumed he was about to comment on Marion, but he had other things on his mind.

'I need a favour,' he said, adding, 'I need to question someone, and I want you to be present.'

'Any particular reason?'

'You're a psychologist.'

The police had their own psychologists, and they were notoriously suspicious of those they didn't know and trust. 'You must have access to any number.'

'I do,' said Tate. 'But what I need right now is a *paranormal* psychologist.'

'What's going on?' said Audrah.

'You'll find out,' said Tate.

33

The past twenty-four hours had been a living hell for Guy. Yorkshire Police had studied footage from the closed-circuit television cameras that covered every inch of Leeds Infirmary and the surrounding streets. There was therefore a fairly comprehensive picture of the route Rachel took as she made her way out of the hospital.

She left by the main doors and walked towards a shopping precinct in Leeds. The main arcade was covered, as were the streets beyond it, but Rachel then headed into a part of Leeds where there were fewer cameras monitoring people on the streets below. It wasn't known where she went after that.

Now he and his father were in the room at Rippon Gardens. It hadn't been cleaned in over two weeks. What a dump it was. Strange how you could live in a place and somehow grow immune to the conditions. All it took was a taste of civilised living to bring you face to face with the reality of the way you were leading your life. They might be broke, but it was no excuse for squalor.

His father sat on the edge of the bed, as if terrified he might contract something incurable merely by breathing in too deeply. 'Maybe you should think about moving in with me.'

'What about Rachel?'

His father didn't answer.

'I can't walk out,' said Guy. 'I thought I'd got that through to you.' Before his father could reply, someone shouted from somewhere deep in the house. 'Guy. Phone!'

Just for a moment, he allowed himself to imagine it might be Rachel. He lifted the receiver, a mixture of relief and rage tying him up inside. But it was the police, and the floor started rolling again. Last time he got a call from them, they were asking him to go to Leeds Infirmary. Maybe, this time, they were asking him to go to the morgue.

'Detective Inspector Tate,' said the voice. 'Northumbria Police.'

The conversation went something like the one he'd had with Wilcox but it culminated in Tate saying:

'Your wife has been taken to the station in Hexham. She's asking for you.'

Guy was aware that his father had followed him down the stairs to where there was a communal pay-phone tucked into a recess off the kitchen. 'Can you hold a minute,' said Guy.

He put his hand over the receiver and said, 'Rachel turned up at Lyndle. The police want me to go to the station in Hexham.'

His father shook his head as if to say he thought Guy was making a big mistake. But he said, 'Use my car.'

Guy took his hand from the receiver. 'Tell her I'm on my way.'

Instead of heading straight for the station, Guy made for the village. It was only a matter of weeks since he'd last been there, but he would hardly have recognised it. Back then it was at least populated, if only by a handful of diehards. Now there was no one. The shop where he and Rachel bought a sandwich was boarded up, not just for the summer but for ever, as was the petrol station with its two meagre pumps.

On seeing the cottage again, he was reminded why the agent felt they would have a problem selling it. He walked inside to find the rubble deeper than he remembered, the smell of rotting timbers more pervasive.

He thought back to something Rachel said at the hospital. No matter how many times he thought it through, it made no sense. On the one hand, she was trying to convince him she'd seen a ghost. On the other, she was trying to tell him she didn't realise until she got back to the cottage that she'd seen anything at all.

'I told myself it couldn't have happened – not really. It was all just an impression, something that somehow registered at the back of my mind.'

He didn't know how to handle this – whether to admit that he had no idea what she meant, or to humour her. Before he could decide, she added:

'You know about adverts – how they work, I mean.'

He felt a kind of sickness sweep over him. 'Rachel,' he said, softly, 'what do adverts have to do with what you just told me?'

'But you do, don't you – you *do* know how they work?'

He knew a certain amount. He certainly knew how to make them. Whether or not anyone was ever going to give him the chance to prove it remained to be seen. The way things were going, he'd be lucky to get a job as a runner.

'One of your tutors said he didn't see what commercials had to do with making films, but in the end he gave you good marks.'

She was talking about an essay he wrote that focused on the impact images had on the subconscious. He remembered discussing it with her now, but he still didn't see what it had to do with what she'd just told him.

Rachel said, 'Remember that company who came up with an idea for an advert for a particular brand of cigarettes?'

She started to cry, and it added to the difficulty of trying to understand her.

'But as the ad . . . advert was being shown, an image relating to a particular brand of matches was flashed on-screen.'

This is for the rest of your life, Guy – the rest of your life.

'Anyone who saw the advert, next time they bought the cigarettes, they found themselves buying the matches, and not really knowing why. Even if they had a lighter, they found themselves buying matches they didn't need.'

He remembered how appalled she'd been when he told her, and rightly so. It was a form of advertising that worked on a particularly insidious principle: the image was flashed up so quickly the person watching didn't even know it had been projected. Their conscious mind didn't register it. But their subconscious did.

'People complained,' said Rachel. 'They thought they were going to end up walking round like zombies – buying things they didn't really want.'

He suddenly wondered whether she thought she was being brainwashed. 'It's all right, Rachel. The practice was banned. They're not allowed to do it any more.'

She wasn't listening. 'That's what happened to me when I reached the cottage. That was when I realised I'd seen a woman crawling through the undergrowth. I didn't see her at the time. It was only when I got back I realised.'

Either she had seen something or she hadn't. He was tempted to tell her to make up her mind. Instead he kept his mouth shut. Too terrified of tipping her over the edge.

'People have it all wrong.' Her eyes were almost wild with the revelation, as though she'd discovered a secret that very few people knew. 'A ghost isn't something you see, not the way most people mean – a ghost is something that registers at the back of your mind. Do you understand, Guy? Do you see?'

The wooden peg sat stiff and cold in his hand. When he found it, the certainty that some father had whittled it for a child had charmed him. Now it was a reminder that his marriage was breaking down. He threw it back into the rubble, as if by doing so he could put an end to some kind of curse, then he set out for the station.

Tate had shown Guy and Rachel into an interview room that was comfortably furnished. With its sofa, curtains and coffee making equipment, it looked more like somebody's living room. It was reserved for people who were in a state of shock and Rachel, with her dark frightened eyes, looked like the kind of person who was more than entitled to sit there.

Audrah's immediate impression was of a girl who looked younger than nineteen. She also looked as though she might have been sleeping rough.

Tate introduced Audrah to them. 'This is a colleague of mine – 'Dr Audrah Sidow.' He now spoke to Guy rather than to Rachel. 'I asked her to be present while I talked to your wife.'

When he heard the word *doctor*, Guy seemed reassured. He looked at Rachel. 'Is that all right with you?'

'I don't mind,' said Rachel.

Tate spoke to her as if she were a child. 'You're not in any trouble, Rachel – all we need to know is, what brought you to Lyndle?'

Her reply of 'Nothing' could barely be heard.

'It's a long way to come for nothing,' said Tate.

Guy squeezed her hand. 'Tell them—'

She shook her head, and he added, 'Rachel, you *have* to tell them.'

After some moments, she finally said, 'You tell them – I can't,' and he explained that back in the summer Rachel's aunt had died and left her a cottage. At the end of the previous August, they had come to take a look at it, and for reasons he wouldn't go into Rachel had had a few problems since then. A couple of days ago, she'd ended up in hospital. He wouldn't say why – that was private.

What Guy had told them explained what had brought them to Lyndle in the first place, but it didn't explain why Rachel had returned.

'So what brought you back?' said Tate.

Again, Guy looked at Rachel, and when she didn't reply, Tate added, 'You said yourself that Rachel has only just come out of hospital. It must have been something important to make her want to come back at a time like this.'

Before Guy could reply, Rachel suddenly blurted out: 'The woman in the pipe.'

'What about her, Rachel?'

She began to weep; great racking sobs. She could hardly get the words out: '*I saw her die.*'

*   *   *

It took some time for Tate to draw the story out of her, after which he felt that she had been through enough for the moment. He arranged for the Harveys to be taken to a guest-house.

Once he and Audrah had the interview room to themselves, he asked her what she made of it. Audrah replied, 'Before I answer that, tell me – how much of what Rachel told us tied in with what you know to be true?'

'All of it,' said Tate. 'We know the remains are those of a woman. We know her killer wouldn't have found it possible to insert her body ten feet into a pipe that was only just wide enough for her shoulders, so we can only assume she crawled into it. That information hasn't been released yet. There's no way Rachel could have known unless she saw what she says she saw.'

As far as Audrah was concerned, there obviously *was* a way, otherwise Rachel couldn't have known. 'She witnessed that woman's murder.'

'Then how come she didn't just say so?'

Audrah replied, 'Sometimes, when people can't understand what they've seen, they explain it away as a supernatural experience. If Rachel isn't able to accept that she witnessed a murder, she might well convince herself that what she saw was a re-enactment of it.'

'What would be the psychological advantage of that?'

'It puts it at a distance,' said Audrah. 'It makes it safe, because it places it in the past. It also places it in a realm that has nothing to do with reality. Therefore it makes it controllable.'

'And that's what you think happened?'

'I certainly think it's the most likely explanation.'

Tate said, 'What if I were to tell you that what Rachel just told us might explain what happened to a woman who went missing from Lyndle some time ago.'

'How long ago?' asked Audrah.

'Eighteen years,' said Tate.

34

The first thing Audrah said was, 'That's not possible.' It was an understandable reaction, and Tate let her list the reasons why. There hadn't yet been a post-mortem. Perhaps someone went missing more recently than eighteen years ago and there were further remains out there, waiting to be found. Maybe Rachel had woven a fantasy that just happened to be uncomfortably close to the facts of a known case. Maybe she'd heard somebody talking about a murder that had actually taken place.

Tate was about to throw her a challenge. Before he did so, he felt it only fair to let her know what Veronica Lundy told him earlier.

The minute she mentioned Margo's, Tate had recalled the name. At first he couldn't remember where he'd heard it, then he remembered Williams, the security guard who came forward to say he was told to evict Francis Herrol from the premises of a modelling agency.

Veronica said, 'Margo was in her sixties when I was signed. And when she died . . . well, the agency died with her. But at the time, it was *the* agency to be with. We knew we were lucky.'

Veronica was the original Naomi Campbell – perhaps not quite as stunning, but not far off. She had his complete attention as she went on:

'Girls today are taken on when they're little more than children. It isn't uncommon to find twelve-year-olds modelling clothes aimed at the over-twenty-fives. But things were different then. There wasn't a girl on the books younger than sixteen, and most were older. I was sixteen,' she added. 'Fresh out of school. I didn't know a thing about a thing. Fortunately, Margo was terribly protective. At the time I thought it was

sweet. Now I realise she was simply looking after her invest-
ments. Some of us were going to be worth an awful lot of
money to her one day.'

Tate suspected that Veronica turned out to be worth more
than most.

'She referred to the younger girls as her "babies", and her
"babies" had to sign contracts with the kind of clauses reminiscent of 1930s Hollywood. You know the sort of thing – I
swear by Almighty God that I will be home by ten o'clock at the
latest. We weren't allowed in certain clubs and bars – especially
around Soho. We weren't allowed to move in with our boy-
friends, or they with us, and so on. To tell you the truth, I think
I had more freedom at convent school.'

A vision of Margo appeared before Tate as surely as if she
were standing in front of him. She was a diminutive woman,
slightly overweight in her old age, but wearing extravagant
clothes and strand upon strand of pearls, like Coco Chanel.

'How did she manage to enforce it?'

'Easily. For a start I, and girls like me, were just sixteen.
Margo regarded herself as being *in loco parentis*, and our
parents were only too relieved that she cared enough to insist
we played by her rules. It was, after all, for our own good. Pity
there aren't more like her today.'

The vision of Margo faded as Veronica went on:

'It wasn't the thought of any of us getting pregnant that
worried her. It was 1985. Abortion was an option. It was more
that she'd seen how easily men can manipulate women –
especially girls who were living away from home for the first
time. So she liked each of her babies to flat-share with one of
the older girls until she found her feet. That way, as well as
keeping one another company, the older girl could look out for
the younger, and tell Margo if she thought she wasn't coping,
or was getting into drugs, or was seeing men who were likely to
have certain plans for her.'

That sounded sensible enough. Beautiful girls were vulnerable at the best of times. Even more so when they lived alone in

a city. The idea of them living two or more to a flat was good security. 'I expect it also kept the expenses down.'

The comment had embarrassed her. 'Margo had only the best, Mr Tate. We earned a great deal of money. And I could afford a place of my own. But Margo was right. Girls of sixteen are better off living with someone. Preferably not a predatory boyfriend – all too many turn out to be pimps in our business. So she introduced me to Nina.'

'Nina?'

'Bencini,' said Veronica. 'She thought we might get on. We had things in common – like mothers who weren't English, for instance. Nina was half Italian. She was slightly older than me. I forget exactly – about twenty-four, I think.'

'Not exactly a woman of the world, then,' said Tate.

'No, but she knew more than I did. And I looked up to her. She was a successful model by anyone's standards. I wanted to be like her. And I listened to her. If Nina told me something, I made a note of it.'

'Sounds as though she was a good friend.'

'She was,' said Veronica, softly. 'I didn't know it then, but I do now. In an industry like ours, you meet thousands of people over the years who claim to be your friend. The hangers-on. The wannabes. The people who rub you for luck. But you don't make many friends – I was lucky to know her.'

She had grown quite emotional over the past few minutes, and Tate gave her a moment to collect herself. 'But Nina had a secret – something she was desperate to keep from Margo. She had a child.'

'How old?'

'Three, I think. Not much older, if at all.'

'Who was the father?'

'A photographer,' said Veronica. 'Italian, and very highly regarded in the industry. Nina hadn't had any contact with him since before the child was born.'

'Any particular reason?'

'I think, at first, he denied he was the father. But when he realised she wasn't about to try to screw him for maintenance, he stopped denying it. He never tried to see it, though.'

'That must have been hard.'

'I suppose it was at the time. She didn't talk about it much.'

Something occurred to Tate. 'Bencini,' he said. 'Was that her maiden name?'

'No, it was his.'

'Women don't usually take their partner's name unless they're married.'

Veronica smiled. 'She stole it,' she said. 'Nina Bencini sounded an awful lot better than Nina Kelsey. And image is everything in our profession.'

Tate could imagine it would be.

'Nina loved her child, Mr Tate, but she wasn't a very good mother. She used to look after it now and again. Mostly she left it with relatives.'

The existence of an illegitimate child shouldn't have been a problem in 1985. 'Why was she so worried about Margo finding out?'

'She just didn't want to risk it. For all she knew, Margo might have been fine about it. But Margo had what some might say were fairly old-fashioned ideas. It simply wasn't possible to guess how she'd react to something like that. She might have decided she didn't like the idea of having a single mother on her books. And it hadn't been long since a girl was stripped of the Miss World title when it came out that she had an illegitimate child.'

Tate could suddenly see why Nina, whose career, whose *life* in fact, was more or less controlled by a powerful and probably highly unpredictable matriarch, might want to keep it quiet.

'So Margo didn't know,' said Veronica. 'And by the time she found out, it didn't make much difference. Nina wasn't on her books any more. Something happened to make her leave the agency.'

Nina was introduced to Francis Herrol. 'He invited us down

to Lyndle for a summer party. It was quite an event. Tent on the lawn. Free champagne. We stayed the night.'

'Where did you sleep?'

'We didn't. It was a party.'

It was years since Tate had last been to an all-night party. He suddenly felt old.

'And the following morning, we left.'

That was it? That was all that happened?

'It was after we got back to London that something happened.'

Francis Herrol followed them back. And because he didn't know Nina's home address or telephone number, he hung around the agency in the hope of seeing her. 'But people don't realise – just because you've signed with an agency doesn't mean you live there. Weeks could pass without any of us needing to go in. *Months*, sometimes. Margo did most of her business by phone, sending us here and there. So he started to hassle the staff for Nina's number.'

'I take it Margo wasn't impressed.'

'At first, she was polite. She pointed out that she really couldn't have him practically camping on the doorstep. But after a couple of days she had him thrown off the premises. She threatened to call the police if he came back.'

'Sounds a bit extreme.'

'You don't understand – he was married and, as I said before, Margo had some very old-fashioned ideas. The thought of a married man travelling four hundred miles to hang around one of her girls didn't amuse her.'

'What did Nina think of it all?'

'No idea. She never mentioned him. But I'm assuming he must have managed to get her number eventually, though he certainly never phoned when I was around, and he didn't go to the flat when I was there.'

Before Tate could ask what made her so sure Francis had finally managed to get Nina's number, she added: 'Then Nina left the agency. She just walked out one day – not only on

Margo, but on me. Left everything. Just like that – and she was the last person I would have thought would do a thing like that.'

'Where did she go?' said Tate.

Veronica reached for her bag and pulled out a letter. She handed it to Tate, who found that it had been written from an hotel on the outskirts of Rome.

'She wrote to tell me she'd heard from the father of her child. He'd asked her to go back to Italy to see if they could make a go of things.'

'What did you think about that?'

'I didn't think it was true.'

'Why not?'

Veronica replied, 'Because she'd never mentioned him much, and when she did, she didn't sound particularly bitter.'

Tate couldn't quite grasp what she was trying to say.

'People don't try to resurrect relationships when they're indifferent.'

'Maybe it was an act?'

'I don't think so. A few months earlier, there'd been a photograph in some magazine – it might have been *Harpers*, now I come to think of it. Anyway, there he was on a podium, collecting an award for his work. And there, on his arm, was a fabulous-looking woman.'

'And?' said Tate.

'And Nina said the dress was a Galliano. That was about as much interest as she had in who he was with. Don't you see? She wasn't in love with him any more.'

Tate now saw exactly what she meant.

'And why stay in an hotel?' said Veronica. 'Why not move back in with him?'

Again, he could see her point.

'She promised to write again as soon as she could let me have a more permanent address.'

'And did she?'

'No,' said Veronica. 'That was the last I heard from her.'

215

Tate could see how the fact of Francis Herrol's name having recently been reported in the press would have brought all this back to her. But he couldn't see what bearing it had on the current investigation. He was just about to say so when Veronica continued:

'It may seem strange to you after I just said we were close, but there were certain areas of her life that I knew nothing about, and I didn't ask. She was an intensely private person. That didn't mean we weren't close.'

Tate agreed that you could be close to someone without knowing all there was to know about them. Veronica went on:

'For instance, I knew she had a child, and I knew who the father was. But I didn't know where her relatives lived, so I had no means of getting in touch with her. I hoped for months that I'd hear from her. I kept thinking how wonderful it would be if we could meet in Italy and spend a few days together. Childish, I know.'

Tate wanted to tell her that caring about what happened to people wasn't childish. Nina had been a friend to her. But he still couldn't see what this had to do with the current investigation.

'And then it turned out that, just before she . . . vanished, she did something unforgivable to her child.'

What kind of unforgivable? he wondered. He hoped she wasn't about to tell him that Nina had harmed it.

'She dumped it somewhere she shouldn't have. Just dumped it and left it.'

'Where?'

'Heathrow Airport.'

Pictures of a child left wandering around one of the terminals formed in his mind. 'Whereabouts?'

'In a . . . cubicle,' said Veronica.

'A lavatory, you mean?'

She nodded. 'Terrible, I know.'

It was indeed a terrible thing to do, but desperate people did desperate things, and it occurred to him that Nina must have been desperate to do a thing like that. 'You say that after this letter you never heard from her again—'

'Nobody did,' said Veronica. 'And after a couple of months, people got worried – it turned out I wasn't the only one who hadn't heard from her.'

The Italian police had launched an investigation into Nina's disappearance. They questioned the father of her child, but came to the conclusion that he had no motive to want her 'disposed of'. 'In the end,' said Veronica, 'they had to let him go.'

'Did anyone ever discover what happened to her?'

'No,' said Veronica, quietly. 'You hear of these things – of people going missing – but you never think it could happen to someone you know. Someone you . . . love.'

Tate had heard this so many times during the course of his career.

'And then, when I heard that remains had been found at Lyndle, and that it was already known that they couldn't be those of the girl you were looking for, something just clicked into place.'

Veronica clutched the letter harder than she'd meant to. It crumpled under the pressure, and he watched as it was crushed.

'I was sixteen when Nina and I came here. When I said I didn't know a thing about a thing, it was true – I didn't. It was only as I grew older that I thought about a look that passed between them at that party – a fleeting look. It couldn't have lasted more than a second, and yet it lasted a lifetime. *That's* why Francis Herrol came to London. *That's* why he was hanging around at Margo's.'

'What are you saying?'

'I'm saying that Nina didn't return to Italy, other than to post a few letters perhaps – she came back here. She came to Lyndle to be with Francis Herrol. But he was married. Presumably neither he nor she wanted it known that they were involved, so she lied about where she was.'

'Are you saying—'

'She came to Lyndle to be with him. And then she disappeared.'

After giving Audrah the chance to absorb what he'd been told, Tate added:

'After I spoke to Veronica, I put a few people on to it. They came back with the information I needed, and it all checks out. Some months after Nina wrote that letter to Veronica, her relatives both here and in Italy reported her missing.'

'What took them so long?' said Audrah.

'The relatives in England assumed she was over there, and vice versa, but after a while people began to get worried. The Italian police did their best to prove the father of her child was somehow involved in her disappearance, but there wasn't a shred of evidence against him, and nobody could see what motive he might have. By then he was involved with somebody else, and he seemed to have no interest in getting custody of the child.'

When Audrah made no comment, Tate threw her the challenge:

'Some days ago you told me there was nothing on earth for which there was no rational explanation.'

'What about it?' said Audrah.

'Well, now's your chance to prove it – if you can. Tell me how Rachel Harvey could possibly have witnessed a murder that happened eighteen years ago.'

35

The following morning, Tate was called to a cottage fifteen miles outside Otterburn. The word 'cottage' conveyed an impression of thatched tranquillity, but there couldn't have been anything tranquil about living in a property built for a farm labourer at the turn of the last century.

The farm it belonged to had sold it long ago, and it was now in the hands of a landlord who rented it to a family on income support. It stood alone on the side of a slope, moorland sweeping away at the back to a series of low-lying hills. It was bleak, and it was lonely. Above all, it was cold.

Tate stood on the weed-choked path and hammered on the door. Seconds later it was opened by a woman in her thirties. Her plain, round face was deeply and prematurely lined, her lanky hair tied back in a rubber band.

Tate produced his ID and she let him in. The door gave immediately on to a downstairs room that was strewn with washing. A clothes horse had been placed in front of a gas fire, moisture rising from the clothes to cling to the walls and drip down the flaking plaster.

These were the conditions in which Jacqueline Edmunds, her two young children, her elderly parents and her husband were attempting to survive. And 'survive' was the operative word. You couldn't call this living.

She was embarrassed, she said, that she couldn't offer him anything more than instant coffee – black. 'There isn't no milk.' And she was embarrassed that the sofa was smeared with Farley's Rusk. 'I meant to give it a wipe before you come.'

It was all right, Tate assured her. He liked his coffee black.

And she ought to see what his own kids did to the sofa back home.

His Geordie accent reassured her. 'You're not like the copper who come earlier. He spoke posh.'

The copper who had investigated after Jackie phoned the police was a Manchester lad, but Tate supposed he might have sounded like the Queen Mother to someone like her.

As if glad to have someone to talk to, she suddenly started going at it nineteen to the dozen. 'You can't imagine what it's like trying cope with this lot.'

Tate knew only too well how hard it was to bring up a family in conditions such as these. They weren't too far removed from those he'd been raised in himself. 'What brought you out here?'

'Dave and me was born round here,' said Jackie. 'Besides, there might be work in Newcastle, but there's drugs as well – and we've got two kids coming up eleven and fourteen.'

Better to starve. Better to freeze on a slab of moor than wonder who was approaching your kids as they walked out of the school gates of an afternoon.

'It's hard, though,' she added. 'If Dave was in work, things might be different, but that's not the way it is.'

Tate agreed that, if Dave was in work, things might well be different. They might be able to rent a larger house, for a start – something with enough rooms to accommodate two growing adolescent kids who, by rights, ought to have had rooms of their own by now. Life was difficult enough without the additional strain of having to look after elderly parents, one of whom was bed-bound, and the other too active for her own, or anyone else's, good. 'She wanders off, Mr Tate. There's no keeping her in.'

Tate was aware that Jackie's mother, Edith, was in the habit of wandering out of the house, taking a bus to Otterburn, then trying to walk it back to save the fare. According to police records, Edith had been reported missing several times since she and her husband came to live with their daughter. She was usually found within a couple of hours, largely because she moved slowly and stuck to the roads, so it wasn't so much that Edith wandered off that was the problem. The problem was that Edith was losing her marbles. 'Honest to God, Mr Tate, you can't believe a word. A couple of weeks ago, she told everyone she'd been offered a major role in *Coronation Street*.'

Tate smiled.

'And only last Christmas she phoned the *News of the World* and claimed she'd had an affair with Matt Monro.'

Tate was laughing now.

'So you see,' said Jackie, 'we didn't take that much notice when she said she'd found a body.'

Tate was reminded of why he was there. He stopped laughing as Jackie added, 'Week after week she gave us a running report on how it was doing. First, it was just dead. Then it was decomposing. Then it was starting to stink something dreadful. I didn't take much notice. Well, you wouldn't, would you?'

Tate stared down at a letter that Jacqueline Edmunds had shown to the Manchester lad who called when she phoned the police. Her mother claimed to have found it on or near a body. Jackie didn't know whether it was genuine, but she'd read in the papers about what was going on at Lyndle, so naturally, when she read the signature, she called the police.

'Where's your mother now?' said Tate.

'Upstairs.'

'Do you think I might have a word?'

Edith Edmunds descended the stairs with surprising agility. She was remarkably fit for her age. She was also remarkably mad.

'So, she's snitched on me, has she?'

Tate admitted that, yes, her daughter had in fact snitched on her, but that Edith wasn't to be cross. He fully appreciated that the body had been her little secret, but once her daughter saw the letter, she realised she had a duty to tell the police. 'Do you think you could show us where you found it?'

Immediately Edith looked at him rather slyly. There was nothing malicious in the look. She was having a game with him.

'What's in it for me?' she said.

'What are your favourite sweets?'

'Pear drops,' said Edith.

'I'll buy you a couple of ounces.'

'Four,' said Edith, sharply.

'You'd have my last breath,' said Tate, and his teasing won her over.

'I wouldn't show just anyone.'

'No, I'll bet you wouldn't.'

Normally it took her a good hour to walk up the hill at the back. Today she and Tate travelled in style, the 4 × 4 depositing them close to an outcrop of rocks.

This, she said, had been one of her favourite places as a girl, and when Tate saw the view that stretched out before him, he could understand why. He could also understand why she repeatedly tried to escape the cramped, depressing conditions of the cottage: the kind of arrangement that threw three generations of a family together in circumstances such as those in which the Edmunds family were living was very often hell for all concerned. But Tate wasn't there to contemplate what motivated Edith to escape; he was there to find a body, and now he asked where it was.

Edith, all wide-eyed innocence, replied, 'He's right beside you, pet.'

Tate looked around, but all he could see were rocks. 'Edith,' he said, 'I don't see a body.'

She pointed to a group of small boulders. Tate peered between them and saw what looked like a sheep's ribcage poking through the snow. But it didn't belong to a sheep – not unless the sheep had taken to wearing human clothing.

A jacket lay close by, scavengers having ripped it from the remains. As Tate walked over to it, he said, 'When did you find it, Edie?'

'Shortly after we moved in with our Jackie,' Edith replied.

Tate recalled Jackie mentioning that her parents had moved in a month ago. *She couldn't cope with looking after Dad, so I didn't have much choice, did I?*

She resented the loss of valuable space for the kids. Her husband resented the loss of privacy. And Edith resented the loss of her home, and her independence. Almost immediately, she started taking long, solitary walks. And almost immediately, she found the body of Francis Herrol.

Ever since finding it, Edith had been returning for a chat. He was a good listener, she told Tate. Her daughter couldn't seem to spare her a moment any more, but Mr Dead Body seemed glad of her company. There came a point when the animals had pulled the clothes from the bones, and that was when she ran a hand through his pockets. Not to steal, she hastened to add, but to see whether there was anything he might want her to look after. All she found was a letter. She took it home and hid it under the bed. Her daughter found it when she pulled the bed out to hoover round the skirting.

From all that Edith had told him, Tate felt able to form what he felt was probably a fairly accurate picture of Francis Herrol's last few hours of life. He came up here and sat with his back to the rocks. He then committed suicide, having written a note that explained the situation.

Tate made his way back to Lyndle in the knowledge that, after breaking the news of Francis's suicide to Claudia, he and Audrah were scheduled to break some equally shattering news to Rachel. Audrah had contacted him that morning:

'You threw me a challenge,' said Audrah. 'I'm ready to meet it.'

36

After leading the Harveys into the interview room, Tate warned Rachel that what Audrah was going to tell her might come as a shock.

Immediately she looked nervous, and Audrah tried to soothe her. There was nothing to worry about – it was merely that, as a result of some of the things she told them yesterday, she and Tate had been able to piece together an explanation for what she saw.

It was an approach that failed to reduce the air of tension. Rachel reached for her husband's hand, found it, and held it tightly.

'What you saw related to the murder of a woman who died some time ago.'

'How long ago?'

There was no easy way to break this. 'Eighteen years.'

It took a moment for the implications to register, and when they did Rachel stood up. 'Let me go.'

'Rachel—' said Audrah.

She started to shout: 'Guy – make them let me go!'

It took a lot of soothing to calm her down. Here was a psychologist, in the company of a senior police officer, who appeared to be confirming what she suspected all along: that she'd seen a ghost.

'There was a particularly sad aspect to the case,' said Audrah, carefully. 'She had a child. We believe that child was with her the day she was murdered.'

Guy said, 'What does that have to do with what Rachel saw?'

Audrah replied, 'We knew she crawled into the pipe to die.

What we didn't know was why. We now know she was trying to escape her killer. And we know it because . . . Rachel saw it happen.'

'I can't have,' said Rachel. 'Not if happened eighteen years ago. And I didn't see a child. There *was* no child.'

'I'm afraid there was,' said Audrah.

'No – I'd have seen her.'

Audrah broke it to her gently, cutting across her insistence: 'You didn't see a child because you *were* the child.'

The news was met, as Audrah had anticipated it might be, by denial. Rachel insisted she must have got her facts wrong.

'Guy, tell them.'

'She was your mother,' said Audrah.

'No,' said Rachel. 'You've got it wrong. My mother died in a hit-and-run. And prior to last August, I'd never been to Lyndle in my life.'

'I'm afraid you had,' said Audrah.

'I'd remember.'

'You were three years old,' said Audrah. 'You can't be expected to remember on a conscious level. Subconsciously, though, you remembered a lot of things, like the gap in the trees that led to the sunken road.'

Rachel was shaking her head. It couldn't be true. She wouldn't *allow* it to be true. Guy, however, was willing to explore the possibility.

'Rachel,' he said, 'I don't think the police would be saying all this if they hadn't checked their facts.' As if, having said this, he suddenly needed reassurance, he added, 'Would you?'

Tate replied, 'We checked.'

'No,' said Rachel. 'What I saw was a ghost.'

Audrah supposed that, in a sense, she was right, though whether what she saw was what most people would think of as a ghost she couldn't say. Her subconscious memories of what had happened to her mother were stirred when she returned to the cottage. Perhaps without even realising it, she was drawn to walk through its garden and down the lane that led to the sunken road. And once she neared the pipe, despite the fact that it was hidden now, her subconscious began to regurgitate long-buried memories of what had happened the last time she was there.

But the subconscious could sometimes be kind. It sometimes allowed such memories to seep through little by little. Sometimes they came in the form of dreams. At other times, they surfaced as flashbacks. And very occasionally the person experiencing the resurfacing of memories long buried believed that what they were experiencing were supernatural phenomena.

'Why would Ruth say my mother died in a hit-and-run if it wasn't true?'

'She was probably trying to protect you.'

Audrah was guessing now, but she thought it likely that, as the years went by, and as hope that Nina might return finally faded, Ruth probably forced herself to face the facts: either her sister was dead, or she had abandoned Rachel. Whatever the case, she probably decided to protect her from what she thought was something she was better off not knowing. She added:

'It's possible something you said made Ruth suspect you had witnessed an event she would rather you forgot. And you did forget. Very young children invariably do.'

'Only they don't,' said Guy.

'No,' said Audrah. 'They don't. None of us do. We bury our memories deeply. Sometimes we recall them as we grow older. The very old sometimes recall their childhoods with greater clarity than their middle and later years.'

Guy, at least, was finding it possible to accept that this might be true. Rachel, however, was still in total denial. 'But you'd think I'd remember *something*.'

She was appealing for an alternative explanation, and Audrah suspected that if she were to concede that she had in fact seen a ghost, she would somehow find this far more believable than the truth. Rational explanations were not always the most palatable, or believable. Sometimes they took a little getting used to.

Finding that explanation, piecing it together, had kept Audrah awake until the early hours of the morning. And it wasn't merely the challenge thrown by Tate that made her determined to find it: on the contrary, she needed to find it for herself, because had she been confronted by something she couldn't explain, she would have been forced to consider the possibility that certain alleged supernatural experiences might be genuine.

The personal implications of that would have been too disturbing. It would intimate that she might yet make contact with Lars, and the knowledge that he might yet be restored to her would keep her in a kind of emotional bondage. There would never be room for anyone else to enter her life. The space they ought to occupy would be filled by his ghost. It would prevent her from living her life in a normal way, for who could be asked to share their world with a ghost? Was it even reasonable to ask it of herself? Small wonder positive proof of an afterlife evaded people. Few realised how emotionally destructive it would be.

Tate said, 'What made you suspect that Nina might be Rachel's mother?'

Audrah replied: 'I knew that, whatever else Rachel saw, it certainly wasn't a ghost, and it was obvious she couldn't have read news reports relating to the circumstances surrounding Nina's disappearance because nothing was known about it. The only reference the press ever made to it stated that an English model had gone missing in Italy. No mention of Lyndle, or flowers, or pipes. Yet Rachel was aware of all these. Also, her reaction, her behaviour, was very much in keeping with what we know of the way children react when traumatised—'

'What made it so hard for her to deal with the idea of seeing a ghost?'

Audrah replied, 'Parapsychologists get to see a lot of people who claim to have seen a ghost. We soon learn which are the ones who really believe it, because they're the ones who can't cope with it. Suddenly, they know for a fact – or maybe I should say they *think* they know for a fact – that there's a spirit world, and it throws their entire value system into chaos. It makes them question every aspect of their lives. They see almost everything they're striving for as superficial. They want to make big changes. Often, that means shedding everything about the way they currently live – partner, job, environment, *everything*. It's the ultimate in the life-altering experience, and people don't actually want it. The thing they keep coming out with is, I didn't ask for this. I didn't go looking for it. Why me?'

'The Road to Damascus experience.'

Wober was the expert on religious visionaries – which reminded her: he'd left a message on her mobile. He'd spoken to Goldman. Could she call him.

There were certain things they would never know, such as what Ruth thought when she discovered that her sister owned a cottage in Lyndle. But Nina was a model, and men gave gifts to beautiful women all the time. Cars, clothes, jewellery, horses, holidays and houses. Maybe she thought nothing of it, which was a pity, because if she'd told the local police that her sister disappeared shortly after someone gave her a cottage, they might have looked into who gave it to her, and that would have led them to Francis. That didn't mean they would have found sufficient evidence to build a case, but it would at least have pointed them in the right direction. As it was, Ruth appeared not to have followed it up.

The cottage had been on the market several times over the years. No one made an offer. The local community was fragmenting; there was no work, and Lyndle wasn't the kind of place that tourists flocked to for a holiday. The cottage, along with the neighbouring properties, fell into disrepair, and because she couldn't sell it and didn't know what to do with it, Ruth left it to Rachel. She couldn't possibly anticipate that

Rachel might want to see it, and even if she had, she couldn't have foreseen that returning to the area would trigger traumatic memories.

'There are still a couple of things I don't understand,' said Audrah.

'You're going to ask what happened to Rachel after her mother was murdered.'

'Yes,' she replied. 'It was obviously thought too risky to leave her wandering around – if somebody found her locally, her mother's connection with Lyndle would have been realised. That would have led the police to the cottage, and Francis. But why go to the effort of taking her anywhere? Why let her live? Where was she taken? Who by? These are the questions I haven't been able to answer.'

'Maybe Claudia Herrol can answer them for us.'

37

Claudia sat in the study at Lyndle Hall. Outside, police were loading equipment into the back of the vehicles. Soon they would drive away. The snow would come, and the tracks they left would be covered. It would be as though the police had never been there. But nothing would be the same. Soon, she too would leave. Though not of her own volition.

It was only a matter of hours since she had been told about Francis, and Tate regretted having to do this at what must be a terrible time for her.

Audrah stayed in the background, but Tate sat down beside her. The contents of the suicide note revealed who killed Nina, and why. Therefore he assumed she knew what was coming.

'Do you have a lawyer?' he said. 'Someone you'd like me to contact?'

She raised her hand, the slightest of gestures, but one that was sufficient to let it be known that she cared neither one way nor the other for a lawyer. Then, after some moments, she said: 'I could well understand what he saw in her. She was beautiful, you know. And she, of course, was charmed by him. Francis was terribly charming.'

Tate could well imagine that Francis was charming.

'He made her his mistress. He was quite open about it. He couldn't understand why there should be a fuss. We were all adults. It was perfectly possible to be civilised. Plenty of women, from all walks of life, simply got on with it. Why couldn't I?'

You do understand, I have to have her. I love her.

'You must have known there was a risk we might find her,' said Tate.

'I think I knew from the moment you started looking for Ginny.'

Tate made no comment, and she added, 'I've heard it said that people who kill often feel the need to talk about it. All these years I've wanted someone to understand.'

Tate remained completely silent.

'She never saw it coming, you know. I rather regretted that. A part of me wanted to confront her face to face, and make her beg. I didn't have the courage. I was frightened, you see – frightened I'd lose my nerve. I could imagine myself ranting and raving and threatening her, but not actually stabbing her. And if I'd lost my nerve, I think she might have laughed. So in the end I stabbed her in the back.'

Tate closed his eyes.

'She just sort of staggered forward. And then she turned round, her hand reaching up behind her. I honestly don't think she knew she'd been stabbed at that point. "Oh, it's you," she said. Such an odd thing to say. She must have thought I'd slapped her on the back. And then she looked at her hand, and there was blood on it. And she realised.'

Tate imagined her walking along the sunken road and feeling what she must have thought was a violent shove in the back. She would have turned and seen Claudia, and straight away she would have suspected that this was some kind of showdown. 'How did you lure her there?'

'I didn't have to. Francis gave her the cottage as a token of his commitment, but whenever they thought I was out, they used the conjugal bed.'

'You'd stabbed her,' said Tate. 'What then?'

'It was all a bit of an anticlimax, to be honest. She stood there, and so did I, and you wouldn't have thought that anything had happened. She kept reaching behind her as if she couldn't believe it. Maybe she thought it was paint, a joke of some kind. And then I think the pain kicked in. She suddenly said, "Oh," but that was all.'

'And what about you?'

'I'd lost my nerve, much as I feared I might. I almost said I was sorry. I almost sat her down and said, "I'm sorry, I can't imagine what I was thinking of. You stay here, and I'll get help. Try not to move if you can." Then I realised that, already, there could be no going back. People weren't simply going to say, "There, there, Claudia. You must have been under stress." No matter what the provocation, as they say, nothing could possibly justify stabbing another person in the back with a six-inch blade. The press. The embarrassment. The inevitability of prison. But most of all Francis, and me in a situation where there was nothing I could do to prevent him from divorcing me. I'd have lost everything.'

It was as if, after all these years, she needed to reveal how it had been done.

'I know this sounds stupid, but this is the way it really was. She started backing away, and all the while I took little dancing steps towards her. Now and again I'd slash at her with the knife. But nothing deep. All superficial. I didn't have the nerve to . . .'

To move in. To do what a trained soldier might do and get the job over with quickly. She didn't know how to kill, so she did what young predators do: she played at it. She experimented. She railed at her own inability to inflict a fatal wound in a single bite or blow. But she carried on trying.

'I read something rather terrible once,' said Claudia. 'A woman walking alone in a national park in America. There are bears, you know. Horrible things. Forget all that sentimental rubbish about what a marvellous thing it is to be able to reintroduce them to the wild. You might as well say much the same thing about dinosaurs. They belong to an era more savage than we can imagine. But bears are here and now. And one of them attacked her.'

Tate caught Audrah's eye. They wondered where this was leading.

'A black bear, I think. Not a grizzly. A grizzly would have killed her within seconds. It just kept coming back at her. She held out her arm, and it stripped it of flesh completely. She lost her arm. But by staying calm, she saved her life. That's what I call courage, and presence of mind. Nina had presence of mind. She stayed completely calm. She even tried to engage me in some sort of conversation: "I can see that you're very upset, and it's obvious to me that nobody has been taking your point of view into consideration. Let's talk, shall we, and sort this whole thing out?"

'Then Rachel came running up. I didn't know she was with her. "Mummy," she said. "You're all bleeding!" And Nina told her that she and the lady were talking. She asked her to go and play.' She paused, then added: 'Children aren't fools, Inspector. She stood there, and she watched as I finally plunged the knife into her mother's stomach. That was when she fell. That was when she crumpled to the ground. She rolled on her stomach and lay there. But after a moment, she started to crawl away.'

Tate recalled what Rachel had said about turning round to see a woman crawling through the undergrowth.

'The pipe was several yards away. And she crawled so very slowly.'

'Did you stab her again?'

Claudia shook her head. 'I couldn't bring myself.'

'And where was Rachel?'

'Standing a little way away. Silent, the way they are when they don't understand, and they're frightened.'

'And when she reached the pipe?'

'It was like a dream. One of those dreams in which people do very strange things. And after she was gone, after she'd . . . crawled into it, you can't imagine – within moments, I had to convince myself she'd ever been there at all. If not for the blood and the child—'

'You didn't kill Rachel. Why?'

Claudia replied, 'I might be a killer. But I'm also a mother. Nicholas was barely two years older. I couldn't . . . I just couldn't do it . . .'

'You dumped her at Heathrow,' said Tate. 'That's quite a drive.'

'I didn't know what else to do with her. I knew that Nina had a sister, but I didn't know where she lived. And I couldn't leave her wandering round the wood. She was three. Anything could have happened to her. But nor could I risk her being found anywhere near Lyndle. I think I hoped people would assume Nina had dumped her and flown off somewhere.'

'What about her belongings?' said Tate.

'I went to the cottage and cleared it.'

'Weren't you afraid that people might see you?'

'People did,' said Claudia.

'Didn't they ask what you were doing?'

'No.'

'Why not?'

'Because I am who I am, and it wouldn't have occurred to them to ask. They might have wondered, but they wouldn't have asked. And people knew the cottage belonged to us. Everything did. The school, the church, the shop. They probably thought I'd put my foot down and forced his mistress out.'

'And Francis,' said Tate. 'I take it he knew what you'd done?'

'That was the end of our marriage. He never came near me again. Hardly ever spoke to me. Couldn't stand the sight of me at times.'

'And yet you stayed married?'

'There was Nicholas to consider. Francis didn't want him affected by . . . by what I'd done, and . . . It was honourable of him in a way – he was prepared to take his share of the responsibility. After all, he'd brought her here. He made her his mistress.' After a moment, she added, 'But he never went near that road again unless it was to lay a bunch of flowers by the pipe. He . . . he never forgot her . . .'

'And last August,' said Tate, 'he saw Rachel in the trees.'

'He knew straight away who she was. She looks like her mother, apparently. Tall, and dark, and exotic. He thought she'd remembered. He thought it had brought her back.'

234

'Did you know he intended to kill himself?'

'I guessed.'

Tate recalled that Francis had died looking at a particular view of the moors. 'I take it he chose to die in a place that held some particular significance for him?'

Such wonderful light. I thought I might spend the morning on the moors.

You're going to meet her.

I don't have the time, or the patience, for histrionics.

I'll kill her . . . I swear to you, Francis . . .

'Yes,' she replied.

38

Cranmer had decided to return to the States. Earlier in the day, Tate had called at the Grange Hotel for a word before he left. He was packing. When Tate turned up, he asked reception to send him up to his room. It was dominated by a four poster bed. Tate sat on it as he said, 'Yesterday, the psychiatrist treating Nicholas had a meeting with someone called Wober. He's Professor of—'

'I know who Wober is,' said Cranmer, abruptly.

Something about his tone of voice – maybe psychics and parapsychologists were naturally wary of one another. The psychic would know that the parapsychologist was out to prove them a fraud, and the parapsychologist would know the psychic was out to prove that, at best, they believed themselves to be possessed of psychic powers.

Tate couldn't make up his mind about Cranmer. As Goldman had said, maybe he was psychic. Maybe he was schizophrenic. Or maybe he was a con man pure and simple. If the latter, then his guesswork had paid off. But as Audrah pointed out, when a girl went missing from a house like Lyndle Hall, it didn't take a genius to work out that it would make better sense to hide her body somewhere in the wood that surrounded it rather than in the house itself or the moat. Tate said:

'I thought you might be interested to hear what Wober had to say.'

'You're obviously going to tell me anyway.'

Tate cast his mind back to Audrah's account of Wober's meeting with Goldman. Having seen Goldman's office, it was easy for him to visualise where the meeting took place, but not having met Wober, he had to conjure an image of the man from

236

the little he knew of him. Even so, it wasn't too difficult to picture an erudite academic standing in front of the shelves that lined the wall behind Goldman's desk.

In his hand, he held the book that Goldman had shown to Audrah the previous day. It had fallen open at a page depicting Joan of Arc being burned at the stake, her eyes almost wild with terror and defiance.

Cranmer would no doubt have claimed she was a medium. Wober had claimed that Joan of Arc was a transsexual schizophrenic.

According to Audrah, Goldman was amused. 'And what about my patient?' he said. 'What would you say is Nicholas Herrol's problem?'

Nicholas had been too heavily sedated for Wober to be able to talk to him, but the case notes made for interesting reading. 'If accurate,' said Wober, 'then Nicholas suffers from a form of psychosis that is even more rare than transsexual schizophrenia.'

He pointed out that extremes of emotion invariably resulted in a physical reaction of one sort or another. Sometimes the manifestations were as gentle as a blush, or as natural as an erection, but they could be as radical, as inappropriate as the stigmata. Historically, if the wounds took the form of holes through the hands and feet, the victim was hailed as a person of sanctity. If not, then they were believed to be possessed. 'If Nicholas were a religious person,' said Wober, 'then his wounds might correspond more to Christ's suffering on the cross. In the absence of a religious vocation, the wounds are taking a very different form.'

As he listened to this, Cranmer folded his cashmere sweater and placed it in his case, and when it became clear that he wasn't about to comment, Tate said: 'I'd be interested to know your opinion?'

Cranmer snapped his suitcase shut. 'If you think I'm going to tell you Nicholas is at the mercy of a malign entity, then I'm afraid I have to disappoint you. Psychics don't automatically assume that everyone like Nicholas is possessed. Some people are just ill. He's one of them.'

Tate was slightly disappointed if he were honest. He felt that Cranmer owed it to people to wander around the countryside proclaiming that this or that was haunted or possessed. What else was he paid for? After a moment, he said,

'You don't have a problem with parapsychologists coming up with a rational explanation?'

'I only have a problem with it when they try to find a rational explanation for everything,' said Cranmer.

It sounded fair to Tate. 'You think most parapsychologists are out to discredit you.'

Cranmer replied, 'You know . . . it took me a while to realise it, but after years of subjecting myself to their scrutiny only to end up being insulted by most of them, I came to the conclusion that a lot of parapsychologists are frustrated psychics. They resent those of us who have a genuine gift.'

He reached into his pocket and drew out a rubber ball. He tossed it to Tate, saying: 'Whenever you're tempted to think I'm a fraud, ask yourself how I know what Audrah told you.'

Tate was taken aback – but only for a moment. 'You were listening,' he said.

'Was I?' said Cranmer.

There was no way Tate could be sure. And that was just the problem. Proof of an afterlife would result in most people having to change the way they lived. Proof that death was the end would result in social chaos.

Now, he stood in the courtyard with Fletcher and Bevan. The doors to Lyndle Hall were closed and bolted and he intended to ensure that an eye was kept on it until such time as a decision could be made with regard to its future. Not that a police presence was strictly necessary. Once those massive doors were closed, Lyndle was impenetrable. Barbarians might gather at the gate, but their chances of getting in were no better now than they were six hundred years ago.

In his opinion, houses like this ought to belong to the nation.

They were, after all, built and maintained by the sweat of the underpaid. The fact that they could still be privately owned was, he felt, an insult to every decent working-class man in Britain.

There were grants available for their restoration and maintenance, and though part of him thought it diabolical that people like the Herrols could apply for them yet still retain ownership of the property, another part of him thought it even more diabolical that they hadn't bothered. As Bischel had written, Lyndle was an obscenity, an offence to all that was right, and good, and clean. But it was also possessed of a sinister beauty. It deserved better than to be left to crumble away to nothing.

39

Marion stole up the path to a house she had never seen before. In many respects it was similar to various of the houses Reeve had lived in since Kathryn's death – a small, rather dark semi with a simple bordered lawn.

She had never had the slightest difficulty finding him. His downfall had always been his desire to work, to cling to some semblance of the life he led before she embarked on her campaign to bring him to justice.

The last time she tracked him down, she poured petrol through his letterbox. flicked a match in after it, and stood well back to watch the conflagration. This time she rang the bell.

Reeve answered, and the minute he saw her he pressed a panic button next to the door. It said a lot that the authorities had thought it essential to equip a full grown, able-bodied man with a device that would alert the local police in the event of a woman half his size turning up on the doorstep.

Such devices were usually reserved for the partners of violent men. She, in her leggings and jumper, didn't look much of a threat, but she was seen as one, history having shown her to be capable of behaviour described in court as 'deranged'. As Reeve's solicitor once pointed out to the magistrate who granted the restraining order, all the signs pointed to the possibility that she was a danger. He even went so far as to say that if this had been a country where guns were easily obtainable, his client might be dead by now. And so he might. The authorities weren't altogether confident that he wouldn't, at some point, be found dead anyway. And owing to her determination to turn the entire community against him, there was no saying how many prime suspects there would be. People would point a finger at her, but they would also have to point a finger at every group of parents who had ever mounted a campaign against a convicted paedophile. In addition, there were groups of right-wing extremists who took a very dim view of people like Reeve, and over the years she had seen to it that they were kept supplied with details relating to his whereabouts. It was staggering the number of groups there were that existed for no other reason than to harass or harm, if not an individual then a minority group. And it was alarming just how many of them could be persuaded to direct their anger at something that wasn't connected to their cause. It was almost as if the cause were incidental: the people who comprised these groups merely required an outlet for some private rage. Having recognised this, she had utilised that rage to her own advantage, and it was as if Reeve detected that rage in the insistent way she kept her finger jammed against the bell.

By comparison, the panic alarm was little more than a whining beep. It came and went as he took his hand from the button. 'It takes them two minutes to get here. Two minutes is nothing,' he said.

His voice sounded thin. Not like his old voice at all. Once it was baritone, and filled with the kind of confidence that comes of having a good background, an excellent education, and superb prospects in the profession of one's choice. Now it had lost something of its timbre and was filled with fear for the future.

Two minutes might be nothing, but they were all she needed. It was surprising what one could achieve inside two minutes. A horse shot through the head died in under a second. The impact from a fatal crash killed in less. Two minutes was a lifetime when you were dead. What wouldn't Kathryn give for those two minutes?

He tried to close the door on her, but Marion jammed it open with her foot. It would have been well within his means to crush it, but he didn't try: the pressure he exerted against her was almost apologetic, as if, despite everything she had done, he couldn't quite bring himself to use physical force to rid himself of her. He was gentle, and she had never noticed that before.

'Can I come in?' she said.

He was afraid of her, and Marion, who was afraid of herself at times, was ashamed. 'Please,' she added. 'I need you to forgive me.'

40

As Audrah watched police divers struggle into wet suits she experienced a sensation of déjà vu. It was less than three days since she had seen similar men in similar gear submerge themselves in the moat at Lyndle Hall. This time, however, the divers approached what looked like a hole in the ground. It was the opening to something that had been there for over a century, but there had previously been no record of its existence. There would be a record of it now, for only a matter of days ago somebody lost their life as a result of it being there.

Initially, Steven Harris thought his wife had fallen down a mine shaft. Her cries drew him to a blackened hole in the snow, and he shone an intense beam of light into the depths, expecting to see wooden struts, perhaps the remains of a railway track left at a time when the tin was brought up in trucks.

No tracks. No struts. Just water.

It was a well.

The country was chock-a-block with old forgotten wells, some of them bricked up, but many simply boarded over as this was. Wind had blown soil across the boards and seeds had taken root. Grass and moss concealed it. For years people had walked over it, and the boards had taken their weight. But not even solid oak boards could last for ever. Ultimately, it was inevitable that somebody would one day walk on them, and that their weight would cause them to give.

Paula's weight had caused two broad sections of wood to collapse, leaving a gaping hole. When Harris shone his torch into the depths, he saw his wife floundering in water thirty feet down. He ran to the nearest village to raise the alarm, but by the time rescue services reached her, she was dead. The shock of the fall, the coldness of the water, the length of time it took for people to reach her . . .

Following her conversation with Jochen, Audrah contacted Stafford to let him know she wanted to be present when the well was searched. 'We know it's deep,' he said. 'And we know it's self-contained.'

By that, he meant that it wasn't fed by an underground stream, but that water filtered into it through the walls. The police hadn't stated when they intended to undertake the search because they didn't want the press or the public present. Not that it made any difference. Both were there in force.

It was easy to guess how the press had found out what was happening – there was always someone willing to part with information for money. But Audrah objected to them being there because if Lars's remains were found, the divers intended to bring them to the surface. It would be an intensely private moment for her, and she didn't want her reaction captured on film.

A crowd had gathered as if by osmosis. Among them a woman in a tartan coat, her dog ridiculous in a matching jacket, its tinny bark ringing through the trees.

Jochen and Eva Sidow stood within the cordon, protected from the press and public alike. When Jochen saw Audrah, he gave a slight nod of acknowledgment. Eva, magnificent in a black suit, averted her eyes.

The cordon was manned by uniforms. At one point, one of them approached the Sidows and drew their attention to someone.

Even before Audrah saw the cordon lifted to admit him, she knew it was Cranmer. When she saw him, Eva walked over to him, smiling. Now Andrah knew where Cranmer had got his information about the walnut desk.

A diver was lowered into the well, his fluorescent nylon rope threaded through loops on a harness. His colleagues peered into the depths as he descended, and Audrah, who hadn't yet been able to bring herself to look into those depths, could only imagine what they must be seeing. According to Stafford, if this was where Lars lost his life, his remains would be covered by silt. A diver would have to disturb the debris to find him.

She didn't want to see the debris. She didn't want to see the well at all. She stood a good distance away from it and kept her eyes on trees that were thick with frost. It was several minutes before the diver re-emerged, and he wouldn't look at her. He spoke briefly to Stafford, and after a moment Stafford walked up to her.

She searched his face for some clue as to what he was going to tell her, and saw the answer immediately.

'I'm sorry,' he said.

The dog had set up its barking again, staccato and incessant.

'He wasn't there.'

After making sure she was all right, Stafford walked over to break the news to the Sidows. Moments later, Audrah caught a look from Cranmer. Amused contempt. He placed a hand on Eva's arm, and supported her as she bowed her head in despair.

It was just over a week since Audrah had been here with Jochen. Since then, she had written what she hoped would be her last-ever letter to Lars:

All I have researched during my time at the Institute has proved to me that if there is an afterlife, nobody has yet succeeded in crossing the boundary dividing this world from the next. And so I must let you go, for there are so many things I want to do with what I now believe to be the only life I will ever know.

No one can ever fill the void you left, and nor would I want them to, but I hope to find new purpose to a life that has become devoid of direction, of meaning . . .

Lars, if I am wrong, if you can hear me, forgive me.

She had burned the letter and placed the resulting ashes in an envelope. Now she pulled the envelope out of her jacket. As she tore one corner away and shook the ashes out, she pictured what Lars had looked like the last time she saw him.

The ashes hung on the wind for a moment, then fell to the snow at her feet. They lay there, black and wet. And suddenly she couldn't stand the sight of them. She trod them into the snow and walked away.